PRAISE FOR

"This is a book that deserves to be recognized as not only one of the best self-published books of the year, but also as one of the best Fantasy books of 2018."

— OUTOFTHISWORLD BOOK REVIEWS

"Enchanting, thrilling, and funny...a refreshing departure from most cookie-cutter fantasy realms... characters are fresh and intriguing, instantly memorable...you are going to love this book"

— WAYTOOFANTASY.COM

"Each time I thought the plot had thickened, it just got more interesting...Quick and light...I found myself smiling through a lot of it."

— THE WEATHERWAXREPORT

This is a novel which challenges definitions... a story told with wit, pace, exciting and well-defined characters and in a style that feels so wonderfully relaxed and easy to read. Wow."

— PHIL PARKER, AUTHOR OF THE BASTARD OF FAIRYLAND

PRAISE FOR TALES OF KINGSHOLD

"If you're contemplating reading Tales of Kingshold, don't hesitate, just dive into it. It's a fantastic book...The last short story, "Circles", blew my mind"

— BOOKNEST.EU

"It really is a continuation of book 1 that adds a lot to the story of Kingshold...I really appreciated how Woolliscroft crafted a collection of stories that felt vital to the larger narrative"

— TRAVIS RIDDLE, AUTHOR OF BALAM, SPRING

"Woolliscroft managed to put together a wide selection of genres... Be it heartwarming tale, pirates, zombies, magical creatures or plenty of fights. Tales of Kingshold has them all"

— ROCKSTARLIT BOOK ASYLUM

"Tales of Kingshold is a beautifully crafted series of novelettes and short stories that are both a blast to read and also the perfect way to add rich depth to The Wildfire Cycle series we've all come to know and love."

— FANTASY BOOK CRITIC / WHISPERS AND WONDER.COM

PRAISE FOR IOTH, CITY OF LIGHTS

"Woolliscroft's ability to write characters who don't behave predictably and are multi-dimensional in their makeup is the true strength of this book and series as a whole. You will be hard-pressed to find a better writer of characters and dialogue."

— OUT OF THIS WORLD SFF REVIEWS

"Ioth, City of Lights is a wildly emotional and compelling ride, and Woolliscroft's best yet. The foreshadowing throughout the book hints at something monumental, but let me tell you, it's so much more than I expected,leaving me utterly slack-jawed at the final page."

— FANTASY BOOK CRITIC / WHISPERS AND WONDER.COMC

"I cannot recommend this book highly enough. Six months in to 2019 and Ioth, City of Lights, goes straight into my top spot of Favourite Booksof the Year...It establishes DP Woolliscroft as a first-rate fantasy writer who deserves wider recognition."

— PHIL PARKER, AUTHOR OF *THE BASTARD OF FAIRYLAND*

THE WILDFIRE CYCLE

(READING ORDER)

Kingshold (Book 1)
Tales of Kingshold (Book 1.5)
Ioth, City of Lights (Book 2)
Tales of Ioth (Book 2.5)

TALES OF IOTH

Book 2.5 of the Wildfire Cycle

D.P. WOOLLISCROFT

Created with Vellum

For Haneen. Thank you for all of the magical adventures we have had together.

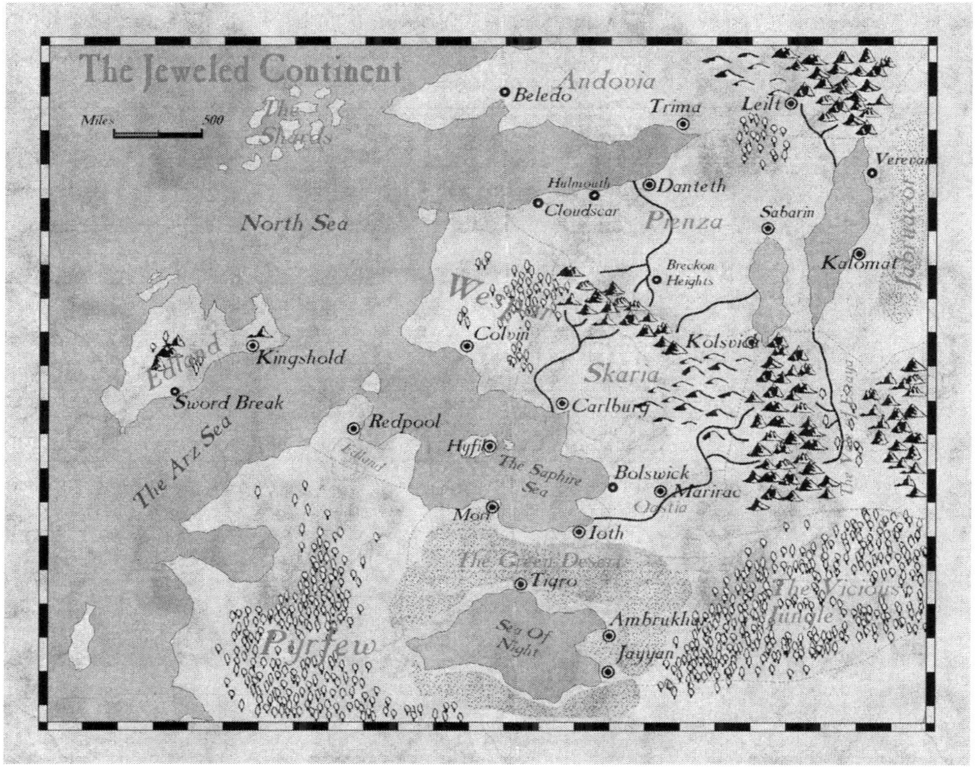
The Jeweled Continent
The Shards
Miles 500
North Sea
Andovia
Beledo
Trima
Leilt
Verevan
Hulmouth
Cloudscar
Danteth
Pienza
Sabarin
Kalomat
Breckon Heights
Colvin
Kingshold
Sword Break
The Arz Sea
Skaria
Kolsvic
Carlburg
Redpool
Hyfil
The Saphire Sea
Bolswick
Marirac
Oastia
Mori
Ioth
The Green Desert
Tigro
Sea Of Night
Ambrukhar
Jayyan
The Vicious Jungle
Pyrfew

AUTHOR'S INTRODUCTION

Though I have titled this tome *Tales of Ioth*, it is not thus called because of the location in which these stories take place. No, this volume is so named because these events take place after the fall of Ioth. Although the city's, and some of its inhabitants', roles in this overarching tale is not ended, those stories are better told later.

It is another place that looms large in these tales. Alfaria, the Wild Continent, is a place unknown to most of us. An unknown people too, though it would soon become clear that our destinies were entwined.

Many of these tales are of both our lowest ebb and of the beginning of our collective climb to what seemed an unlikely end. Loss and uncertainty weighed us down, and while others cast aside their burdens, I'm not sure I can truly say I did so myself. I still see ghosts. Tears still sting my eyes as I read these tales, and as I remember all those we had recently lost and still those who did not reach the culmination of our journey. These are true tales of heroes, though some may be viewed as so only with the passage of time.

These are stories that need telling, that the world as it is today must know the truth of what led it to such a place. How the actions and sacrifices of a few normal people, in far-off places, dark or different, brought good. I only hope my heart can bear to continue with this effort until it is complete.

MARETH BOLLINGSMEAD

THE BEGINNING OF THINGS

I don't think I can sleep, grandfather.

Shhh, they will hear you. Be still.

But I can't. Will you tell me a story? Will you tell me of the old times? When things were better?

Hmmm, fine. But come close so you can hear as I whisper and keep an old man warm at the same time. You want to know about things from long ago? I think it is time you learned about the beginning of things.

~

IN THE BEGINNING, THE WORLD WAS COVERED BY THE ocean, save a small island, where grew a single great tree. Its trunk was wide and strong, and from it stretched long broad branches covered with bright green leaves. The tree had been there a long time, grown from a single seed in the center of the world; and for that long time it was content to be alone.

Until one day, it wasn't content anymore.

And so eight flowers bloomed in its verdant canopy. Great flowers of all the colors of the rainbow that shone with beauty and radiance. In time, four of the flowers wilted and died, as is the way of things, and fruit grew from their essence. Fruit unlike any we have today. Like teardrops of life.

On the first day, four fruit dropped from their branches. One caught in the boughs below it and split open, two winged creatures springing forth to roost in the branches. They were the Thunderbird and the Eagle.

One fruit fell into the ocean, dissolving as it sank into the still, clear waters. The Orca emerged; the ocean waves born of her darting movement.

The two remaining fruit fell to the earth below the tree. From one hopped the Rabbit and from the other slunk the Coyote. The Rabbit moved around the island looking to explore the world, nose twitching. But the Coyote slipped away behind Mother Tree to observe the Rabbit from afar. Rabbit found the island much too small and so dug into the earth to explore the underground. Coyote saw this and was envious. He too thought the island was too small, but he was not a good digger.

"Rabbit," said Coyote. "You are such a good digger. Can you take the earth from where you dig it and put it into the ocean so this land may be bigger?"

"I do not see why not," said the Rabbit, and she set to work. From the hole she dug, Rabbit carried the earth to the edge of the ocean, thumping it down with her hind legs. The island grew in size and Rabbit found that she loved her work.

And Coyote found that he liked to watch others toil.

The small island became a big island, and the big island

became a continent and Rabbit still dug and spread out the land. The hole around Mother Tree became a valley and the tree sat alone on a mountain. Rabbit continued her work until Orca became angry and pounded the shore with her tail. So angry was she that the ground shook. Mountains rose from the land and islands splintered away. Rabbit was ashamed of what she had done to upset her sister and promised to stop.

Coyote traveled, exploring Rabbit's creation, but eventually he became disillusioned. There was much land but it was empty and dark. Coyote returned to Mother Tree and lay down under the great boughs, his head on his paws. He lamented the monotony of creation.

And the tree heard the sad thoughts of her son. Three more flowers wilted and died, bearing fruit. Two of the three fell to the ground. From them came the Wolf and the Tiger. Coyote danced in celebration of companions to share his life. For many years the three were inseparable.

The final fruit of the three fell from the tree. Before it reached the ground, it burst into brilliant flame and the Phoenix emerged. He flew high into the sky, bringing light to the world, and the bird flew for ever more. Reborn every morning, traveling across the land only to die in the evening so that darkness could come once again and his siblings could rest.

Where Wolf, Tiger, and Coyote roamed, the earth bloomed green under the light of the Phoenix and the many creatures of the world emerged. In the seas where the Orca swam, fish of all shapes, sizes and colors were created. To bring sustenance for all living things, the Thunderbird brought the storms and the rains, and the Eagle brought the winds to drive the storms away.

The world was vibrant and teeming with life and nothing died.

One flower remained on the Mother Tree. It was black and had no perfume; and as the flower withered and died, a great round fruit, the color of the sickliest bruise, grew.

For a long time, the fruit hung there in the tree. Rabbit, Coyote, Wolf, Tiger, Orca, Thunderbird, and Eagle came to watch the fruit, waiting for it to fall so that they might greet their new sibling.

The day came when the fruit grew too heavy for the bough that held it. It tumbled to the ground, smashing to pieces. Inside was a great golden seed and all around it were small, black, shiny objects. Coyote, being always curious, wanted to investigate; but he was also afraid, and he urged Rabbit forward. Rabbit hopped close, sniffing the fruit, and she leapt back in alarm as the shapes began to move. Mandibles clicked and wings rubbed themselves free of the sticky juice of the fruit. The sound was enough to set fur and feather on end. Then, as one, the newly hatched creatures rose in a cloud of blackness.

The locusts, for that is what they were, buzzed around the Children at the foot of the tree but did no harm. Instead, they flew into the boughs of the Mother Tree and set to devouring her leaves.

Wolf grew afraid, for he has ever been mindful of his family, and said they must do something. But neither Wolf nor Tiger nor Rabbit nor Coyote nor Orca could climb the tree of their birth, so Wolf begged Eagle for help. The Eagle brought the strongest winds anyone had ever witnessed. The tree bent in the gale but the locusts did not leave their feast, sinking their pointed legs into her flesh until the Mother

Tree was bare of foliage and bark and her exposed wood bled with red sap.

From that day forth, the world knew death.

AFTER THE DEATH OF THE MOTHER TREE, HER CHILDREN left and explored the world in solitude. Even Wolf, Tiger and Coyote, who had been inseparable, went their separate ways. Time passed in this way until one day Wolf called out on the wind for all of the Children to meet at the mountain where they had been born.

They met at night, forming a circle around a fire that the Phoenix had created for light. Rabbit, Coyote, Tiger, Eagle, Thunderbird, and even Orca,who swam a river from the ocean to be there. Wolf padded into the circle once they were all settled.

"Brothers and sisters. Thank you for coming. It warms my heart that we are all here."

"I don't see Locusts," muttered Coyote.

"Brother, must you remind us," said Rabbit. "I don't think anyone would want them here. I wish we could have met somewhere else."

Wolf glared at Rabbit and Coyote to stop their bickering, as he had important news to share. "Here, where we were all born, is where we had to meet. For I have something to show you. I have created life, using part of myself, Coyote, and Tiger. I gave these creatures form and the love of life and family. From Coyote I gave them inquisitiveness and from Tiger I gave them fierceness and strength. I present to you the first-people."

Out of the darkness stepped a score of men and women,

much like you or me, though they were naked under the glittering stars that shone down from above. They passed through the place in the circle vacated by Wolf and looked around at the assembled Children, larger than any animals they had seen before. They smiled.

"These are the Alfjarun. Created to address the void in our hearts."

The Children looked on these strange creatures, the Alfjarun, with wonder. They inspected the first-people closely; they marveled at how they stood on two legs and prodded their strong forms with wing and paw.

"Henceforth, these are my people. And as such I will take their form too." With that, gone was the great grey wolf. Instead he became a broad-shouldered Alfjarun, though greater and more magnificent than the others. "But I would share their joy with you all. If you would agree, I would have them stay with you all and in turn learn from you."

"They cannot fly," said Eagle and Thunderbird. "There is nothing we can teach them."

But Tiger and Rabbit agreed to help, eager for companionship. Coyote agreed, though his heart was jealous at Wolf's creation, as he knew that they were not his and that he would have less attention from his brother. Nevertheless, the meeting ended with a great feast to celebrate the arrival of the Alfjarun into this world.

The Children left the next day. They were eager to be away from the place they were born, but now they had good news in their hearts. Only Wolf and the Alfjarun stayed behind. They traveled up the mountain to the site of the Mother Tree, although the journey was arduous for the first-people. At the foot of the hollow husk of the tree, Wolf told the Alfjarun of how the world was created and their education began. Moga, the first of the Alfjarun, was greatly moved by the story and pleaded with Wolf to allow them to stay at the mountain, to tend to the shell of his mother, and keep the golden seed safe.

"Do you not want to travel with me and see the world? To learn from the other Children?" asked Wolf.

The Alfjarun shook their heads as one. And so they made their home at the foot of the mountain. For a while Wolf stayed with them, but from time to time he would leave to visit with his brothers and sisters to see how the world changed. When Wolf returned to the mountain, he found that the Alfjarun had children, playing in the dust and helping with chores. It gladdened him to see his family growing and whenever he returned, the children would come out to greet him. At their urging, he would take the form of a wolf once more and have them climb on his back so he could carry them. Together they would bound across the mountains and race through the valleys.

But Wolf was not the only one of the Children to visit the Alfjarun. Coyote came and watched from afar, making note of how the first-people enjoyed each other's company and the simple aspects of life.

The children of those created by Wolf had children of their own, and they too had children, and so their settlement grew. Wolf came back one day and asked the same question he had asked many years before. "Do you not want to travel with me and see the world? To learn from the other Children?" Moga and the other elders said no, content to mind the Mother Tree and the golden seed that had not yet sprouted.

But their offspring were not content. Their journeys on the back of Wolf when they were small had created a yearning within many to travel. There occurred a great argument between the first-people, whose elders demanded that their children stay. Some heard those words and listened but others grew more vociferous in their desire to wander.

Wolf stood before his fractured family and spoke. "Come, do not argue. Any who leave may return home. I go to the vast expanse of the plains which you have not even seen. That is where I planned for you to live."

The elders were appeased and soon Wolf left with a group of Alfjarun trailing behind him, waving to their families as they went. Wolf called out on the wind for his brother and sister, Coyote and Tiger, to join him on the journey. They came, each of them taking a similar form to the first-people and for many weeks they traveled through valley and across desert until they reached the wide flat lands of the plains.

Their days passed in contentment. Tiger taught them how to fashion spears from sharp sticks and flints. Coyote taught them how to read the land to find targets for the hunt, and how to set traps to capture prey. Wolf taught them songs and the pleasure of telling stories, and Wolf was happy to be with his siblings and his people.

The plains were vast and wilder then. The Alfjarun hunted and traveled from the cold of the north, where they would huddle at night to keep warm, all the way to the heat of the south, where it was too hot to travel or hunt in the day. As time passed, it was natural for the Alfjarun to find affinity with one of the three Children. The strongest fighters gathered around Tiger, ever eager to hunt or wrestle with each other to see who was the fiercest. The brightest, who thought of all, not only themselves, were attracted to Wolf. And those who found that they were tired of work and of being told what to do, and those who felt that they were not fully appreciated, found a welcome ear for their complaints in the form of Coyote.

It happened on one day that a woman named Shaken, moved by a desire in her heart for one of the hunters, who was partnered with another, spoke to Coyote. Why shouldn't she be happy when others were? Why did they have what she wanted? Other Alfjarun heard Shaken's conversation with Coyote; and they too voiced discontent with their lot. Another man had a better spear. One coveted the headdress of another. The litany of complaints was long. Coyote considered carefully what they said, for he was of two minds regarding how to advise them. Coyote knew that the others had worked hard for their achievements, but he also harbored his own complaints. His jealousy had burned a hole in his heart; and while he had forgotten it for a time, back in the company of his brother and sister it flared with a terrible pain.

"Friends," he said sweetly. "This is nothing to fret over. When night comes, simply take what you want. If they are truly your friends, then they will be glad to share."

Night came and the followers of Coyote snuck through the camp seeking the objects of their desire. Shaken lay with the hunter she coveted. Headdress, spear, shiny rocks, and warm cloak— all disappeared throughout the night. When light came and the thefts were discovered, there was confusion and bewilderment. Never had the Alfjarun been subject to such trickery. Those who had been wounded thought there must have been magic involved to explain such things. Only when they moved to depart were the burglars discovered, proudly displaying their new belongings. The followers of the Tiger were angry and confronted those of the Coyote.

Fights broke out and for the first time Alfjarun fought Alfjarun with weapons. For the first time, the first-people were killed in combat.

Wolf returned from scouting to scenes of bedlam; and he wept. He threw himself between those who fought. His fists were unmindful of side, focused solely on restoring peace. He demanded to know what was happening and even those Alfjarun who were close to Coyote could not bear the looks of anger and grief on Wolf's face, and so they told the truth.

Wolf turned on Coyote. "Is it true, brother?"

Coyote felt the eyes of his brother and sister, and those of the first-people, all looking in judgement at him. What right did they have to judge him? He was their elder. "It is true, Wolf. I am sorry."

The air shimmered around the man Wolf as he changed, becoming once again the great grey Wolf. He snarled, teeth bared. He leapt at Coyote, who changed into his animal form also; and the two rolled in the dust, biting and snarling and raking their claws against each other. Blood flowed from deep wounds and the earth shook with the fury of their attacks. But Wolf was bigger and stronger than Coyote, and ultimately Wolf stood over Coyote's unprotected neck. But Wolf did not strike because he loved all his family, and the piteous look on Coyote's face stayed his attack. Seizing the moment, Coyote kicked and freed himself from Wolf, running off to the west.

Wolf ordered Tiger to capture him for Tiger was the best of all hunters. Next, he looked upon the first-people, divided into their camps, and in his anger, he blamed them for succumbing to Coyote's enticements and creating the conflict with his brother.

"You are all to blame," he called. "Here you shall stay, on

the plains, until I return. Only these poor men and women whose flesh has been sundered will see the mountain again."

Wolf picked up the dead, five in all, and carried them over his shoulder across the plains and to the west, leaving the first-people behind. Where the plains ended and the desert began, the anger that had been brewing inside Wolf boiled over. He stamped his foot against the bare earth and it split. A huge tear ripped apart the land for as far as he could see. Wolf bellowed back to the first-people, "You will forever stay on the plains."

Wolf traveled fast to the mountain, where the Alfjarun were happy to see him until they saw his burden. Tears flowed like rivers from both those who had lost their children and the rest of the first people as they learned of what had happened. Wolf lay the bodies in the same place where he had proudly presented the first-children to the other Children. He called a meeting once more and all came. Tiger too, dragging behind her the bound Coyote.

"You are here to answer for your actions," said Wolf.

"You are mistaken, brother, about where the ill lies," whined sly Coyote. "Yes, I did speak to some and told them to take what they need. I thought family and friends were supposed to share. I never told them to harm anyone. It was the hunters, followers of Tiger, who started the killing. It is there you should focus your wrath."

Wolf looked at Tiger and sadness enveloped his heart; for though he knew Coyote cast those words to sow discord, there was nonetheless truth to them.

"I shall address Tiger after you have been punished."

Coyote cowered. "Don't kill me, brother. I...I fear Locusts."

"Never would I kill one of the Children. But still you must be punished."

Wolf took Coyote up in his great jaws and bounded across the desert to the great chasm. He leapt down into the hole, falling for what seemed like days until he landed at the bottom, Coyote still in his grasp. There he threw Coyote against a wall of rock. His eyes clouded by tears of anger and love, he lifted a great boulder and placed it on top of Coyote, pinning him to the ground. "Here you shall stay."

Wolf traveled back to his siblings and found them deep in discussion. He was minded to speak; but before he could do so, Tiger stepped forward.

"I am sorry, brother," she said, her hand on her heart. "I am also to blame, I accept this. I shall leave here and go into the east, for I shall not be able to look upon you without being reminded of my shame." Wolf heard the words, and his heart ached, but he nodded in acceptance. "All I ask is that I may take with me the fallen hunters that lie here. I shall breathe new life into them, and they will follow me." Wolf nodded again, and then Tiger and the two fallen hunters left.

Wolf slumped to the floor, his anger spent as the sun rose over the horizon. Rabbit tried to console him but Wolf would not listen. Calls from outside of the circle attracted their attention and Moga rushed before them. "Something amazing has happened. You must see."

The Children followed the eldest of the first-people as he led them up the mountain to the husk of the Mother Tree. There they saw it—the golden seed cracked open, long green tendrils growing from it up the corpse of the tree. In the darkest of moments, when the Children turned on each other, and Wolf cast out his people, life had begun again.

THE MOTHER TREE GREW AGAIN UNDER THE WATCHFUL care of the first-people of the mountain. Her vines twisted about the dead shell of her former body, growing thick until they touched each other and merged to form new wood.

The dead was reborn.

Sparkles of light danced between her broad leaves, proclaiming her vitality.

Thunderbird came back to roost in the leafy boughs, bringing with her the storms and the rain. The rain lashed down through the foliage, collecting in pools in the leaves that were as big as men until it overflowed down the trunk of the tree. The rainwater ran with the light of the moon down to the ground and then fell from the mountain in great cascades to the valley below. And still the rains came. Rivers formed, snaking out across the world, reaching all the first-people, the water shimmering with the same light that surrounded the Mother Tree.

The first-people of the mountain bathed in the cascades; and they, along with all those who drank from the new rivers, felt an awakening. Magic had entered the earth. The Alfjarun, for the first time, realized they had a soul. Not only the first-people were affected. New creatures burst from the waters; strange beasts never before seen. Winged lizards larger than trees. Amalgams of tigers and hawks; chickens and snakes; moose and apes. Great shambling creatures, and tiny fairies. Humble beasts of the world drank from the waters too, and those that did were touched with awareness. Some changed and became something more than they had been. They took on the form of the first-people, and they flocked to the Children, and worshiped them.

It had been a long time since Wolf had imprisoned Coyote and Tiger had left. And he had been stricken with despair for all of that long time. He isolated himself from those he loved. But the rains washed away his sadness, and his heart was filled with joy to see new creatures on the plains, so much so that he traveled to visit the Alfjarun for the first time in many seasons. The first-people Wolf had left stranded on the plains had splintered into the first of the clans that we know today. Wolf, Tiger, and Coyote; though they would fracture many more times over the years. Wolf called out on the wind and summoned the clans to meet with him, to come back together once more.

Under the brightness of Phoenix, the Alfjarun saw Wolf and at his back were companions he had gathered on his journeys. One was half buffalo and half man. The other a giant beaver with the head of a lizard. The first-people wept to see Wolf return to them. He embraced each of them in turn, his sadness apparent at their sorry state. But Wolf knew what to do.

"My people. Once I had a plan for you to learn from the other Children, so that you would master this world and show my siblings the joy in life. I say that now is the time for us to do this. Stay here with me and learn and then you may depart."

So the first-people stayed; and to begin their studies, Wolf taught them all he knew. He taught them how to hunt, although he was not as great a fighter as his sister Tiger, or as adept at setting traps as Coyote. Wolf taught them how to build shelters and homes within which they could rest as families. He also taught the clans about magic and the songs and incantations through which they could master the energy that now coursed through the world.

Wolf called on the wind to summon his brothers and sisters. Phoenix came early one morning and taught the Alfjarun to master fire. Eagle showed them how to see prey from afar and taught them the joy of singing on the wind. Orca came up the great river of Umnahack and taught the Alfjarun how to fish. Rabbit came too and showed them how to dig in the earth for strange rocks that could be melted and cooled into weapons stronger than stone, but the Alfjarun did not like to be underground and so Rabbit left with her lessons unheard and a desire to create a people who would follow her teachings.

Wolf was proud of the first-people and their dedication to learning. When the last of the Children left, their teachings complete, Wolf sent the first-people away with a song of celebration, though once he was alone, he was stricken by a sadness once more. It took many moons for Wolf to understand his melancholy. He realized eventually that he missed his brother. At once, Wolf bounded away to the great chasm, leaping to the bottom to find Coyote still pinned beneath the great boulder.

"Brother," he said. "I have missed you."

"I, too," said Coyote in return. "I have thought much on what I did and I am sorry."

Wolf nodded. Those were the words he wanted to hear. He took the boulder in his great jaws and shattered it like a piece of sun-hardened clay. Coyote leapt to his feet and stretched the kinks from his body, delighted to be free.

"Come," said Wolf, "I have something to show you."

And Wolf led Coyote to the plains and showed him what the Alfjarun had become. Clans bound by family, living their lives according to the teachings of the Children. Coyote was impressed although jealous at his exclusion.

"These are great gifts that you and our brothers and sisters have given the first-people. I only wish that I too could teach them."

Wolf smiled. "Your words make me glad. Travel to the clans and show them the best of you. Teach them how to trap and be wary of greater beasts. Show them how to bear great burdens and to be inquisitive. Take care to hide your worst instincts. I will not have my people tainted again." With those words, Wolf returned to the people of the mountain for he had not seen them for a long time and had much to teach them.

Coyote traveled the plains, visiting all the clans. He was welcomed with open arms by all except those from the Wolf clan, who were still mindful of the last time Coyote had been with the Alfjarun. Coyote taught them his tricks and showed them how, through hardship and abstinence, they could learn their true calling. And so the tradition of the Quana was created for all those who come of age.

Coyote told the Alfjarun of his travels and of how his desire to see new things had led him to explore the world. He told stories of great forests filled with creatures never seen before on the plains and of a great ocean where fish greater than the largest longhouse swam the waters. Beyond that, he told of more lands that were home to no people, just the beasts that called them home. In each place Coyote visited, his words caused a desire to wander in some, for the Alfjarun had a little of Coyote in them and many dreamed of seeing these new lands. As Coyote traveled east, many of the first-people followed him, though Coyote tried to send them home, fearful of what his brother might say, but they would not listen. Coyote fled into the forest and those Alfjarun with inquisitive hearts followed him.

Wolf came back to the plains and found his people diminished. Those who had stayed behind to live, and hunt and love, told him that Coyote had taken away their children and Wolf howled with despair. Coyote, far, far away at the other side of the forest, near the end of the land, heard the howl and knew that he would never be able to return home. Wolf in his sadness wasn't sure what to do. Torn between taking his own life to avoid harming his brother again and releasing his tears and weeping until he drowned the world. Wolf sighed as he realized what he must do. He resolved to stop the Alfjarun from leaving the plains and so he once more took the form of a wolf, but one much greater than the world had ever seen. So lengthy was the wolf that he stretched from the seas of the south, to where the world became cold. He lay down, creating a barrier separating the plains from the forest. Slowly, he turned to stone.

Eagle watched her brother's actions; and as he lay down to slumber, she roosted in his highest peaks, there to protect him. And still the Wolf wept. In the lee of the mountains he had become, strange creatures lived, fed by the streams of one of the Children's tears.

And so ended the days of the Children walking with the Alfjarun. All except Locusts of course.

And what of Wolf?

He lies there still. The Great Spine Mountains.

~

Is Wolf still alive?

I don't know, little one. I don't think so. But he is still with us in some ways. For when he sacrificed himself to protect his people, we Alfjarun became blessed by the spirits of our ancestors. We know Wolf loved all of his family and believed that nothing was more important. So when he left us, he parted the veil to the hunting grounds so our ancestors might watch over us. What is more, it is Wolf's magic that gives one person in each clan the gift of a spirit animal.

And what about those who live on the mountain? Are they dead too?

Oh no. The first-people of the mountain live there still, tending to the Mother Tree as she grows. Only one fruit is ever born by each tree; and on the day it falls to the ground, its golden seed spilling on verdant green grass way up in the clouds, Locusts come again. The first-people do not mourn when the tree dies, because they know she will come again from the golden seed, forever until the day the world ends. Thunderbird roosts still in her branches when she is not bringing the great black life-giving storms to the plains. Thunderbird gazes out over the many miles to where the Eagle looks back from her perch atop the body of her brother.

No one from the clans of the plains has seen the Alfjarun of the mountain since Wolf split the earth in his anger at Coyote, or at least none that I know have returned to tell the tale. But we have heard stories over the years. From travelers, visitors who may have been Children in disguise, telling us of how the Children kept their promise to their brother and traveled to the Alfjarun of the mountain to teach them what they knew. Rabbit, Orca, Eagle. Even Tiger.

What about Coyote? Did he ever go back?

Yes, Coyote travels each time the golden seed cracks. We always know when Coyote is abroad on the plains, on his way to keep his promise, for he sows discord amongst the clans. But whenever Coyote reaches the tree he lies there, staring at her forlornly, wishing he could rediscover his initial wonder of the world, and regain the trust of his family.

Now, hush, little one. I can hear the guard's approach and I do not want to be beaten this night for talking after curfew. My bones are too old to heal quickly.

Just one more question...

Quickly then, child.

Why have the Children forsaken us?

They haven't. They gave us strong backs and resilient minds. And one day, I know that Wolf, in whatever form, will free us. Now sleep!

PROFIT AND PLAIN SAILING

The Shards.

A low-down collection of scum from all over the Jeweled Continent in a handful of rough-built towns, all coated in a never-ending deluge of drizzle and fog. And Port, the largest town on the islands, with such a highly original name, was the worst.

But Vin Kolsen wouldn't have it any other way.

Port was his kind of place. A place where there was no law—except that of the rabble—and no taxes, although the prices reflected more than a little bit of a risk-adjusted premium. He'd been there three or four times in the couple of years since becoming Captain of the Juniper. Every time, it had felt like coming home. Like being around *his* people. There was plenty of booze, good crew to be found (assuming you could get them off the booze), and lots of local women who had grown up on the island unencumbered by notions of marriage and propriety.

And today, as Kolsen walked through the muddy, churned-up street, past the meager shop-fronts and roughest inns, the sun shone uncharacteristically down on his red-coated self.

He took that as an omen. A sign of good luck for his wish to share a golden business opportunity.

The postings had been up for a few days all around Port, hand-written by himself as he didn't trust the penmanship of anyone else on his crew, advertising the meeting that would start in a few short hours.

Tired of capturing shipments of tea and spices?
Wonder where all of the gold is?
Join Captain Vin Kolsen at The Squeaky Tiller to learn of an Exciting Opportunity!!
6th bell, Twelfth day.

There are certain taverns that cover the floor in sawdust to soak up the dropped litter of drinking and of the fights that it spawns. The Squeaky Tiller was not such a place. Sawdust was too good for it. The ship planked floor was sticky with the accumulated coatings of the years, and the accompanying odor was strangely welcoming once you got used to it. It was mid-afternoon, so the bar was only half full, with a few empty tables around the cleared area that passed as a stage at the far end of the room. Kolsen wandered over to Rosita, the already half-cut landlady. The years had not been kind to her, but many of the locals told some wild tales about her, so at least she had earned those wrinkles and gaps in her smile. They engaged in a little idle chit-chat while Rosita poured him a good measure of rum, resting her sagging chest on the long wooden bar which had been part of a ship long ago.

"Do you think many are going to turn up?" he asked her

finally, getting to the source of his concern. He expected that most captains would be too proud to follow him, and that, he could live with. What would be a knife to the guts would be if *no one* turned up to hear what he had to say.

"There's a few 'ere already." She nodded in different directions of the room as she worked through them. "There's Behler and Crull. Westrum's in the corner over there. And I don't think they're here for the floor show..." Rosita shook her head as she looked at the wiry man on the stage.

Kolsen smiled, momentarily comforted that there would at least be some audience, and it was only a little past fifth bell. He picked up the clay cup, left a handful of copper pieces behind, and wandered over to a table at the front near the stage. At first sight, he thought he must be watching the world's dullest mime act; because the young man with the wild hair and bones sticking out everywhere was not speaking. He seemed to be mainly paying attention to the floor as he occasionally waved his arms. Only when he took a seat did Kolsen notice the mice scurrying on the floor around the man.

The mice leap-frogged over each other. They climbed on top of one another to form a rodent pyramid. They squeaked in time to the man's gesticulations, producing a passable, if extremely quiet, rendition of Sullen Sally. For the big finale, the man pulled a cat from a carpet bag by the wall. It didn't look happy, its tail outstretched, twitching, as it hissed at Kolsen and the other few members of the audience. *Did he end the act by feeding the mice to the cat?* The performer placed the cat on the floor and snapped his fingers. The cat lay down on all fours, resting its chin on the floor, and opened its mouth wide. A whistle from the showman, and the mice lined up in an orderly fashion, putting Kolsen's own crew to shame, before each mouse in turn ran over to the cat and stood in its mouth for a few seconds. The cat's eyes tracked each mouse as it danced on its tonguc before running away to leap off a chair and into the carpet bag. The cat moved not a muscle even once. That cat wouldn't be much use aboard ship; but it occurred to Kolsen that if you had someone like Mouseman here on board to charm the rodents over the side, then a cat would be completely unnecessary.

Mouseman picked up the cat once all the mice had disappeared, and put it back into the bag as well. He turned back to Kolsen and the handful of others who were watching and bowed. Kolsen found himself clapping. *How had he done that?* Kolsen was just getting to his feet to talk to the animal trainer when he felt a hand clap on his shoulder.

"Kolsen. I thought I might see you around when I spied *The Dolphin's Prize* in a berth."

It was Captain Nini Gilstrap of *The Scythe.* The woman who had rescued him, Mareth, and the boy Karr, who just so happened to be standing behind his old captain.

"Look who I bumped into, Captain Kolsen. I told her you'd be here."

Kolsen conjured his most charming smile. It was showtime a little earlier than he expected. "Captain Gilstrap, it is good to see you!" He clapped her on the arm as if they were old comrades. "But it's the *Juniper* now. Best corsair ship in the North Sea."

"Hah! *The Scythe* is faster than that barge."

"Speed isn't everything. Not when I've got that ballista."

She looked at him agog. "You managed to keep that? How?"

"Cost almost as much as the ship, but it's been worth it."

Gilstrap narrowed her eyes as she looked at him. "You

were a lucky shit winning that treasure on the way to port, enough to buy the ship. What'd you do? Kiss Atarah's arse hole?"

Kolsen threw his hands up in the air in mock surrender. "It's not my fault I'm blessed. In fact, I'm here today because I want to share that blessing with any that will join me." He looked over Gilstrap's shoulder and sized up the gaggle of other captains walking in. "I hope you'll stick around and listen. See if it's something I can tempt you with." He winked, smoothed the wrinkles out of his coat, picked up his cup that Rosita had just refilled, and sauntered over to the stage.

"Thank you for coming, gentlemen. And ladies of course. Let me assure you that drinks are on me once I've finished talking. And I promise to be brief. I want to tell you about an opportunity, that I hope you will allow me to share with you." He paused, scanning the faces that watched him with vague interest.

"There is a land, far from here, full of silver and gold. And Pyrfew is mining and transporting it back across the ocean. Me and my crew have raided Pyrfew's ships and returned to The Shards with precious metals in our pockets." Or at least their pockets were full when they had arrived. Given Kolsen only kept a quarter of the spoils, and that had to cover ship expenses, with the rest shared between the crew, he was certain that most of the treasure was now in the hands of various barkeeps, whores, card sharks and tailors (pirates were, in his experience, like preening birds of paradise).

"Bullshit. It's too far." Someone heckled.

"It's true that it is far, but fortune favors the first. I have walked the Wild Continent, and a wild place it is. Thick forest, mountains that scrape the sky, beasties that lie in wait in the dark, and incomprehensible savages who will trade supplies for worthless trinkets."

"So, if it's so fucking great, why are you telling us?"

"The Pyrfew ships are not packed with marines or fighters, but they travel in convoy, with a single escort ship from their navy. We've had to lurk, waiting for a ship to be separated in a storm. We can't take a ship in convoy with the escort attacking our rear, and if we take the navy's ship first then the rest will be long gone. But if we work together, we can take them all at once."

He could see the cogs turning in the heads of his audience, chins being rubbed, fingers being used for counting as rough sums were tallied.

"What's the split?"

"I take a double share of everything for me and my crew, but otherwise split evenly among whoever joins me. *The Juniper* leaves in two days, what say you all?"

"I'm in," called Captain Crull. Not surprising but not terribly inspiring either. Crull was a particularly nasty corsair who had a higher price on his head from Pienza than his ship was worth. But it was a start.

Some others answered with their feet, pushing their chairs back with an audible scrape before heading out the door. More than a couple stopped at the bar on the way out for one last necked finger of spirits on his tab. *Fucking pirates.*

"What about you Captain Gilstrap?"

"It's obvious you've done well for yourself, Kolsen. However you've done that. But it all sounds too good to be fucking true. And that's a long way to go if it doesn't work out, and a long time without seeing my kid. So I am out, but thank you for the drink." She raised her cup in salute.

"I respect your decision. Family is important." That particular piece of news had been surprising; many pirates had partners and children scattered throughout the Shards but he didn't know Gilstrap was one of them. He filed it away in case that would be useful in the future. But he also needed to stop the public rejection. If too many said no then it would become a cascade. "Think on my offer. Drink and enjoy each other's company. I will be around to answer your questions."

He stepped away from the stage and over the next hour or so made his way around the room. He got a few "fuck offs," one man laughed in his face, and Westrum told him, "I wouldn't follow you even if I really needed a crap and you were the only one who knew the way to the shitter." Pirates could be arseholes.

But there were a couple of maybes and one more to commit: Maldonado, or Trueblood as she liked to be called now. She was originally from Ioth; reputation was that she had been a merchant captain before one day she decided she could get richer a lot faster by just taking the ship and the cargo than ferrying it around the Sapphire sea.

Kolsen ordered another drink. As he took a swig, he saw the Mouseman getting ready to go on stage again. He wasn't sure what it was about him that piqued his interest, but Kolsen called the man over to talk.

"How long did it take you train the animals to do that?" He asked, jerking his thumb toward the stage and the memory of the show.

"I didn't train them. Caught them yesterday. Haven't been here long," mumbled Mouseman as he avoided eye contact. Kolsen eyed him warily, puzzled.

"Then how do you do it?"

"Alchemy. Potions. Magic." Mouseman shrugged and made to walk off.

Kolsen reached out to grab the performer's shoulder and arrest his departure. "How would you like a job?" offered Kolsen, his gut taking over.

"No, thank you. I just need to get some money together and then I'll go to the mainland. I'm not a pirate."

Kolsen clapped him on the arm and smiled. "Well, if you change your mind, come find me on the *Juniper*. We leave in two days."

Axe Blade, a tub of a ship owned by Captain Crull, had already left its berth and waited out in deeper waters for Kolsen and the two other ships to join it. It would be four ships that would make the long journey across the ocean to the coast of the Wild Continent: the *Juniper* of course; the aforementioned *Axe Blade; The Gathering Storm,* captained by Tawfeeq Behler, originally a native of Jabruacor; and a sleek vessel called *Matilda*, owned by Captain Khristina Trueblood.

Three more captains, three more ships. Maybe not as many as he had imagined in dreams where ship after ship from the Shards followed in his wake, but it would be good enough for now. Kolsen didn't know much about the individual captains. Their conversations so far had been brief and perfunctory around the logistics of the journey. Time would tell how well they worked together. And he knew absolutely nothing about their crews.

The Matilda was pulled out of the dock next, three rowboat tugs manned by the strongest of Port, straining to get the ship out to waters where its sail could be raised and they could move on. Kolsen tapped his foot on the deck, impatient to be off but knowing it would be another hour until the *Juniper* would be freed. So he paced the ship, making sure that everything was ship-shape. Barrels of water secured. Provisions stacked neatly in crates. The crew's quarters tidy and any new members with a hammock and a place to store their belongings. They may be pirates, but that didn't mean they needed to live like animals. On board ship, it was essential to be orderly.

Kolsen was back on deck as the ropes from the tugboats were being secured to his ship when he heard a commotion from the dock. Bored and wondering if there might be a little excitement, he wandered over to take a look.

Two men were running along the shore, shouting at someone ahead of them. Kolsen scanned the dirt road, looking to see what they were chasing, only for his eyes to land on a wiry man hastening down the wooden dock toward him. Intrigued, Kolsen moved to the top of the gangplank just as the pursued figure, out of breath and carrying a black leather bag, skidded to a halt at the foot of it. It was the Mouseman.

"Captain," panted the bedraggled man. "I've changed my mind. I'd like to come with you."

Kolsen regarded him and looked back at his pursuers, who had now slowed to a walk, perhaps having grown mindful of assessing whether their quarry had a bunch of friends to back him up. "What did you do?"

"Er... It was the dog fights, Captain. Thought I would earn more money there. Their champion dog is dead."

"By the cat?" he asked, his eyebrows rising as he remembered the docile creature from a few days before.

"No, the mice." Kolsen laughed. "They aren't very happy about it."

"Where are the animals now?" Kolsen didn't see the carpet bag.

"I had to leave them behind. But I have all of my equipment." The Mouseman held up the black leather bag for Kolsen to see; it clinked from the sound of glass things knocking against each other.

The kid was skinny and pale, he didn't look like he'd spent any time working on a ship at sea, and a part of Kolsen asked what use he would be. Could be he would just be another mouth at the *Juniper's* teat, draining supplies. But his gut told him the Mouseman might be useful. Smarts was not too easy to come across in pirates. And besides, if he was a waste of space, Kolsen could always throw him overboard later as a gift to Atarah.

"Welcome aboard, man. You're just in time."

~

THE SWORD WHISTLED OVER HIS HEAD AS HE DROPPED INTO a crouch. He popped back up before simultaneously stamping on the marine's foot and bashing the hand guard of his saber into his opponent's face. The marine fell to the deck before his teeth had finished pirouetting in the air. Kolsen moved on.

A woman, wearing the same green leather armor as her compatriots—painted with gold decoration that seemed to indicate rank—spun with a boat hook clasped in both hands. She'd been one of those trying to push the *Juniper* away as it got close enough to board. She'd also been one of the lucky ones to stay clear of the ballista. But her luck had run out, because Kolsen really fucking hated those boat hooks.

The woman stepped forward, jabbing at Kolsen, and he parried the thrust. He tried to move in closer but she brought the long weapon against him each time. *Now this is just getting annoying.*

"Karr!" He shouted, without taking his eyes off his target. Kolsen gave it one last attempt to get within striking range but it was no good. And then the arrow took her in the eye.

That boy was a scary-good shot. And to think that it was only a couple of years ago that he'd thought that Karr was a mewling waste of space, at best good enough to be eaten as he and Mareth and the boy were adrift on the North Sea. Well, that was one thing he had to remember to thank the bard for. If he ever saw him again. Which he doubted, because he didn't expect Mareth to be sailing at leisure in the waters off the coast of the Wild Continent any time soon.

The female Pyrfew marine fell; and within minutes the remaining green and gold fighters had given up. His first mate, a Skarian man whose real name was Edvard (disclosed one night after too much rum), but who preferred to go by Red Ted, rounded up the soldiers at the far end of the deck. Kolsen stepped over a few bodies to see how the other captains were doing with the remains of the convoy.

There were two Pyrfew ships a quarter mile or so apart. One had been engaged by *Matilda*, while the other had *The Gathering Storm* and *Axe Blade* up against its bows. Fuck. There were four ships in this convoy, where did the other one go? They were going to need to work on coordinating a little better in the future.

"Shall we make an offering, Captain?" called Red Ted, eyeing the captives.

"Not right now. Tie them up. Keep them under guard and strip the ship for anything useful. I need to meet with the other captains. Karr!"

"Yes, Captain," came a voice from the rigging of the *Juniper*.

"Get me a longboat and let's go see how we did."

The ocean was relatively calm, and by the time they made it to *The Gathering Storm*, another long boat arrived from *Matilda*. Kolsen was half way up the ladder when he was hailed.

"Oi, Kolsen! I thought you said we were going to be up to our arseholes in gold and silver." Crull's eyes bulged in his red face as he hung over the side of the ship to yell.

He rolled his eyes, having a sneaking suspicion of what was coming. "Let's discuss it on deck, like *civilized* thieves."

A few minutes later and the conclave of captains had found a small cabin to discuss things privately. They all looked like thunder.

"So, what did we get?" he asked.

"Food. Swords. Arrows."

"Iron bars, and what looks like a disassembled foundry." Behler's eyes narrowed as he stared intently at Kolsen.

"Well, that's a lot better than what was on my bloody ship," said Trueblood, her hands on her hips. "It's full of families, kids, women. Where's the fucking gold, Kolsen?"

"I think you'll remember we got a hold full of silver on that ship last week." He nodded at his own words and the other three slowly followed suit. It had been just the single vessel they'd managed to capture before—their teamwork on the first time of asking having left much to be desired—allowing three other ships to escape. "I think I also remember telling you all that we're only supposed to attack ships that are leaving the Wild Continent, not going to it. What were you doing, Behler?"

Tawfeeq Behler shrugged. "Alright. I got a bit over excited and didn't realize where they were heading. So, what do we do now?"

"We let them go. After we've taken what might be useful for us. Leave them enough food and water to get where they are going, and all being well these ships will be headed back to Pyrfew in a moon or so with plenty of goodies ripe for the taking. But I'll sink the navy ship as an offering to Atarah." Each of the captains pulled at their right ear lobe at the mention of the goddess of the sea. Nice to see they were a superstitious bunch.

"Speaking of water," said Crull. "We're running out, and there's not even any rain to catch. What do we do about that?"

"Smart man," said Kolsen, tapping his temple with his finger. "I have been giving that some thought too. It's about time we set up a base of operations. And I believe that I know the perfect island for it. I stopped there before to forage for supplies. Probably a few days southwest of here, and close enough to the mainland where it will be easy for us to hit any shipments, but not close enough that they'll be able to find us. The island has two forested peaks and there's a cove there that will be perfect. Captains, I think it's time we founded New Port."

~

New Port began as nothing much more than a beach where the four ships threw a party for their crews, once the important task of hauling barrels of water from a nearby waterfall was complete anyway. It was an uproarious affair, something that would be the stuff of legend. The crews came together and mingled in the way that pirates know best; fucking and fighting. And for a while that's all New Port was, a littered beach and a place to store the more mundane elements of their recent haul—things that could be useful when they did actually get around to building something.

The next time they returned to New Port was with a healthy haul of silver, but by then the rum casks were all dry. And when they actually had something to celebrate, there was nothing for the crews to waste their hard-earned spoils on. There were some calls to head back to the Shards, even though the crossing could take months, and that's when Kolsen knew things tottered on a knife edge. If everyone went home now, then he would hardly be ahead of where he was when he started the whole escapade.

So Kolsen set the pirates to work.

Crews were formed to clear the forest of both the tall palm trees and the trees with wide boughs laden with sticky fruit. Other crews foraged for fruits and berries, chasing away families of little monkeys to steal their sweet treats. Wild pigs were hunted and construction started. And fittingly, the first building to be constructed was a tavern, initially little more than a bar covered by a vast thatched roof. A man from Crull's ship by the name of Loftus had been a brewer in the past, and Kolsen had him promoted to Lubricator-in-Chief, ably assisted by Mouse (as he was now known), the animal entertainer from the Shards who had proven to be a fairly miserable seaman. Vats of the sweet fruit were mashed and boiled up, and in a few short weeks everyone was getting drunk again and the shares that each man or woman was allotted was being sold for ten times the price of what it would be in the Shards. Mouse once again resumed his shows, though this time with monkeys and what appeared to Kolsen to be considerably more joy than before.

But no one complained, because there was more than enough silver to go around. What you spent on drink you might win back from dice or arm wrestling. Even though the silver was *officially* changing hands faster than the clap, that was more difficult in practicality as all of the silver was cast into bars. So, to work around it, a complex system of proxy papers that divvied up their shares had been devised.

Over the months that followed, Loftus and a few others stayed back at New Port, keeping the supply of 'juice' flowing, still earning their share in a much less dangerous way as the raids continued. And after each successful raid, Kolsen led his small fleet back to New Port, and hosted the other captains for a return dinner on the *Juniper* while the crews enjoyed themselves.

He was proud of his quarters. They had been reserved for the highest paying guests when the ship was still *The Dolphin's Prize*, the Captain's cabin being much smaller and a deck below. But now they were his, and large enough to house a bed, a wardrobe, a desk, and a table where he met with his captains, all of the furniture of exquisite Pienzan craftsmanship. Karr attended them, bringing a dinner of fried fish and dumplings. As with all of these celebratory dinners, Kolsen had delved into his own supply of aged red wine, something he had been fearful of losing when the booze had run out.

Kolsen raised his glass and looked at the three other captains in turn. "Congratulations to another successful venture. May Atarah bless those we lost and piss on the bastards who did them in."

Crull laughed a laugh that would curdle milk. Kolsen had never met a man who found death quite so humorous. "That's pretty fucking likely as you threw them overboard."

He returned a smile. "It's always good to remember an offering to She who rules the Seas." And for his aunt, he thought. He wouldn't be there if it wasn't for that Selkie Witch. He'd promised to bring chaos to the seas in her name, and he liked to think he was doing a pretty good job of it. And getting rich in the process. Win-win all around.

They clinked their glasses together, though Behler was off a beat. Kolsen turned his attention to the Captain of *The Gathering Storm*. He didn't want any black clouds lingering; best to blow it away. One way or the other.

"Is something troubling you, Tawfeeq?"

The Captain grimaced, as if he was wrestling with the unspoken words. Kolsen didn't think it was from being shy; this one was a cunning one. It was more likely he was wondering how much of his hand to show. "Why did you let the slaves go? We could have sold them in Trima."

Ahhh, that's what was bothering him. Kolsen was not surprised. The last convoy they had intercepted had been different. Four ships in all, one navy, one full of silver, one escaped; but this time the last ship was full of people. People of the Wild Continent, or Alfjarun as they were apparently called by the one captive who could speak Common. They were stacked in the hold like crates for shipment, chained to shelves above floors so full of people that there wasn't room to move. The place stank of piss and shit and they had hardly eaten in the few days they had been at sea. Kolsen had seen his fair share of ghastliness as a pirate, he'd done some pretty nasty things too, but this horrified him. He had considered his brief status as a galley slave, and realized that he'd been lucky compared to those poor souls.

"Firstly," he began, in answer to the question, "we are a long way from Trima. I don't know how those green and gold bastards planned to keep them alive all the way to Pyrfew, but I don't see how you wouldn't be knee-deep in carcasses before long. Secondly, we took three ships and now they are ours. More crew to fill those we have lost. More ships so we can plunder more treasure. Many of them know the seas here, and I am sure they will learn how to sail our ships quite quickly. And thirdly, those that don't want to sail will stay here and build New Port. We need to have more than a juice shack."

"Probably doesn't hurt that they look at you as if the sun shines out of your arse either," said Trueblood. And while Behler undoubtedly had a head full of schemes, it was Trueblood he had to be wary of keeping onside. She was the one with the brains.

"And doesn't it?"

Kolsen laughed first and the others joined him, banging their glasses together in a more meaningful salutation.

"I give them their lives and they give me their service." Or at least, he hoped so anyway. "And as I am feeling especially grateful today, I have gifts for you." Trueblood and Behler exchanged glances, and Crull scowled like he was about to receive a shit blossom. "The three ships we took. They are yours when we return to the Shards for you to sell or do with as you wish, and in the mean-time you will take a share. All I ask is that you hand pick a few of your own to man those ships and teach our new recruits all that it means to be a corsair."

The looks of shock that greeted him were perfect.

"What about you?" asked Crull, his surprise still tempered with distrust.

"There will be more than enough for me in the future. I said I would make you rich and I try very hard not to be a liar. All I ask is that—"

"We call you King?" laughed Trueblood, jabbing Behler with her elbow.

"Well I was just going to ask for you to continue to trust me, but that does have a certain ring to it."

FOR THE FIRST TIME IN A LONG WHILE, KOLSEN AND THE crew of the *Juniper* did not join in the boarding of their prey that day. They'd softened-up the lead ship from afar with Red Ted ordering the ballista to fusillade the deck, and the arrows shot from the rigging had done a decent job too. But he had left the close up fighting to the newly formed crews of the *Liberty*, *Opportunity* and *Independence*, along with *Axe Blade*. Even though no-one had yet to call him King, he had taken the honor of renaming their new vessels, and he tried to impart the meaning in the names he had chosen, but he rather felt that it had fallen on deaf ears.

Fucking pirates. No appreciation of nuance.

It had taken a little while for the Alfjarun crews to become accustomed to sailing their ships, as well as some time to understand how to take another ship at sea. But it was no matter, as they had all the time in the world to train them. Training had been the new ships and their crews against the original four ships, day after day, on an open sea where they felt like the only people in the world. It was a paradise. Food and drink were plentiful. They weren't hunted by the navies of the Sapphire or North Sea realms. The town of New Port was springing up fast around the original juice bar which now had a name—The Green Peaks in honor of the verdantly vegetated twin peaks by the cove they now called home—the freed slaves eager to make places of their own. The forge they had plundered months before was finally assembled and fired-up by Mouse; and even though he was hardly the build of a smith, he was able to train a few others on what to do. And the weather was so much better than the grey smudge that constantly hovered over the Shards.

This had been their first foray out to engage with the Pyrfew vessels, and Kolsen was delighted to see how the new crews had performed. They tore through the Pyrfew marines with a passion borne of a desire for vengeance against the enslavers that was not wise for their long-term health, but it was wholly effective. And even though there had been two navy vessels escorting two laden ships this time—what must be the long-awaited response to their raids—it was a successful day.

When the fighting was over, Kolsen boarded the lead ship and stood before the Alfjarun, bloodied but victorious over the Pyrfew soldiers that were either dismembered on the slippery deck or cowering at the bow. He beckoned to Hunyg, one of the Alfjarun who had learned the common tongue from the Pyrfew administrators who had taken over his home, drawing the man close when he neared. He gestured to what was left of the Pyrfew fighters, dead or alive, and spoke quietly to him. "All of them. Into the sea. For the goddess."

"The Orca?"

"Is that your goddess?" he asked. Hunyg nodded. "We call

her Atarah, but it matters not. For the Orca."

Hunyg turned and spoke to the newly blooded Alfjarun fighters. As Hunyg finished, they smiled and cheered in celebration before beginning their grisly cleanse.

It was three days sail back to New Port, and on the second day Kolsen sent a boat to fetch Hunyg to join him on the *Juniper*. Kolsen wanted to learn more about the Wild Continent, but the first thing he heard was that the Alfjarun were delighted that he knew of their gods. That was somewhat surprising as he hadn't the faintest clue about their gods, but it was quickly apparent that Hunyg was a canny man, telling stories that cast Kolsen in a flattering light. He was someone to keep close. For the rest of the journey, Kolsen made sure to learn what he apparently already knew.

They navigated the final leg of the journey to New Port by the stars, and the lights of his burgeoning town welcomed them as they dropped anchor in the cove. *Give it about an hour and the whole town will be at the Green Tits.* He boarded the first boat to the beach and it was only as he escaped the bustle of the ship and the sound of Red Ted's barked orders that he realized that New Port was quiet. Quiet and pirates didn't go together.

A gaggle of thirty or so people, a mixture of old crew and new, greeted him at the beach— torches in hand, worried looks on their faces. He spied Loftus at the front and strode over to him, his hand on the hilt of his blade. Had Crull or Behler arranged a mutiny? Had those bastards decided to stab him in the back after all he had done for them?

"What's going on?' he demanded.

"Fucking savages came out of the forest a few hours back. Killed Callan and took one of the new boys."

"Which one?"

"Scar, I think 'is name is."

"Skah?" asked Hunyg as he came alongside Kolsen, his eyes darting around the crowd looking for someone in particular. "That boy has no parents. I was caring for him."

Loftus shrugged. "They came out of nowhere. Must have been a hundred, all with spears. They looked at all the new boys and picked Scar. Then they were gone, back into the trees, but they were shouting something as they left. Sounded like 'Towka'."

"Towka?" Hunyg repeated the word to himself. "Was it Taioka?" Loftus shrugged again helplessly and looked at Kolsen, the meaning evident that he didn't really know.

Hunyg turned to face Kolsen. "Taioka is Fire Bird. God of flame and good luck. Captain Kolsen. They are going to burn the boy."

Fuck. How did this uninhabited paradise end up being not so uninhabited after all? How long had whoever-it-was been watching them?

It didn't really matter.

What did matter, was that one of his people were gone, and if he didn't address it, it would be seen as a sign of his weakness by both their attackers and the crew who now looked at him expectantly.

"Nobody attacks my town," he declared loudly. "Bring everyone together. I want defenses organized here and a squad to come with me to get the boy."

~

THE ISLAND ON WHICH THEY FOUNDED NEW PORT WAS approximately tear drop shaped, the top of which curled back on itself creating their sheltered cove under the shadow of the twin green mountains. Kolsen had been all around the island by sea, and saw no sign of any other human or Alfjarun habitation; while they had not explored all of the island, he had no reason to believe that they had neighbors.

That was until the neighbors came around and kidnapped a guest of his.

Kolsen led the way through the dark undergrowth, the light of the dipping moon filtering through the branches overhead, leaving a myriad of shadows that had him constantly on edge. At his side was Hunyg and Red Ted, and behind came two score of handpicked, seasoned and terrible pirates, all doing their best to stay quiet but failing miserably. At least it was not too difficult to miss the path that their neighbors had taken—there had obviously been enough of them to trample the vegetation as they came and went. At least he hoped he was following the path they had taken, trying multiple times to brush away the thought that maybe he was blundering after some terrific beast that was laying in wait for them.

Their way led toward the heart of the island, but before reaching the hill that formed its center, the path curved around to the left and began a gentle descent. All around were the sinister sounds of the night; animals rustling unseen through the undergrowth, the leathery thwack of bat wings as they flew overhead. Kolsen was not a fan. It was a cacophony compared to the quiet night sounds that he was used to; the thud of the waves against the hull of the *Juniper*, married to the creak of wood against wood. The trail ended at an escarpment of bare earth, the ground falling away at a steeper angle where only small trees clung on. It looked like they could get down it, but Kolsen wasn't so sure about how to get back up. But there was no turning back now.

Down they went. More than a couple of pirates skidded down on their arse, careful of not impaling themselves with their swords or accidentally releasing their crossbows. Kolsen tried admirably to stay on his feet, not wanting to dirty his long red coat. The night sky was starting to lighten, but there was no immediately visible trail to follow once they had reached the bottom. After a moment of collective uncertainty, Kolsen plowed ahead again, assuming that there must be some sort of settlement and chances were that it must be close to the coastline, even if they hadn't noticed it before. Soon their blades were in action, cutting away at vines and branches that barred his way, his anger at being put in this position, at someone daring to fuck with his developing plans, finding a temporary release.

Then they were free of the forest, a cliff edge before them, and the sight of the sun peeking over the horizon. The undulating ocean stretched out beautifully before him, the light of dawn bathing it in a soft orange glow. He basked in the sight of the moment, before a tug on his arm from Red Ted directed his attention to where the cliffs stepped down to a bay that curled around, sheltered by a great hill of a rock bigger than three ships. He recognized this place from when they had circled the island at sea. It had been a good option for where they could land, but the fact that this side of the island faced the ocean made it a less desirable place to anchor than the cove where New Port was now situated. When he'd seen it before through his looking glass, it had appeared uninhabited, like the rest of the island, but from this vantage point he saw the small congregation of huts sheltered at the foot of the hill.

"That must be it. Down we go, friends. Be ready for a welcome."

Skirting the edge of the cliff, they descended down to the bay and as stealth was no longer their aim, by the time they neared within a few hundred feet of the little village, the locals were assembling in a dusty dirt square. They gripped long stone-tipped spears probably more used for fishing than fighting. They were a mixture of men, women and older children, more than fifty but less than a hundred. More than his group, but then he didn't intend to fight.

Intimidate. Talk. Get what he wanted. That was the way of a pirate. And he knew his squad looked the right kind of scary; the missing teeth, the curled lip, and what he always found to be the most important thing of any fearsome visage, eyes slightly dead and glassy, like they were eying you up as a butcher regards a side of beef.

Stopping within crossbow distance, Kolsen had his squad line up either side of him, their best snarls already on display.

He nodded to a man that stood by one of their huts and spoke to Red Ted. "See that one there? Hit the wood by the side of him. Just don't fucking accidentally shoot one of them." Red Ted lifted his crossbow, sighted and shot just as he had requested. The crossbow bolt thudded into the hut and the locals ran back to the far side of the empty space near the big rock, shock on their faces. Kolsen nodded in appreciation.

"Hunyg. Translate what I say," he said to his new friend, before shouting out across the space between them and the village. He made a note that he was going to need to start working on speaking the language after he'd got out of this mess. "We don't want to kill you. We are neighbors here. But you took one of ours. We want him back."

A man stepped proudly forward from the group, forgetful that he had just ran away along with everyone else, and brandished his spear in their direction. Kolsen couldn't understand what he was saying so focused his attention on the man's appearance, noting his seal skin trousers and thinking that Aunt Xataniel would be happy for this one to become an offering to the goddess.

"He says that they took him as a prisoner of war to give to the Fire Bird," translated Hunyg. Kolsen knew his interpreter was angry, he'd been venting about the boy the whole walk across the island, but he was happy that Hunyg was controlling his emotions now. There was a job to do, and there would be a right time to be angry. The man with the spear turned and pointed at another man, bent in the back and using his spear to hold himself upright. "He says that one recognized his tattoo as from a tribe they are at war with."

"War? When was this?"

He waited for Hunyg to convey the question as Kolsen scanned the rest of the group. He didn't think there was a fighter among them, they all looked scared shitless, not the type to be at war with anyone. He guessed that the raid on New Port was opportunistic, or a mistake. The old man was the one who looked most defiant, maybe he was behind it. Even the children hid behind their mothers, and he'd seen more than his fair share of young boys who thought they were warriors. One little girl was backing away further to a small dark cave in the rock...

"He says time is not relevant," the words of the elder translated by Hunyg. "The Nawaxowen, the tribe the boy comes from, forced them to flee from their home when he was a child."

"But the boy was not even alive then?" Kolsen asked Hunyg.

Hunyg shrugged. "It does not matter. War is not over

until peace is made." It was interesting to see Hunyg's stance change; it was as if the actions of the pisswater village were understandable now.

"Do you think they realize that these Nawaxowen probably did them a favor by getting them away from Pyrfew?" Hunyg stared blankly back at Kolsen. Apparently, irony was not a big thing on the Wild Continent.

Kolsen turned back to face the leader of the village. "I understand you being at war. And I understand that you want revenge." He paused, waiting for Hunyg to translate, and found his gaze drawn to the small cave once more. There was something about it that looked strange and also extremely familiar, all at the same time. It made him look at the rest of the huge rock behind the village in a different way. The smooth curve of the surface. The symmetry of it that he now only just noticed. It certainly looked like what he thought it was but how could that be? He realized that Hunyg had stopped translating and was looking at him, waiting for further instruction. "But the boy... He is the last of his clan." Kolsen had no clue if this was true but it fit the narrative he wanted to tell. "And so, he is your last chance to make peace. He can stay with you, your guest now. Treat him well, but know that if you come uninvited to my town again, I will take *my* revenge. But if you are good neighbors, we will be good neighbors too."

Hunyg's mouth hung open below a furrowed brow, but Kolsen waved him to get on with his job. Kolsen turned his back on the village of hovels and started back up the hill. "Come on, boys. I'm sure Scar will be perfectly fine. I have something to think on."

KOLSEN PULLED UP HIS TROUSERS AND THEN PULLED ON A boot, flicking off some specks of mud from the night before. He'd dismissed most of the questions from the squad on the way back to New Port with diversions like "it is important to encourage peace with our neighbors", and simply waved away those that approached him when they had returned, heading straight for a boat to take him back to his quarters and his bed.

After getting dressed, he had breakfast in his room and then turned through page after page of the books that he had inherited with the state room, a collection that was supposed to bring wonder of the sea to those who traveled in it. It was after lunch by the time he wandered up on deck and spotted a few idle deck hands to row him ashore. Kolsen strode up the beach, Red Ted getting up from his table at the open-air bar of the Green Peaks to intercept him.

"What's up, boss?"

"Going to see a man about a cat. Keep everyone the fuck away from me, will you?"

"Aye, aye."

New Port was already bigger than the village they had been to the night before, at least thirty rough huts dotted around the clearing they had created behind the beach. He strode with intent to one on the outskirts of the settlement, its location matching its inhabitant. He swept the fragment of sail that was used for a door to one side.

"Mouse. I want to talk to you," he said, as he stuck his head inside. It was not what he expected to see. Inside the small hut, open crates were stacked from floor to high above Kolsen's head, sealed clay jars were grouped in clusters on the floor or any other flat surface, and the animal entertainer—and the most useless pirate he had ever met—was perched on the edge of a palate bed. Mouse had the head of a small monkey in his hand and was administering drop after green drop of some liquid down the creature's throat. Mouse jumped at the interruption, dropping the monkey, who landed on the floor, squatting on its haunches, snarling.

"Captain Kolsen!" he exclaimed, like a boy caught with his hands down his pants by his mother. "What can I do for you?"

Kolsen's eyes narrowed as his gaze went back to all the stuff stacked in Mouse's home, his original purpose for being there slipping his mind for a moment. "Where'd you get all this?"

"I bought it, sir. With my shares. It's all stuff no one else wanted. Tinctures. Ointments. Oils. Containers. Useful things, if you know what to do with them."

"Hmmm," he wondered. He'd have to investigate who was selling this stuff, but for now it was a good enough, though cryptic, answer. "Do you know a lot about creatures?"

"I know a great deal about many things, Captain."

"Good. Put your boots on and come with me. And you can leave that thing here."

The walk back through the forest was quite different in the light of day, and though Kolsen knew he was taking a risk going alone with someone who would be useless in a fight, he was happy not to have to deal with the shadows and sounds of the night. Mouse trudged along behind him as Kolsen's long strides propelled him along the trampled trail they had followed before. There was a sound behind them and he turned, raising the crossbow he carried and ready to stick a bolt in whatever approached.

There was a blur as a small brown creature leapt at

Mouse. *The bloody monkey*. Mouse helped the creature onto his shoulder.

"I told you to leave the little fucker behind," he growled.

"He wants to protect me, Captain. He can't help it." The monkey hissed and Kolsen took a step back. He scowled back at the tiny face, imagining the kind of bite those sharp teeth could do.

Giving up the argument, he continued to lead the way. When they reached the escarpment, he took a different path than the night before. It was slower going, and he had to cut his way through the undergrowth, but he didn't want to be seen. And he wanted a different view. Eventually they reached a point where they had a good view of their neighbors' bay and Kolsen called a halt.

Kolsen pulled his looking glass from where it was tucked into his belt and looked down at the village, seeing signs of indigenous industry. It didn't look like they were planning any further attacks. He scanned the strange looking rocky hill, seeing signs of a bonfire that still smoldered at its peak, something blackened and twisted at its center. *Looks like the boy met the fire bird after all.* He beckoned Mouse over to join him and handed him the looking glass.

"Take a look at that hill down there. Really closely. Look past the patches of vegetation and focus on the ridges around the edge. How the curvature looks symmetrical. That cave at the front that looks odd, and how there's another one on that corner. What does it remind you of?"

The looking glass traced the air as Mouse followed his orders silently. He brought the instrument down from his face and tilted his head in thought.

"What does it look like?" asked Kolsen in exasperation.

"Well, sir. It looks like a turtle shell." Kolsen laughed and slapped his thigh in delight. "But it's huge..."

"I know!"

"But I didn't think they really existed..."

"Me neither. Haven't seen one before, but certain events have opened my eyes to the possibility that there are plenty of things I haven't seen before. What do you think? Ready to take your act up a notch?"

"Is it alive?"

"Don't know. It might be just hibernating. If it's alive, could you wake it up and control it?"

The smile that slowly grew over Mouse's face scared Kolsen a little, the mad little eyes sparking at the possibility. "The theory should be the same. If I can administer the potions directly into the blood. I'll need some supplies..."

"Whatever you need." Kolsen paused, momentarily uncertain about his own plan. "Are you sure?"

"Oh, yes," said Mouse nodding, the monkey on his shoulder mirroring the motion.

There was something about Mouse's confidence that was not contagious. *But fuck it. If you're going to die, then trying to capture a mythical monster was probably a good way to go. If only Mareth was around to turn it into a song afterwards.*

~

IT HAD BEEN MONTHS.

Months of Kolsen going to visit their new neighbors that had started their relationship by burning alive a boy that was under his protection. Months of Kolsen encouraging members of all crews to collect whatever it was that Mouse wanted without an explanation as to why. There had been a couple of successful sorties during that time, but he knew that the other captains were wondering what was wrong with him. First, he'd freed the Alfjarun slaves, then he'd given them ships, and now he was trying to befriend a small tribe that had acted with impunity against New Port. Behler was whispering poison, he knew this as word made its way back to him. The idiot not smart enough to consider who he brought into his circle. He wouldn't be surprised if Trueblood was thinking about leaving, running off with whatever she considered her share.

Months of apparent weakness that led up to this evening.

When all would be set right.

Kolsen and the other ships had just returned from their latest adventure and for the first time, their holds matched their imaginations, gleaming with gold. The gold had been split between the ships, no one trusting the other to hold the stash. He knew that the other captains would be keeping careful count of where each other was during the evening. But that was not Kolsen's concern; he had gone to see Mouse when everyone else had headed for the Green Peaks for some cautious celebration. The animal tamer gave him the nod that he was ready—three small casks full of some type of liquid, a big hand drill, a knife, and a length of metal pipe, all stacked by the door and waiting for Kolsen's return.

Yes, he knew that some of the crews, had been whispering about what they saw as his strange behavior. And he knew he was adding oil to the galley fire by sending Hunyg to the neighboring village to invite them to join the good citizens of New Port for a celebration. Neither the pirates nor the Alfjarun were particularly keen on it, but he told a few of the more loose-lipped pirates that he'd been working on a surprise and there would be something that made it all worth it later that night.

He met the tribe as they arrived through the dark of the forest and into the anarchic sight of New Port, the beach lit up with bonfires, half naked pirates dancing and cavorting. Karr thrust a drink into each of their hands, young or old, as he said whatever came to mind, knowing they couldn't understand what he said anyway.

Kolsen enjoyed a cup of sweet rum—Loftus really was getting the recipe to be pretty good—before he and Karr found Red Ted and dragged him, complaining, away from the celebration. They swung past Mouse's hut, and between the four of them they picked up the young man's supplies and set off across the island.

Red Ted complained the whole way about missing out on the party. "This is going to be bigger than any party," spat Kolsen, exasperated at Red Ted's lack of imagination. His first mate knew the plan, knew what they intended to do, but still his first mate whined like a baby away from the teat. "This'll be a story you can trade for free drinks in any tavern for the rest of your life." Fucking pirates. At least Karr bounced with excitement about what Kolsen had planned. Of course, that was dependent on the whole thing working.

The village was quiet when they arrived, and Kolsen led them past the huts and up to the side of the great rocky hill. He clambered up first and then offered a hand to the others to help them over the lip. They crested the rock, and up close it was unmistakable that this was no normal hill or outcropping; it was smooth save for where interlocking plates met. Over time there had been an accumulation of soil and stone next to the 'rock', which had become home for a variety of trees and plants to grow. Even at the top, where the fire from the sacrificial bonfire had still left a mark, mosses and weeds grew in clumps.

Mouse started with the hand drill, normally used for opening casks or when repairing ships, but now used to drill a hole into the ground below them with a bit almost as wide as Mouse's hand. Small shavings curled up as he twirled the handle but it was slow going. Kolsen ordered Red Ted to take over. Progress became faster and the drill bit disappeared into the rock. Red Ted's face become ever more puzzled as the rock was drilled quite easily. Kolsen bent close to where his first mate worked, concerned the drill wasn't going to be long enough, as it was nearly all of the way in, when all of a sudden it slipped, resistance gone, and a spurt of dark liquid leapt out of the hole and splashed Red Ted in the face.

"What the fuck?" exclaimed Red Ted as he sat bolt upright and Kolsen almost laughed. But unfortunately, the blood on his face was the least of his worries as a knapped stone spearhead emerged through his right breast.

Kolsen scrambled backwards, exclaiming Red Ted's words himself, only to see the old man of the village, the one who had insisted on taking the boy, twisting the spear, an evil leer on his face. Mouse froze, staring dumbly at their skewered comrade as Karr fell backwards, dropping his crossbow which skittered down the side of the incline until it lodged in a small bush. The spear came free of Red Ted's back and the wrinkled village ancient made to raise it again, babbling something that Kolsen couldn't understand, even though he'd been taking some lessons with Hunyg. But their frail attacker swayed on uneasy feet.

Mouse responded first, whipping the length of metal pipe around and into a pair of kneecaps swollen with arthritis. The elder fell backwards onto his arse. Kolsen pulled his sword free from its scabbard and Karr reached his crossbow, all at the same time. Kolsen advanced on the ancient spear-wielder, but paused as the point waved menacingly in his face. This was starting to seriously piss him off now. Red Ted, a bloody good first mate, even though he liked a whinge at times—and who doesn't—was on the floor between Kolsen and their attacker; eyes open, staring accusingly up at him. He was certain that there was going to be an account that needed settling now and this tarnished old copper of a man wasn't going to be enough. Kolsen looked around for Karr who held his crossbow, apparently waiting for his captain to do all of the fucking work.

"Karr?"

"Yes, Captain?"

"Will you please shoot this fucker? Now."

A twang of string. The satisfying wet thud. The used-to-be-ancient collapsed, a quarrel's fletching sticking from his chest. "There you go, Captain."

"Good. Thank you. Now, remember to keep a fucking look out!" he screamed. Karr blanched, turning almost luminescent in the dark of the evening, but he made a show of loading and arming the crossbow and patrolling around Kolsen and Mouse.

Kolsen turned to Mouse, "Let's get on with it."

Mouse nodded and inserted the long knife into the hole. Blood bubbled up to the top of the shell. Kolsen couldn't look away as Mouse took the metal pipe and inserted it into the hole, pushing down with as much strength as he could muster. He looked up at Kolsen, that crazy grin and wild look in his eyes again.

"Blue, red or green?" he asked Kolsen.

"For what?"

"Potion. Which one shall I try first?"

"Don't you know?"

Mouse shook his head. "It's always a little different depending on the creature. I'm sure they'll all do something though."

Something. Mouse's lack of specificity was concerning. "Blue," he said finally.

The cork came out of the top of the cask with a pop and as Mouse struggled to lift it over the funnel he had placed in the pipe, Kolsen leaned over to help. A decent slug of blue liquid disappeared down the pipe, but nothing happened. They looked at each other and waited for a minute but still nothing, so Mouse poured a bit more.

There was a gurgle underneath them that made the 'ground' shake.

A knocking sound came from the edges of the rock-shell.

And then the ground in front of the rock, where the village was built, erupted into the air. Dirt, stones, bits of hut and meager belongings rained down around them. A serpentine neck and massive draconic head emerged from where it had been buried. The creature's mouth opened and a huge blast of fire and sand emerged with a roar, flattening the tall palm trees around the remains of the village.

The turtle reared up on newly emerged flippers and slowly pushed back into the bay. Kolsen wasn't sure whether to laugh or shit himself—it looked like Karr had definitely gone with the second option—so he grabbed the tamer of turtles in an embrace.

"Mouse, you fucking genius."

GENIUS MIGHT HAVE BEEN OVER PLAYING IT A LITTLE.

Over the following, craziest, hour of Kolsen's life, as the newly awoken Draco-Turtle raged like a toddler who did not want to go to bed, it became clear that Mouse was really doing everything by trial and error. At one point it looked like the turtle was going to dive underwater, and it was only a quick application of red that kept him on the surface; but strangely that caused the creature to spin around clockwise.

Kolsen encouraged Mouse to figure out how to get a handle on the creature out on the open water before they headed back to New Port. He had no interest in accidentally destroying their town, or worse, looking a fool as the creature did something unexpected. He and Karr sat not too far behind the head of the beast, whose scales shimmered blue in the reflected moonlight, allowing Mouse some space to work.

"Captain, can I ask a question?"

Kolsen looked at Karr, noting how much he had grown up over the past couple of years. It seemed like just yesterday that the lad had been signing up with the pirates who had attacked his home town just to be close to a boy he had a crush on. Karr had served under four different captains since then and all before he really needed to shave. He'd filled out a bit from the skinny little whiner he once was, even if his whiskers kept getting blown back in by the wind. Kolsen nodded.

"What are you going to do now?"

A simple question, yet so full of possibility. "First of all, we need to get even for poor old Edvard, not to mention that boy they burned. Then, I think it's time for us to *really* take over."

INTERESTINGLY, THE DRACO-TURTLE CREATED A MIST wherever it went. So, as the pirates of New Port and their guests of honor boozed and sang, they thought nothing of the light fog that rolled in off the bay.

At least until the head of the Draco-Turtle pierced the veil, Kolsen standing on top, a hand resting on one of two horns for balance. Those on the beach dropped their cups or their jaws in awe.

"Friends!" called Kolsen. "What do you think of my new pet?"

One pirate, a great fat man from the *Axe Blade,* squealed and ran away.

"There is nothing to be afraid of." Kolsen stepped down the snout of the Draco Turtle, until he reached the end, taking a seat near a massive nostril. He breathed deeply and forced a smile, willing himself to ignore the hot breath coming from the nose or the long ivory fangs he could feel beneath his legs. "Or at least not from this good boy anyway." He paused for a moment, bringing a serious expression to his face before continuing. "Pirates! I have bad news. Our dear old Red Ted has gone. His heart pierced by a spear."

"What! Who did that?" called someone from the beach.

Kolsen pointed to where Karr was propping up the dead body of the ancient villager. "He did. And they burned their guest, the boy we left with them. I think it's time that we show these neighbors of ours what happens when you cross the North Sea Corsairs!"

The light of the bonfires gleamed on the murderous grins that greeted him. *About fucking time*, was what he expected them all to be thinking. Whether it was from the drinking or the entrancing sight of the Draco-Turtle, no one moved.

"Well, get on with it!"

The sweetest music he knew filled the air—the whistle of a sharp edge slicing through the crisp night. And before long, New Port was once again the only habitation on their island.

THE NEXT PYRFEW CONVOY THEY ATTACKED WAS A TRAP.

Eight ships, twice as many as usual, but Kolsen had chalked that off to the convoys just being provided the adequate protection that they deserved.

Unfortunately, all of the ships were full of the green and gold marines.

It was apparent something was definitely amiss when their prey, instead of trying to run, changed course to intercept them. The whole of Kolsen's fleet was out. All seven ships and almost every soul from New Port. They were outnumbered and up against combatants who were a lot more zealous than his crew.

He really hated zealots.

More than pirates.

It was going to take a miracle for them to get out of that situation.

It was lucky that he already had a miracle on hand. A fog-shielded miracle that the approaching ships didn't notice. Kolsen maneuvered the *Juniper* alongside the Draco-Turtle's shell, jumping across once he had butted up close. Mouse was all alone on the Draco-Turtle's shell. He considered using the beast to destroy the Pyrfew force, but he knew the casualties on their side would also be great. It wasn't worth it.

Kolsen ordered Mouse to burn away the fog.

The sight of a monster from legends looming behind the

pirate ships must have given the captains of those Pyrfew vessels a stroke. They turned on a hairpin, and Kolsen couldn't help but laugh as they ran with their tails between their legs.

THEY MAY NOT HAVE TAKEN ANY TREASURE THAT DAY, BUT they had escaped a Pyrfew trap without suffering any casualties. For Kolsen, that was more than enough reason to celebrate with a dinner in his cabin for the other captains. Unfortunately, they were not sharing his happy opinion.

"What is wrong with you three? Have I not made you rich? What's with the walrus faces?"

Trueblood took a gulp of wine. "It's been good going alright."

"Aye," said Crull. "Too good to last." These didn't sound like Crull's words. The man was happy enough with a different person to murder each day. He'd been speaking with someone else.

"What are you talking about?" asked Kolsen.

"The beast has woken up," said Behler as he slapped the table. "And not the Draco-Turtle," he clarified for the confused Crull. "Pyrfew! It's woken up to us; the annoying wasps buzzing around and spoiling it's picnic, and it's not going to stop until we've got squished." Kolsen couldn't help but laugh at the tortured analogy, but he didn't do his best to keep these captains happy for their erudition.

But Kolsen knew where this conversation was going. He had been planning to steer it in the same direction himself, and so this would be easier now.

"You think it's time to go back to the Shards? Well,

you're right." The other captains looked surprised at Kolsen's agreement. "But we're not going back to live the same old life again. We're not giving this up. We need to share the wealth with our brothers and sisters back in the Shards, and when they see what we have accumulated, they'll be lining up to join us. With more ships, the Pyrfew navy won't be able to swat us."

"We've seen this before Kolsen. It will escalate. They won't back down." Trueblood shook her head. He knew it was her he needed to convince and the other pair would follow.

"Look, I don't want a war. That's not good for us. But I'm not sure they won't back down. They have a lot of gold and silver, but what are they short of?"

"Ships?" ventured Crull.

"Exactly. We come back here with a pirate fleet big enough to make them piss themselves, give them a bloody nose, and then we make them an offer they can't refuse."

"And what would that be?" asked Trueblood, hanging on his every word.

"They pay us to leave their ships alone. Treasure for nothing."

Pirates are a bunch of lazy shits. That's why they weren't merchants or sailors or another job where people would use the phrase an honest day's pay for an honest day's work. They wanted the maximum amount of money for the least amount of effort. And he could see that this offer was appealing to those he shared the table with.

"You'll sign a treaty with 'em?" Kolsen nodded to Behler's question. "Normally its Kings what negotiate treaties," he added.

Kolsen held up his hands. "I never said nothing about no

king. We'll just need some way to make it official. What do you think? You in?" He held out his hand palm up. Trueblood's hand joined his first, then the other two captains and a fifth hand topped the pile. Karr, who had been waiting attentively for any needs. Kolsen coughed and Karr quickly withdrew.

"It's going to be a shame to leave New Port behind," said Behler. "Who knows what will be left when we get back."

"Leave it? We're not going to leave it. We're taking it with us."

~

IT WAS QUITE A SIGHT.

One that never failed to impress him each and every morning when he strode on deck for the first time.

The lord of all he surveyed, there in the middle of the ocean.

It was a far cry from when he had last made this journey back to the Shards. Just his ship, his crew, barely enough profit realized to hatch his crazy scheme.

Now there were six other ships that made up his fleet. The three of those captains who had taken a chance on him, and the three other ships they had taken from Pyrfew. And looming behind them all, the town of New Port, lashed to the back of a monster controlled by a man who made mice dance.

Who was going to be able to resist his call?

Who wouldn't want to travel in the wake of someone as lucky as him?

Who wouldn't want to call him King?

DUNDENAS

DUNDENAS I

TERRIBLE NEWS AND A RIDICULOUS PLAN

The Darting Seal bobbed at anchor off the barren stretch of Edland coast. Here was where the mountains met the sea, and the rocky walls plummeted down to a small sheltered beach. Fin knew that this was where they had been heading for almost a week now; not going back to Kingshold. Alana had confided in her once the odd couple—which was how she thought of Motega and Trypp now, without Florian they didn't seem to make sense together—had spoken to her about the witch's magical visit. It was time to leave, a longboat waiting to take them to shore, and Alana was breaking it to the Admiral that they wouldn't be coming back.

The past couple of weeks on board ship had been a strange and emotional journey. Everyone that escaped from Ioth was distraught by the big fighter's self-sacrifice, and though she was thankful, she had other concerns as she watched her childhood home go up in flames. Her father was there somewhere, and she didn't know what had happened to him. Surely some of the citizens had survived? Maybe he had dived into the grand canal outside his very door or perhaps he had hidden in a basement until the flames had gone. She didn't know, and in some ways, that was worse than knowing he was dead.

Fin watched Alana's back as she spoke with the Admiral. He tried to move close to her but she took a half-step backwards. Eventually she relented and let him hold her hand. Fin was far enough away not to be able to hear what they were saying—she didn't want to be rude—but she was quite a good lip reader, so she knew at least one side of the conversation that began with him asking why she had her belongings with her if the plan was to collect Neenahwi.

Fin watched as Crews listened to Alana's response and then read his reply. "I don't understand. Why can't you go back to Kingshold? The Lord Protector will be waiting. And your sister."

Alana patted the back of Crew's hand. They knew this was going to be a difficult conversation, why only three of them would be leaving—counting only herself, Motega and Trypp. Fin was sure Alana had brought up how dangerous it would be in Kingshold for anyone that had been in Ioth with her, because she had thought that Fin would be going back to the Syndicate. But it had been a number of days since Fin had already decided that she was going to see out her contract, no matter what.

Alana either needed to get back to Kingshold, or the Lord Protector needed to say the contract was satisfied; and Fin was a stickler for fulfilling what had been agreed. Besides, that was not even taking into account that she was actually enjoying Alana's company; she was bright, a quick and diligent student when it came to fighting... and she liked the feeling she got in her stomach when she was close.

"Can't you tell me any—" mouthed the Admiral before he was cut off by Alana.

"Fine," he replied once she had finished interrupting him. "I will be careful. Of things not being what they seem." He said this last part in a way that reminded Fin of the actors that she'd seen on feast days as a child, stiff and parrot-like.

"Is she nearly ready?" asked a voice over her shoulder. Fin turned to see Motega and Trypp dropping their packed bags next to hers and Alana's. All of their gear was new. They hadn't had a chance to pack up before leaving Ioth, and neither had *The Darting Seal* been fully stocked for a long sea voyage. So, they'd gone the widdershins route around the sea and stopped at Colvin on the way. It was by no means a Kingshold or an Ioth in terms of merchants available, nor even a Redpool for that matter, but they had been able to get a few changes of clothing and some much-needed supplies. Behind them stood the tall figure of the Pyrfew soldier that Motega had captured, hands still chained together though his feet were free.

"It looks like it," said Fin, as Alana walked over to them with Crews at her side. Crews still had her hand clasped in his, and Fin noticed an uncomfortable and uncommon feeling inside her at the sight. It had definitely been an emotional couple of weeks.

"Gentlemen," said the Admiral to Motega and Trypp. "I trust you will look after this very fine lady."

"You don't need to worry, Admiral. The Ravens are going too." Morris, along with Midnight, Cherry, Forest and Syd, tossed their bags on the increasing pile. Fin looked to Motega with an arched eyebrow.

He shrugged his shoulders. "He heard us all packing and wondered what was going on. Can't stop him from coming."

"In for a penny, in for a crown," said another voice from behind Trypp. Dolph's belongings joined theirs. "If you'll have me, miss."

Alana nodded, a sheepish grin on display for the group assembled on deck before her. "I think we'd better be getting off the Admiral's ship. Let him get home." The crew lined up to chain their bags down to the boat waiting off the port deck. Fin almost averted her gaze as the Admiral swooped in to kiss Alana, but instead of landing on her thinned lips he got a taste of cheek instead. Alana's quick reflexes made Fin irrationally happy.

~

MOTEGA LEANED OVER AND SHOUTED SOMETHING TO Trypp and Alana, but the words were taken away and carried out to sea by the wind that whipped across the bow of the longboat.

"What did you say?" shouted Alana.

"I said, I thought Neenahwi might have flown over to meet us." Motega's falcon was clinging to the man's shoulder, the sharp talons digging into his thick wool cloak for purchase. Apparently, deciding that fighting the wind was the worse option compared to soaring in it, the bird flapped its wings and launched itself skyward. "I guess Per isn't going to wait with us either. Can you see her?" Motega asked.

Trypp nodded. "I think so. There's another man there too. And a few of the Dwarves. Not much of a welcoming party. Are you sure about this?"

"Of course he's sure," interrupted Alana. "What else are we going to do? Mareth and my sister will be there too. Can you see them?"

"I don't know. Maybe that's Petra and Mareth I can see? We'll know soon enough."

Fin watched the exchange without comment. They would be there soon enough, and she was happy that Alana would be able to see her sister again. It was obvious that her ward had really missed Petra while they had been away. At first, it had gone unsaid—when she had been getting to know her as Jill—but she could tell that Alana had found being away from her home and what was left of her family to be a jarring change. Over the past few days, Alana had become more and more excited at the thought of seeing her sister again and being able to introduce her to Fin.

A steady drizzle angled into Fin's face and she swept her hair back from her forehead, rivulets of rain streamed down her nose to drip from the tip. A call went up from ahead; they had almost reached the beach. Two sailors at the prow jumped into the water with ropes in hand and dragged the boat ashore.

Fin climbed over the side and down into the shallow freezing water just behind Motega, Trypp, and Alana. The two men strode off ahead up the beach, pushing their prisoner ahead of them, while Alana waited for Fin. They set off toward the waiting figures, Dolph and the Ravens trailing behind.

Fin hadn't met Neenahwi before, but she had met Petra before they had departed Kingshold, back when she was still Jill, and this was definitely not Alana's sister. While Petra had struck Fin as a bright summer's day, her blond hair a corona around her smiling face, this woman had the look of a thundercloud; purple and liable to explode. When Motega left the Pyrfew soldier in the care of Trypp to run the last few yards between them and grab the waiting woman in a deep embrace, it basically confirmed her identity.

Fin and Alana stopped a little way away, out of respect for their reunion. Motega eventually peeled himself away from his sister, wiping his eyes with the back of his sleeve before falling into the arms of an older taller man who was standing nearby. He didn't have a family resemblance to Motega but she would still have him pegged as being from the Wild Continent too. Dolph, Sergeant Morris, and his Ravens waited with them until the extended family reunion was over.

Neenahwi crossed the patch of sand to stand before them, her brother and Trypp trailing behind. She turned to face Motega. "You've brought more than I expected. What happened to it just being Alana?" Fin thought it strange that the woman was talking about Alana as if she wasn't there. In fact, Fin was pretty sure that she hadn't even looked at her yet.

"They wanted to come," said Motega simply.

"Where's Mareth?" asked Dolph. Neenahwi fixed him with an appraising look before answering.

"He's inside." She hooked a thumb over her shoulder in the direction of what looked like an unremarkable cliff face. "We should all get inside too. We've got places to go."

"Is Petra there?" Alana had finally piped up. Fin found it strange to see her show such obvious deference to someone else. They must have some history that she didn't know about.

Neenahwi finally faced Alana, and Fin couldn't tell whether it was the biting wind or something else that was bringing the tears to her eyes. "Oh, Alana," she said, as she reached out and grabbed Alana's free hand in hers and pulled her gently away from the group. Fin watched as Neenahwi leaned in close to Alana, the intimacy of the moment ruined somewhat by the expression on Neenahwi's face. She saw Alana's legs give way before anyone else noticed, and though she sprang forward, Fin couldn't catch her before she fell to the ground in a faint.

BEHIND THE CLIFF WALL WAS A SMALL DWARVEN OUTPOST. Fin had never been to Unedar Halt before, or even seen any of the Deep People for that matter, but she had learnt about them in Heraldry and History class back at the Syndicate. She had no idea if this place was similar to the rest of the dwarves' city; carved from the mountain it was all clean straight lines—large functional rooms that could probably be used to both give soldiers instructions, as well as being a place for them to sleep.

There were a few smaller private rooms too, and that's where Alana was taken once she had come round on the beach. To see Mareth and get answers as to what happened. Fin offered to go with her but she politely refused, one hand on the doorknob, saying she needed to do this on her own. Fin's heart twisted looking at the pain evident on Alana's face, wishing she could be with her. When Alana went in, Fin caught a glimpse of who she could only believe was the Lord Protector sitting on a low bunk. He didn't look well; his skin was sallow, his scalp bare.

Alana was gone for some time. The others made a space for themselves in the big room, and so Fin found a quiet corner for herself and waited. She saw Motega and Trypp come and go, speaking with some of their hosts. Even

Sergeant Morris appeared to know some of the other people there. Fin did not, and it made her wonder what she was doing there. Did Alana really need a friend like her when she was surrounded by so many others that cared for her? And did she need this? So many people around, with existing, meaningful, relationships. She had purposefully chosen a career where wanting to be a loner was an attribute, not a hindrance.

She didn't have too long to think about it as Neenahwi and a gaggle of dwarves entered and set to making the room orderly for a gathering. Benches were dragged to one end and arranged around where Neenahwi was doling out instructions. Fin stayed back, watching the wizard interact with the dwarves; she seemed confident enough but there was something a little manic, a little anxious, about how she was giving out orders. If Fin had been able to check, she was sure Neenahwi's heart was racing.

Eventually things were organized to her liking and Neenahwi beckoned for everyone to take a seat, before she strode out of the room, muttering about needing to find the others. Those who had come with Fin from *The Darting Seal* were there, all except for Alana. Fin took a seat at one of the benches in the rear of the room, unsure of her place now with these people.

Neenahwi returned with Alana and Mareth in her wake, along with a pair of dwarves. One she recognized as the Keybearer who had greeted her when they had arrived, but the other dwarf, visibly younger with the smile of a child who had been invited to dine with the grown up, she had not met. Trailing behind the dwarves was a young bespectacled man. He had wild hair and eyes to match that darted around the room in stutters before returning to the floor.

The Lord Protector had to be helped into a seat. Once Alana had done that she came over to Fin, reached for her hand, and with a nod of her head guided her over to a place at the front near the sickly man who had hired her.

Motega's sister stood in front of the audience like one of her old school teachers, and now Fin got a chance to see another side of her. Prepared for her role, aware that everyone would be watching her, Neenahwi was an intimidating sight. A rod of steel dressed in purple silk, without adornment or jewelry, save for the leather belt around her middle where a shriveled human head hung from a long tassel of hair. Fin could have sworn that she saw the head blink. Next to Neenahwi stood the Keybearer, but the younger dwarf and the wild-eyed man who she had escorted in took their place on a bench across from Fin.

"I'm not going to mince words with you all," said Neenahwi, a sudden hush falling as the faces around the room turned to look to her. "Things are seven shades of fucked-up right now. Kingshold has fallen. A Pyrfew doppelganger of Mareth sits on the throne, with one of Llewdon's wizards at his side. I blame myself, but no one knew that Lady Grey was not who she seemed to be. I know for a fact that my father had no idea, or I am sure he would have addressed the issue. In the interests of full disclosure, the situation in question is somewhat more complicated. Grey is as ancient as Jyuth. They shared the same teacher before she was drawn into the service of Llewdon.

"And as I have heard, Ioth burns. Who knows what remains of the city or how many escaped the inferno, but it is clear that the City of Lights was always part of Pyrfew's ambitions. They have killed the Saint and taken the reliquary."

"How were they able to do that?" asked Alana, leaning forward in her seat. Fin looked at her intently. Alana's eyes were red raw, and though she had positioned herself to be sitting close to Fin, she hugged herself tight. Fin could well imagine what she was going through. If she too knew that her only family was dead, if she had evidence that her father had perished, then even though she had declared the Syndicate her only family, she too would feel like the ground had been ripped away from her. But was she just kidding herself? What were the chances that her father had survived? It amazed her that Alana seemed to be able to think somewhat rationally. "How did they kill the Saint? How could they resist his magic?"

"They took my master's things." Fin started at the words that came from the severed dangling head. Assassins and death were bedfellows, but victims didn't usually talk back.

Neenahwi looked down at the speaker hanging by her skirts and continued the story. "Arloth was once a wizard named Myank. He was my father's teacher, and the teacher of the Librarian here. Somehow, he ascended to be a god. It seems that those who wore Myank's own personal effects were protected from the magic that came from his old body. This is important, as I believe it is the root of what drives Llewdon."

"Does this come back to your vision?" asked the tall man who sat by Motega. He had been introduced to her as Kanaveen, older than either the brother or sister. There was barely concealed anger contained in his clenched jaw.

Neenahwi nodded. She looked around the room, and Fin was certain she saw the same quizzical expressions as her own. "I saw in a vision how the elves died. Llewdon tricked them to give him their life force; his intent was to use that power to ascend as Myank had done. To prove that he was the equal of his old friend. But Llewdon failed and all the elves died. It has taken him centuries to build his empire, taking the lives of his people on the way, but I believe that he has not fore-sworn his intention of matching Myank's achievement.

"He is subjugating the place you know of as the Wild Continent. Bringing my people into his sway. Converting them to his own religion, enlisting the young to his armies as the ones you saw in Ioth. Enslaving those who disagree. He tried once to use the lives of many people to power his ambitions, and I am sure he would do so again."

Neenahwi paused and looked around the room. Her fists were held in tight balls at her side. "You have all lost those you know and love to Pyrfew's schemes. Friends." Fin saw Trypp nod to himself, his hand clutching his knees tightly. "Family." Alana shuddered. Fin attempted to rest a hand on her arm comfortingly but she found she was gripping tightly, thinking again about how the soldiers in green and gold had devastated her home.

"What do you propose?" asked Sergeant Morris. "Do we fight?"

The wizard nodded. "We fight. We take the battle to Pyrfew in a way they won't expect."

"Good. That bitch took the only woman I ever loved. We have to take back Edland and muster the armies," croaked the Lord Protector. "Egyed, will the dwarves help?"

Before the Keybearer could speak, Neenahwi answered the question herself. "I have secured the Forger's help. But for now, we must leave Edland." There was a chorus of disagreement and confusion in response but she raised her voice to speak over them. "We are too few to fight what appears to be the rightful leader of the realm. You must see that. I will not have the blood of innocent Edlanders on my hands. And it would only make matters worse if the dwarves, and I would never ask them to do this, were to do the fighting for us. We have had many years of peace between Edland and Unedar Halt and now is not the time to shatter that."

"So what are we going to do?" asked Fin, before she even realized she had opened her mouth to speak.

Neenahwi didn't miss a beat responding, even though these were the first words they had exchanged. "We are going to the Wild Continent. To free my people. If we have need of an army, they will be it. If they are instrumental to Llewdon's plans then we will stop it at the source." She pounded a fist into her other palm to punctuate each point, "we need to think differently than facing him here in the Jeweled Continent if we are to solve this problem. His plans are too well-framed here; his agents hidden in places we can't suspect."

"But we just sent our ship away. Should we signal for the Admiral to return?" asked Alana.

"No. Edland rules the waves, and who knows if Crews will side with us? No. We will not go across the sea. We will go under it."

"Begging your pardon, miss," said Sergeant Morris. "But that sounds fucking ridiculous."

Neenahwi gestured for the timid young man with the wild hair and the dwarf sitting at his side to stand. "This is Mouse, the man behind the Draco Turtle's assault on Kingshold this summer." There was a gasp from everyone except Motega and Trypp. "And this is Kyle, a friend of mine who has offered to help us. Together they have devised a way for us to travel. We're going way under the ocean. Through the tunnels that line the world. We shall travel by purple worm."

~

FIN TRACED HER FINGER ALONG THE CRISSCROSS OF SCARS on her forearms from where the demon dog had mauled her. They had healed reasonably well considering that she'd been afraid that the wound could have become infected—who knew what taint existed in the mouth of such a beast.

She was in the small cell that had been given to her as a place to rest and have some solitude. It was a square room with a short bed, though still just about long enough for her, a trunk, and no other adornment or furniture. A far cry from what awaited her back at the Hollow House as a full partner. But it's sparseness, coupled with the quiet of being inside the mountain, was a blessed relief after weeks at sea with everyone on top of each other. She'd spent much of the past day in quiet reflection, wondering what on earth she had committed to do now that she had heard the wizard's plan—which quite frankly seemed absurd.

She knew she could leave if she asked. She could return to Kingshold and what she had worked so hard to achieve. It would be so simple, to go back to the business of the syndicate. There were always people that needed killing, and it didn't have to be *complicated*. The plan seemed ridiculous but everyone had nodded along. And there was something about the wizard that set her teeth on edge but she couldn't figure out what it was.

Not being able to figure something out was incredibly frustrating for Fin, so she spent the rest of her self-imposed isolation focused on training. She didn't need a partner, or space to move, or even her weapons. She closed her eyes and pictured a fight that had happened, thinking through each move, each motion, that she had taken.

The scars brought back that night in stark relief. She remembered the Pyrfew soldier who had faced her. His eyes were as green as his armor, but she could see the fear in them. The fear from seeing his friends and comrades falling around him. He'd stabbed out from behind his shield with his sword, but Fin slipped to the side, momentarily pitying the man and where he had found himself. Pity. A strange emotion, but one that was taught at the Hollow House. For if the assassin could not feel pity for its victim, at whatever cruel circumstances had led to that moment, then who would? She danced forward, left hand striking out but her blade was parried on the shield. Right hand came up, quick as a scorpion, behind the shield and sliding into the soldier's armpit. There was a cough of blood. The snort of the drowned and as she pulled her blade free, he was falling to the floor.

She had been taught pity, but never remorse.

That's when she'd seen the dog closing on Motega. And that's when she'd made her first mistake. Fin had taken two steps and leapt onto the back of the dog, burying her Sai into either side, already thinking about the next target. But it wasn't a dog that she was fighting. Dogs didn't appear magically from smashed glass balls. Dogs didn't go around without fur or skin, displaying their insides. And the demon was much more difficult than a dog to put down. That's when the demon dog had mauled her, and if it wasn't for Motega turning the tables and saving her, she might have lost the arm.

She stepped backwards through the scene to the moment

before she jumped. This time she hacked at one of the demon's rear legs, hoping to sever it. There was a crack and the bone broke, the dog's snarl swinging to face her as it became distracted. The head snapped forward, apparently unmindful of its injury, but Fin was ready and her other Sai flashed forward into its neck. She saw the tip of the blade appear out of the other side, but the dog still came, its weight wrenching her weapon from her hand. The long teeth, dripping with saliva, loomed large as they approached her face and she flung her other arm up in protection. She screamed as the dog bit down and tore at her flesh.

Fin opened her eyes. A different tactic and the same result, only a different arm. Not good enough.

There was a knock at the door that pulled her away from the Sanctum. The door was pushed slowly open and Alana's head peeked warily around the door.

"Fin? Can we talk? I haven't seen you in a while."

"I thought you might want some space." Fin patted the bed beside her. "But I've been wanting to talk with you."

Alana sat down, and even in the dim light, Fin could see that her eyes were still red. Hardly surprising.

"I'm sorry. I haven't been feeling very sociable. But I thought I should tell you what happened to my sister—"

Fin held up a hand to stop her. "You don't have to. The others told me. I'm so sorry. How are you taking it?"

"I... I don't know." Alana rubbed at her eyes wearily. "At times I can't believe it. That it must be a horrible mistake. But mostly I'm just angry." She balled her fists so tightly that Fin could see the whites of her knuckles. "Really, really angry. I haven't felt like this before. Oh, I was mad when my parents died. I blamed Arloth for it, but that was mainly anger at the futility of everything. This time..." Alana looked

Fin in the face, her gaze like granite. "I want revenge, Fin. Like Neenahwi said yesterday. We've got to make Llewdon pay. For Petra. For Florian. Have you felt like that before?"

She thought about it for a moment, and then shook her head. "I don't think so. Back at the Hollow House, revenge is not something that is encouraged. If we fail, then it is our fault, not someone else's. Revenge is only good for creating opportunities for contracts. We're taught to be completely neutral. It doesn't matter the motive for the contract, it's just the contract that matters." Fin paused for a moment as she remembered standing at the railing of *The Darting Seal* as she watched the city of her childhood aflame, wondering what had happened to her father. "But I think I understand. I want to do something too."

Alana nodded and reached out to hold Fin's hands. Fin felt the connection at her touch.

"But is this the right thing to do? Going so far away when we could do something now?"

"I don't think there is anything else we can do," said Alana. "You heard Neenahwi—"

"Why don't we just go back to Kingshold and hire Chalice?" interrupted Fin. It wasn't that she didn't want to follow the wizard, it was that she didn't think there had been enough discussion of other options. "She could kill the Chancellor and the fake Mareth and everything would be back to normal."

"Chalice can't do that. Firstly, why would she even believe us. And then if she did, Mareth himself reiterated the rules that the Hollow Syndicate now has to follow. She would have to go rogue and the whole city would be against her. Not to mention that they will be watching for us, especially now while they are on guard."

"Well, we can do it then. Me and you. If we're disguised. We both know how to go unnoticed." Fin was serious. She knew it would probably mean her death, but she would do that. For Alana.

"Two of us against a whole city? We should go with Neenahwi and follow her plan."

"Not sure the odds of twelve against an empire is any better." Alana laughed at what Fin hadn't meant as a joke. "What is it with how you react around her anyway?"

Alana's brow furrowed at the question. "What do you mean?"

"You're so deferent to her. You'd have a million questions if this plan came from someone else. Remember you're a leader too. The Ravens. Me. We're here because of you."

"I don't know." Alana paused as if she was trying to get the words in the right order before speaking. "Maybe it's because she seems so in control. So powerful. It's what I've always wanted to be. I guess it's hard to stop remembering that I was a servant not long ago; that's what I was when I met her. But thank you for saying that, I'll try to remember it from now on."

"Good."

"I have to ask you. One last time and any answer is fine. Mareth will release you if you want to go home. Do you still want to come?"

That was the time when she had to finally make up her mind. And though she had pursued something her whole young life, something unexpected had come along and tossed all of her old priorities into the air. She squeezed Alana's hand tight. "I'm not leaving you. If you're going, then I am too."

"You don't know how good that makes me feel," said

Alana. But Fin did know, because she felt it too. "In that case, it's time. Someone will come and get your things. Will you walk with me?"

Fin smiled and stood, helping Alana to her feet. They passed out the door of the cell, a dwarf ducking in behind them to collect Fin's things. They walked a long passageway and out into the central common area of the dwarven outpost, the others of their group milling around as if they had been waiting for Alana and Fin. The old dwarf called the Keybearer looked at them both and clapped his hands like a man eager to be about his work and get back to his breakfast.

"We're all here. Time to go. Follow me."

The Keybearer led them along a series of winding corridors, all hewn from the rock with perfectly smooth precision. Motega and Trypp nodded in greeting and presented what amounted to a smile between them but didn't come over and talk. Fin wasn't sure if it was because they didn't have anything in particular to say to her, or if they didn't want to bother Alana. Fin and Alana followed in silence, hand in hand, each of them focusing their attention on their strange surroundings.

Eventually their course led them to a great cavern, naturally occurring by the rough nature of the walls and the stalactites that hung from the ceiling. Mosses of many colors covered much of the cavern floor like a patchwork, but that wasn't what drew her eye.

No, it was the pair of monsters that waited patiently in the center of the open space. When Neenahwi said they would travel by worm, she had no idea what the wizard meant. Now that she saw the purple worms, easily twelve feet high and sixty feet long, her mind still struggled to comprehend what her eyes were telling her. Fin's legs wanted to stop where they were, but Alana, turning to show her the broadest smile of wonderment that she had seen on her friend's face for many weeks, pulled her eagerly onward.

The worms had segments, much like a normal earth worm, but each segment was dotted with sharp spines, almost like horns. And each creature had been harnessed in a series of leather belts and buckles that crisscrossed its length up to what appeared to be a saddle behind the worm's head. She hoped that they wouldn't turn so she wouldn't see what their faces looked like. There was only so much someone could handle at once. Waiting a little distance behind each of the worms were long metal boxes on runners, attached to the harness by metal chains that spooled on the floor. She supposed these were their carriages.

"It's very nice to meet you both," said a voice that dragged Fin's attention back to where she stood. It was the dwarf that had been with Neenahwi when they met. "I'm Kyle." He shook Alana's hand vigorously and then reached out for Fin's. "You'll both be traveling with me. Come on over and meet Karcan."

Alana and Fin followed obediently. Karcan was apparently the name of the worm, and standing a dozen paces away was plenty close enough for Fin. She could feel the heat that came from the worm's body, and her nostrils bristled at the smell that hung around it. Alana touched the beast, her eyes wide as she took everything in. Moments later, the Keybearer was shaking her hand as well and wishing her luck and she was ushered to the rear of the carriage. Their belongings had been stowed beneath the long metal benches that lined either side and Mareth, Morris, Dolph and Forest waited for them inside.

Fin sat opposite Alana and the rear door was swung up and secured behind them. There was a shout from someone outside and the worm started to move, a few seconds passed before the carriage lurched into life once the slack of the chains had run out. She looked around at the cramped conditions, suddenly realizing that life aboard ship was not as bad as she had been thinking. There wasn't going to be a lot to do each day except talk to each other or run through fights in her imagination.

Only one choice really.

Fights it would be.

She knew she would be ready the next time she met a demon.

DUNDENAS 2

THE VOICE BETRAYS

He saw her face as he floated beside her. Petra had stumbled down on her hands and knees, quivering with weakness at the exertions of simply walking. Mareth floated. His eyes adjusting in and out of focus, head feeling light, like he hadn't eaten in days—or like someone had taken a part of himself away. So, it had taken him a moment to realize that he truly was floating, stretched out like on a raft on a lake, but with nothing but air to support him.

People were talking all around him, but he couldn't see anyone else other than Petra. He tried to reach out but his arm was weak and he could hardly move it more than a few inches. A face loomed above him suddenly. A man, close-shaven cheeks and the crown of his head hidden under a metal helm. He looked familiar.

The face disappeared and Mareth rolled his head around looking for his observer. Mareth remembered that his name was Grimes. He finally picked out the Commander amongst other armored soldiers; Grimes was talking with a lady. Mareth's mind was still working slowly and even though he wasn't sure who she was, some part of him really wanted to retreat from her, to slide away and hide in a dark corner and hope that she wouldn't see him.

But it was too late for that. She caught his eye and Mareth's brain screamed. He clenched his eyes shut and turned his head away from her. He heard her call out, not in a lady-like way, more how you would hear a town sheriff calling on the executioner to do their work. He gave it a moment, sure that he must be facing in a different direction from her, so he opened his eyes once more. A shriveled head, dangling, disembodied, greeted him.

The head winked.

Mareth's eyes widened in horror.

The soldiers moved.

His life raft disappeared.

And the ground was a hammer to Mareth's skull.

Mareth awoke with a start and scream. The back of his head throbbed from where it had hit the wall of the metal sled. He rubbed it as he leaned forward over his crossed legs, breathing deeply to bring his heartbeat back under control, all the while thinking back to the sight of Petra. Sleep was not coming to him whenever the dwarf decided it was night, and though he longed to be in his dreams with his happy, beautiful Petra that he had loved so much, he found that it was only these fitful sleeps during the day that would grant him her vision. And only ever the worn and weak Petra that he barely recognized from the dungeons and their escape.

He felt an arm around his shoulder and looked up to see Alana considering him, a concerned expression on her face. "You saw her again?" she asked.

Tears, snot, and a sound like a cow being butchered erupted from him all at once as he nodded his head. Mareth brought his knees up to his chest and clutched them tightly. Alana held him and brought his head to rest against her shoulder. He closed his eyes, waiting for the moment to pass but also not wanting to meet the gaze of anyone else onboard their sled.

There was Dolph, his old bodyguard who he wasn't sure if he should trust anymore, along with Sergeant Morris and Forest of the Ravens. And then there was Fin, the assassin he had hired to carry out his wishes in Ioth but who had come back as Alana's shadow. He knew what they were all thinking. Why they didn't want to be caught looking at him. *Can't he hide his grief? Don't you see how Alana is handling it?* But he didn't care what they thought.

He never told anyone he was strong.

He had hidden from having anyone rely on him for a long time for exactly this reason.

The sobs subsided and Alana released her grip on him so he could bring his sleeves up to his eyes to rub away the tears. "I'm sorry," he said.

"It's fine, Mareth," said Alana as she slid back over to the other side of the sled and leaned her back against the smooth metal side opposite him.

He forced a little smile for her and surveyed their moving home. A long sled, made of iron, twenty feet or so in length with a canvas roof that could be opened to look at the passing scenery. The space inside was plain. No seats or table. Just two long benches, a few cubby holes to store their things, and enough room on the floor of the sled for them all to lie down with their bed rolls if there wasn't a good place to camp.

It had been ten days since they had left the outpost of Unedar Halt with the cheers of the Dwarves in their ears, excited at the sight of Mareth and the others speeding off into the tunnels below the earth—into the Dundenas, as they called it—hitched behind massive purple worms.

At first it had been a good distraction for his withered old soul. He would lie back on his bedding and watch the roof of the tunnels pass by overhead, whether old or freshly chewed, there seemed to be a never-ending variation in color and pattern, or maybe something sparkling that would make him think that it could be a precious stone. But always it was gone before he'd really processed it.

At times they would pass from tunnels that had been created by worm into large caverns or chambers, either natural or created by some different type of beast entirely, and he would gaze on the geological delights. Twinkling seams. Rocks of strange shapes. Even insects that glowed in the dark, some much bigger than similar above-ground species. All of this distracted him for a few days until he realized that there really wasn't an endless variation. It was the same all the time.

And it was going to be the same for a month or more—who knew how long it took to go under an ocean—and the sled that was their home began to feel like a cage. Like he was a floppy white eel, swimming round and around in the dark of a barrel, not knowing the moment when a hand would dive in, pluck it out and dash its brains on the side of a table. Maybe the immeasurable weight of stone and water above them was causing his brain to squish under the pressure. Or maybe it was because it felt like Grey's doppelganger had taken the best parts of him.

Or maybe it was simply because he'd given the best parts of him to Petra for safekeeping and hadn't thought to ask for them back.

Mareth closed his eyes, biting the quicks of his fingers, as he attempted to force away the awareness of where he was.

~

Hours must have passed, though he had no real way of knowing other than a dull pain in his stomach, but eventually they stopped for what would be classified as the night. Neenahwi's sled had been in front of their worm, and as Mareth clambered out of his purple-powered human-sized coal scuttle he took a look at the chamber that had been chosen for their camp.

Before this expedition, he hadn't given too much thought to these kinds of spaces that existed way under the surface of the world. He'd seen a few like them before, but he had no idea there were so many, and how they had been formed was something that hadn't occurred to him to ever find out. This particular dark hole was not remarkable; it was just big enough for the worms to rest side by side, letting their bodies cool after the day's exertions, and still provide enough space for the companions to be able to stretch their limbs and talk with each other.

Mareth watched as Motega and the older Alfjarun man, Kanaveen, walked the perimeter rock walls with Kyle. It was the same for every stop; the dwarf would point out what was safe to eat and the three of them would think about how secure their resting place was from possible unfriendly attention. When it came to food, that particular area of the Dundenas seemed to be home to a plethora of foot-long hairy red caterpillars. He had wondered whether eating something so big and so red was a good idea when it had first been served to him—the memories of long walks with his father's game warden teaching him nature lore came to mind—but the meat inside had been soft and smooth like a fat marrow bone and he'd gobbled it down.

Mareth leaned back against the stone wall away from the others, feeling the warm rock on the palms of his hand. He slumped down until he was sitting upright and he wished for a drink.

Not for the first time, he thought that a nice whiskey would help improve matters. Put a fire in the belly and a dullness behind the eyes. He'd hoped that the Forger might have packed him something before they left. After all, he'd shared his good stuff with him. But no, the little shit had said he didn't think that was a good idea. Mareth had noticed the quick glance that the old dwarf had given Neenahwi. Why, he would even settle for a beer around now. Something crisp and bitter, anything would be better than the underground water they had been topping up their barrels with.

Yes, a drink would be nice. But Mareth knew, deep down, the Forger was right. It wasn't a good idea. If it wasn't for the drink, then he maybe wouldn't have been captured so easily, and Petra would not be dead. He knew it was the fault of the booze, and he knew it was his fault for succumbing to temptation and the illusion that things were better with the world. And that's why he wanted a drink.

"Gather round, children. Time to get educated," said Kanaveen. The same joke every night that heralded their lessons. Mareth would have preferred to skip the session on how to speak the common strain of the language used by the Alfjarun, the people that called the Wild Continent home. And it wasn't because he didn't think it was important to be able to speak their language when they eventually, if ever, made it to that far away land. He knew it would be useful.

His biggest complaint was that some people proved to be so horrendously slow at picking it up. Mareth had always had a natural talent for languages, but the Ravens (besides Morris who was doing passably) and Dolph were living up to the standard warrior stereotype and their constant ability to mix up the names for breakfast and latrine, while initially funny to some, was causing him physical pain.

But the time passed by quickly. Mareth watched Motega turning the caterpillars over in a pan perched on a dwarven oil stoves, and he recited the words as they went through their vocabulary drills without really paying too much attention. Kanaveen eventually dismissed everyone after noticing most were getting restless in their seats. They'd all been cramped in their positions all day, and most were eager to get some physical activity. Alana paired off with Fin, who had taken on the role of her instructor since Florian's death; it didn't seem like Dolph had been asked to resume his prior caretaker position. From what he had seen, the young woman seemed to know what she was doing. Though her approach did differ; she was not interested in teaching Alana how to handle the rapier which she was already adequate with, but instead a much more physical approach to using twin knives; constant movement, attacks from oblique angles and sharp kicks.

The Ravens went through their drills and Motega and Kanaveen practiced with wooden clubs while their dinner slowly cooked. Even Neenahwi and Trypp moved in a slow synchronized movement of balances and stretches, apparently something he had picked up in Ambrukhar. But Mareth had no real intention of doing anything. Though he was feeling physically stronger now, his mental burden weighed him down. Watching in silence would be the best he could hope for.

"How are things, Mareth?" asked Dolph as he sat down next to him. Once again, the gods had no intention of letting him have peace to wallow in his own misery.

He turned and glared at his former bodyguard, unable to forget that Dolph had been foisted on him by Lady Grey during the election—and now knowing that she had all along been a Pyrfew traitor, what did that make Dolph? Mareth was a little surprised that Neenahwi had allowed Dolph to come on the journey, but there he was. He eyed him up like a random acquaintance in a tavern who all of a sudden, thinks he's your best mate.

"I'm grand. How about you? Missing your boss?"

"I told you already. I didn't know who she was." Dolph shook his head. Yes, he'd said that before, but 'a lie told thrice don't make it nice' as his childhood nurse used to remark. "It was Hoxteth that hired me, I just got passed down when he died. I might never have been in the army, but I'm an Edlander. I wouldn't work for Pyrfew."

Mareth locked eyes with him, wanting to see if there was anything that would give him away. "Tell me, Dolph. If you were a Pyrfew spy, would you say anything else?"

Dolph stood quickly and wielded his finger in Mareth's face. "Fuck you, Mareth. Fuck you! We know it hurts you, but we care about you. We cared about Petra too. Look at her," he said, gesturing to Alana who had stopped sparring with Fin to see what all of the commotion was about. "She lost her sister."

"I loved her, you prick!" spat Mareth, his face red with anger.

"Yeah, well, Petra was the only family Alana had and she's trying to get on with it. We've all got bigger fish to fry. You need to work through it, man. Talk to someone about it, even if it's not me. Fight me if you want. Or write a bloody song. Whatever it is. But you've got to lance this pain or it's going to fester."

Mareth gritted his teeth before responding. "Leave me alone."

Dolph flung his arms in the air and stalked off to the other side of the dimly lit cavern, passing Alana by with a shake of his head.

Mareth resumed looking at the floor, suddenly ashamed of his actions. He was fairly certain that Dolph had nothing to do with any of Grey's schemes. After all, he had been away in Ioth while all of that had happened, and Alana had made it home safe and sound. He'd even protected Alana when there had been an attack on a ball she attended. No, he knew it was nothing to do with Dolph, but it was difficult not to see the former chancellor standing over the man's shoulder. Mareth just couldn't believe that he'd not spotted anything wrong with her.

"Are you going to shout at me as well if I sit down next to you?" said a woman's voice by his side. He looked up to see

Alana, flushed and with a visible sheen of sweat. Mareth shook his head sullenly.

"He was just trying to be a friend you know," she said.

"I know. I'm sorry. I'll tell him that later, promise." He looked into her eyes, searching for a trace of Petra in her sister's face but remained disappointed that he couldn't be reminded of her. They were so different, just a little similarity in the shape of the face and her green eyes, but that was all. "How are you managing?"

"I don't know, Mareth," she said shaking her head. "None of this makes sense. I keep thinking that I'm going to wake up and the past year is going to be nothing more than a crazy dream. I really can't believe she's gone." She broke off and wiped at her eyes with the back of her hand, streaking tears across her cheeks.

"I'm so sorry. I wish it would have been me that Grey killed."

"It's not your fault, Mareth. Or Neenahwi's. I know she feels guilty too because she's been trying to avoid me." She paused and wrapped her arms around her chest like she was huddling from the cold, even though it was always warm there in the dark. "Look, you asked how I'm managing. I'm trying to stay occupied. I'm trying to be ready for when I can make a difference. Petra was the person who started this whole thing, and I'm not going to have her die for no reason. What Pyrfew has done is personal now. For all of us. And in the Narrows, you don't let anyone get away with hurting your own folk."

Mareth closed his eyes and lent his head back against the cavern wall. "I...I don't know if I have it in me to fight any more."

"Then don't. Do whatever you need to do. Write a story.

Compose something. Just stay busy. It's what I did when my mum and dad died. Sometimes me and Petra would cuddle and have a good cry, and then get back on with things." Alana smiled at him as he opened his eyes. "And I'll be here for you if you want to do the same. Alright?"

Alana turned and walked away, back to where Fin was cleaning her blades and putting them away before dinner was to be served. The young assassin put her arm around Alana as she approached.

Mareth remained still for a moment thinking on what his friends had said. He knew they were right. He wouldn't ever move on from Petra, but he did need to start living again, even if it was just doing the smallest of things for now. He was still supposed to be Lord Protector for fuck's sake. Maybe not having a funeral didn't help the situation. Petra's body was being preserved by the dwarves, which had seemed like a good choice at the time, but now he wasn't so sure. There needed to be something that remembered the mark she had left on the world. Florian too, he now realized. No-one had been able to recover his body.

Well he'd start by living up to the promise that he'd made Petra when she left to go to the Bard College. He'd finish the poem that would declare his love.

And then he would find the perfect place for them all to commemorate their lost friends.

MARETH DASHED DOWN THE STAIRS FROM HIS STUDY TO the front door of Bollingsmead Manor. From the window of his study he had seen the carriage and didn't want to keep the driver waiting, but he knew he was forgetting something.

He looked around the hallway at the stuffed bears standing guard either side of the door, and patted at the pouches that hung from his belt as he tried to remember what it was.

"Here, father," came a voice from the doorway to the sitting room by the hallway's great hearth. "Are you looking for your journal again?"

He snapped his fingers in pantomimed recognition that it was indeed his leather-bound notebook that he should have with him. How else was he to capture the stories that he heard or scratch down the lyrics that popped into his brain? He walked over to his little girl, eight years old this past spring and tussled her hair. "Thank you, Esme. Whatever would I do without you?"

"You'd have no one to tickle if I weren't around."

Mareth stopped her with a finger in the air, and narrowed his eyes—just a little— at her. "Have you been playing with that kitchen boy again? It's 'wasn't', not 'weren't'."

"Sorry, father."

"That's quite alright, my dear, I know you don't have too many friends your own age around the estate. Now, where is your mother? I don't suppose I can sneak out of the house now that you spotted me."

Esme grabbed hold of his hand and led him through the sitting room to a room almost completely glazed with large —and expensive—panes of glass. The light of the sun poured through the windows, casting beams of light on tiny airborne dust particles and shooting small rays of rainbow across the floor. He was not surprised to find his wife in the center of the room, for Petra loved to gaze out onto the rolling green fields, working variation upon variation of the same landscape in oils. She stood with her feet planted shoulder width apart and her back arched, all to ease the discomfort that came with the large swelling that had taken over her stomach. She didn't turn as Mareth approached from behind, taking hold of her shoulders and tracing three small kisses down the side of her bare neck. Any more than three would hardly be appropriate in front of their daughter of course.

"Stop it, Mareth. You're going to have me make a mistake." She said, with a smile on her face and laughter in her voice and Mareth wondered, as he did every day, why he was so lucky to have her.

"I'm sorry, my love," he said. "Esme caught me creeping out the door to go into town and I knew the game was up. Gonal is staying at The Badger's Set and I was hoping to hear some new stories."

"You should invite him for dinner. He's more than welcome." Mareth nodded his agreement, hoping that he was going to be able to escape without any errands being placed on his shoulders. "But while you are there, would you please pick up a few things for me? I made a list there on the table." Petra waved a brush to a small, delicately folded piece of paper that contained items written in Petra's great looping scrawl. Mareth drooped at the ask, but he was hardly going to ignore his pregnant wife's wishes.

"Of course, my darling. It would be my pleasure. Alright, must go. See you later."

Mareth pecked Petra on the cheek and trotted toward the main hall, his boots making a tippy-tap noise on the wooden floor.

"Wait, father," came Esme's voice behind him. "You forgot your journal again." She ran up and handed it over to him. "What did mother ask you to get? Can I come with you?"

"Oh, I am afraid not, little one. I will be talking with a

friend of mine for a while first. It will be quite dull. The list is not much more interesting either," he said as he pulled the paper from his jacket pocket and unfolded it. "Hmm, how strange. I could have sworn that this was the list." Mareth turned the paper over, back and forth, looking for his wife's distinctive hand writing but the paper was blank.

"There isn't a list?" asked Esme. Mareth shook his head in confusion. "Well, maybe that makes sense."

"Whatever do you mean?"

"Mother is dead after all. How could she write a list?"

Mareth took a half step backward. Dead? Yes, he supposed she was after all. "I guess that is true, Esme. You are always so perceptive. Just like your mother."

Esme smiled and it did his heart good to see that. "But I have another question for you then, father. If mother is dead, how is it that I am here?"

The words fired into his face like hot needles, one after the other, leaving him reeling. He took a moment to realize that Esme was once again right, as she slowly faded away before his eyes, an expression of pity on her face. The walls of the manor dissolved around him in turn until in the distance he could see the crystalline shell of the sun room, the easel unattended and the canvas blank.

~

His head lolled forward and the sensation of his chin hitting his chest woke Mareth from his fitful nap.

He'd spent all of last night writing by the light of a glow-stone lamp when he knew he should have been sleeping, but he finally had something to take his mind of things. Dozing while being pulled along by the giant worm was a predictable side effect.

Mareth rubbed at his eyes, squinting at the unexpected rays of light that pierced his vision. He shaded his eyes as he stood up to look out of the open roof of their sled, his jaw hanging loosely in disbelief at what he saw.

They were in an enormous cavern, many times higher than the purple worm that pulled them; and wide enough that he could not see where they were destined. But the thing that was taking his breath away were the crystals that covered the walls and ceiling of the cavern, hanging down in great shimmering facets that sparkled and shone with the reflected light of the small glow-stones from the sled.

It reminded him of the sun room of his dream; brilliantly lit and oh so empty.

"Stop," he muttered. His sled mates looked quizzically at each other but he ignored them. He squirmed his way to the front of the sled to see the long leather straps and chains leading to the back of the purple worm where Kyle was harnessed to the back, administering Mouse's potions as needed. "STOP!" he called again, much louder and cupping his hands to his mouth so the dwarf would hear. He saw the young dwarf, lying on his front in the strange saddle, turn his head to look behind him. Mareth waved his arms and called a halt again.

Moments later the worm slowed, eventually to a stop. The sled they were in careered gently into the back of the soft purple fleshy rings.

"What's wrong, Mareth?" asked Alana in concern as she got to her feet.

He looked down at her briefly as he made his way to the back of the sled. "Here. This is the place. It's perfect." He could see the other worm approaching apace; Mouse always wanted to see how fast the creatures could go. He called and waved for it to slow down too, and for a moment Mareth had the feeling that this crystal cave was going to be not just the perfect place for a memorial ceremony but also his final resting place. Thankfully, Mouse noticed him and moved the worm to the side to avoid crashing into the back of their sled, before skidding to a halt. Neenahwi and those in the other sled peeked their heads above the side. Mareth walked purposefully over, sensing the puzzlement of the companions from his sled right behind him.

"What's wrong, Mareth?" asked Neenahwi. "Is something the matter with your worm?"

"No," he said as he neared close enough that he could talk without shouting. "Everything is fine. It's this place." He gestured with both arms to the cave around them. "This place is perfect."

"What for?" asked Trypp. "It's too soon to camp."

Mareth smiled. "It's perfect for us to remember our loved ones. Petra, and Florian. We haven't had time to commemorate their lives and we need to do it before we go much further. This place is so full of light compared to the rest of the Dundenas. You have to admit that it's perfect."

Trypp visibly winced when he'd mentioned Florian's name. Motega's brow was furrowed in consternation too, and Mareth could tell that he'd hit a nerve. He hadn't been feeling himself ever since the doppelganger, and he wasn't sure whether he was right yet, but he could still read people.

He puffed himself up a bit and looked Motega's sister in the eye. "Neenahwi. I insist that we stop here until tomorrow. We will have this ceremony."

She looked at the others around her and those standing

behind Mareth before eventually speaking. "Of course. That is a fine idea."

"Good," said Mareth, clapping his hands together. "I will call you all together in a few hours when we are ready. If you'd like to prepare any words then that would be ideal. For now, I must go and see our resident Chiseler."

EVERYONE WAS STOOD IN A CIRCLE AROUND THE engravings on the cavern floor. Kyle had been only too happy to help—losing friends and family was a solemn occasion to the dwarves of Unedar Halt and it was no secret what all of them had been through before they set out on this journey—and his craftsmanship was outstanding. The dwarf had taken to the task with relish as well. Maybe he missed his usual role in Unedar Halt, Mareth could imagine how strapping yourself to the back of a purple worm day after day might wear a little thin. He could vouch that traveling in the sled was quite mind numbing.

First, Kyle had laid out his tools on the ground before getting started. There were bottles of various liquids, large devices that looked like hand drills or grinders, and then a series of delicate chisels and awls. He had smoothed the ground while Mareth watched, using liquid from one bottle, but then the dwarf had shooed him away. He didn't want anyone hanging over his shoulder while he worked.

So now Mareth, along with everyone else, was able to see the beautiful work of the Chiseler, for the first time. On the floor were three engraved plaques. Each was bordered with delicate scroll work and ornamental details fitting to the person they commemorated, and in the center were a few simple words remembering them. Florian. Petra. And the fallen Ravens.

It was strange. As Mareth stood there looking at the names of those they had lost, the love of his life, the friend he had asked to help him with a mission, and the men and women that he had sent to their deaths, he felt his load begin to lift. Was he regaining his sense of self after what the doppelganger had stolen? Or was he just starting the process of healing? Water welled at the corner of his eye and he brushed it away.

"Thank you for agreeing to pause for a while, here in this place," he said to the circle of people around the engraved floor. These were the only people who knew what had happened to Kingshold and Ioth, and were going to try to do something about it. Just a few people in a dark hole going in the wrong direction away from the Jeweled Continent. He carried on quickly before his thoughts ushered back a cloud of despair. "This has been a difficult few weeks for everyone. We have all lost friends and loved ones. But we have a difficult job ahead of us, so we must carry on." A mean little voice in his mind pointed out that everyone had seemed to be doing alright, and that it was only him that had been struggling. "And this may not be the last time this happens, but we should always remember the fallen."

"Lord Protector," said Morris. "Thank you for including the Ravens. We lost good men in Ioth. I know most of you didn't know them too well, so I hope you don't mind if I just take a moment and commit their names to this place?" Mareth nodded for him to continue. "Molely. Been with me a long time. Never knew how to do anything else but good soldiering and bad deeds..." The remaining few squad members repeated the name and spat on the plaque, much to the obvious annoyance and mystification of Kyle. "Crabs. Scourge of every Kingshold whore house but he would always have your back. Bors. Best hunter we ever had and a damn fine cook. Joe. Always wanted a nickname but we never gave him one. Good lad who grew up into a good man. Morrissey. He was a miserable fucker."

Mareth waited for a moment to see if there was going to be anything else that Morris would add to the memory of Morrisey's, but after a few seconds it was obvious that there was nothing else. He lifted his bowed head and said, "Thank you for your sacrifice. May the grass be green and your trees shady in the next." That was a common prayer where he had grown up in the west of Edland and where the country was a lot of hills and sheep pasture. He wasn't sure that it was the most fitting for those men he hadn't known, but it was the best he had right then. No one seemed to notice and the others around the circle said their own versions of similar prayers.

All was quiet for a moment and it became obvious that everyone was looking to him to be master of this particular ceremony. Is this what was expected of a failed Lord Protector or was it because it was his idea? He moved on regardless. "I don't know how I can do justice to the memory of Florian. He was a man big enough to blot out the sun, but with enough kindness to fill the Sapphire Sea. He saved Kingshold from the North Sea Corsairs with Motega. He saved my life when I walked into Eden's trap and agreed to the duel. And could he fight! Florian, I only knew you for a short while, but you were the best of men."

Trypp was stood next to Mareth and he coughed to clear his cracking voice as he began to speak. "I can't believe that Florian is gone. He was my brother for the last ten years and more, and it came about because he caught me trying to steal from Neenahwi. I'm sure this bastard," Trypp pointed a thumb at Motega who stood next to him, tears sliding unashamedly down his chalk-white cheeks, "would have just strung me up or handed me over to the guard. But Florian was different. He saw someone, closer to child than man, though not too much younger than himself, and wondered why I was doing what I was doing. Not the usual situation for a burglar and I remember at first thinking that if I could just keep the dimwit talking for a while then I could make a run for it when he let his guard down. It took me a while to realize that it was his own story, of ending up in places that you hadn't planned, that was why he wanted to talk instead of fight. And somehow, he won me over. I don't regret a day I knew Florian. He was a constant reminder to me and Motega that we can be better people than the world has made us. I don't know what we'll do without him, but sleep tight my friend."

Once Trypp had finished he looked over to Motega, but the man waved his arms to pass him by as the tears continued to streak down his face. Trypp wrapped his arms around his friend, resting his chin on Motega's head as he gave into the embrace.

Morris picked up after Trypp. "We lost three good people on that wharf in Ioth. Twins, Hameth, and Florian. I knew Twins longer than all of you. I taught him how to fight and he learned pretty good. I taught him how to look after his squad mates and his friends and he was good at that, so you're welcome," he said with a sad smile to Motega and Trypp. "I taught him to follow orders and be a good soldier, and I was never prouder when he stood up to me and said it was all bollocks and that he quit. People underestimated

Florian. They'd think a big man wouldn't have much wits. But he always knew what was right and he gained the courage to do it, whatever it took. Without what he did, who knows how many of us would have got out of Ioth. Florian, you'll be missed."

Mareth nodded, acknowledging how much worse it could have been without Florian's sacrifice.

Neenahwi was next in line and she was lost in her own thoughts for a moment, staring down at the engraving before she spoke. "I remember when Uncle Uthridge brought Florian to the palace to keep my brother company. Jyuth had me busy with lessons and studies, and it was his idea to see if there was someone who could keep Motega out of trouble. Florian was a few years older than him but they hit it off right away. I think Florian enjoyed the chance to be someone other than a soldier. Now, of course, if they hadn't met then my brother might not have run away and gone missing for years, but I guess it was more likely that he would have eventually been thrown in prison otherwise. Florian was a dependable presence for Motega and whenever I thought about them after they had gone, I felt a little more at ease knowing that Florian was with him,"

Trypp raised his hand. "For the record, I've tried to keep them both out of plenty of bad situations."

"I'm sure you have," said Neenahwi smiling. "But I'm also fairly confident that the pair of them wouldn't have done quite so much 'extracting' without you on the team."

Trypp chuckled and nodded, unable to argue.

Neenahwi was silent for a moment. Mareth saw her wipe a tear away too. He wondered if she was going to comment on the fairly obvious attraction that Florian had for her. "I wish you were here, Florian," was all she added. He'd have to ask her about that one day.

The eulogies from around the circle became briefer as the Ravens and Dolph added their thoughts, but most of them didn't know him well. Alana was the last person in the circle.

"Mareth, you mentioned how Florian was responsible for you winning the election." He nodded. "Well maybe you wouldn't have even been in that situation if he hadn't saved me from Win on the first night we met. Who knows what Win would have done to me, or what Aebur would have done once he knew what we had planned? We could all have spent the rest of the election in the cells. Florian was instrumental in our victories. And he helped stop our defeats from becoming unmitigated disasters. I know that without his training, I would not have even escaped the attack on the ball, much less made it through that Wintertide night. Not having Florian around scares me. I hope, wherever he is, that he'll be looking over us."

When Alana was done, Mareth looked over to Motega who was busy still wiping his face. "Ready?"

Motega nodded, sniffed again and began to speak with a cracking voice. "When I was young my family was taken away from me. All I had were my sister and Kanaveen. But for all of my adult life, I've had the best two brothers that a man could wish for. Florian stood up for us both. He got into trouble with us. He was a better man than either of us and I can't believe that he's going to miss seeing my home. Florian leaves behind a lot of good friends, a lot of worse enemies, and more than a few admirers, including one particular lady assassin back in Kingshold. If I had a beer right now, I would raise it to you my friend, so instead I'll pour you one out every tavern we hit. There won't be a day that goes by when I won't miss you, you stupid bastard."

Trypp wrapped an arm around his friend as Motega's voice broke at the end.

"Florian, may the doves guide you and the crows forever stay away," said Mareth, wrapping up the fighter's remembrance. Not that he wanted to rush forwards. Now his head was starting to feel compressed at the pressure of thinking about Petra. He took a deep breath. "We lost good people in Ioth, and a few of us lost someone we love in Kingshold. Alana, would you like to talk about Petra first?"

She had her eyes closed, and she too took a deep breath, blowing out slowly before nodding. Her words came out slowly, as if she was carefully considering each one. "My sister and I didn't often see eye to eye. For those of you that knew us both, you probably realized that we were quite different people. She was the oldest, the prettiest, the one that everyone wanted to be friends with. She shone the brightest. Sometimes it was hard being her sister, growing in her shade. But I know when our parents died, she took it worst. She didn't know what to do, while I carried on." Mareth noticed her looking at him as she spoke, and he wasn't sure if she was telling him these words as succor or pointing out how similar he was to Petra. "She railed against the injustice of the disease that had taken them, and how the church blamed it on their not living a pious life. But I know some things now since Ioth. I know there's no master plan from Arloth. He's not involved in what's happening here. All we have are the memories of the people we loved that we need to cherish.

"So I'm going to remember how she was always so much more confident in me than I was in myself. How she would always help our neighbors. Brushing each other's hair and talking about the future, a future she won't get to experience now. Another supposed friend of ours was responsible for her death, Lady Grey, and I'm not going to rest until she is held accountable for what she's done." Alana gripped hold of Fin's hand and squeezed it tight. "Petra, somehow I'm going to make it up to you."

He noted Neenahwi looking at Alana, distress plain on the wizard's face. Mareth knew that look well. He'd seen it in the mirror way back in Unedar Halt before he had to talk to Alana. It was the look of anguish from wishing that you could have done more. "I truly am sorry for your loss, Alana. And you too, Mareth. I wish there was something else I could have done, somebody else that could have helped me. Grey had me fooled. I never thought she was a wizard and it was that complacency that left everyone in trouble. Petra didn't deserve it. She was a good woman. I'll help make it up to her too."

"Thank you, Neenahwi," said Alana.

"Yes, thank you," said Mareth. He paused and took a deep breath before launching into the words that he had given so much thought to. "Petra was the only woman I ever loved. Our time together was a whirlwind. It's been less than a year, but when she was around it felt like she was the other part of my soul that had been missing for so long. It was bright, sweet, confident Petra who thought we could try to do something in the election. It was her outgoing personality and tireless pounding of the streets that got people on our side. She gave me the confidence to be strong in front of all of you, and she listened to me when I was wracked with doubt and worry. I loved her with all of my heart and I never told her." He looked down at her name carved in the stone. "Why I never told you, I do not know.

"Now I don't feel quite right. Parts of me are gone; that creature who is pretending to be me has made me...hollow, and Petra's absence has made it so that my heart may just decide to stop beating so it can be with her. But I know that now is not the right time.

"When she left to go to the Bard College, I told her I would finish writing my song for her. I didn't then. But I have now, and though I fear my voice is not strong enough, I hope you will bear with me."

Black days of winter chased me,
Dark, and drink, and death they claimed me,
Abyss and void, memory, sorrow and regret,
But the sun came and it brought you
My rose.

Clouds left the sky,
And bitter winds fled,
All because you brought life to the dead.

Mareth closed his eyes as he sung in a soft low voice to begin, more to test his vocal ability. His throat felt raw and scratchy already, and whereas usually when he sang, he could feel the flow of power in the words, the tune rippling up his body to his throat in soft waves, now it felt different, like bursts of sharp wire against his skin. He had to resist the urge to wince more than once.

The rose brought spring,
And love burst forth, a shower on my soul,
Cleansed and made strong, I followed you,
Your words filled my mind like perfume,

My sweet rose

The world shook
Swords, knives and beasts
But none could harm because you held back death.

Our summer came as the nights grew short,
My love blooming as your beauty shone,
You guided my hand with no need for thorn,
Though my voice betrayed me, I was yours
My brilliant rose.

Then the dark came
Chains, traitors and schemes
When it mattered, I couldn't hold back the dead.

It was not getting easier. He'd hoped that as the words flowed his voice would return, but the opposite was true. He knew the last verse would be a challenge as the pitch increased.

Now no more seasons,
The world has ended,
How can I go on when you are not here?
The one thing I know
Is I will avenge you, my one and only rose.

Plucked
Scattered...

His voice cracked as he reached for the higher note and then disappeared entirely. He looked around at his audience, the concern on their faces evident. He screwed his eyes shut to escape their pitying looks; he didn't need that. He needed Petra to hear these words.

Mareth took a deep breath and started the verse again but his voice faltered in the same place. He forced the sound up his throat, the exertion sending the blood to his face as if he was starved of breath. And then, as if a blockage was removed from a pipe, his voice was free. But it wasn't his voice of old, the voice of a song-weaver. It emerged as the sound of a thousand nails being dragged across glass.

The sound was unbearable. He clamped his hands over his own ears as he saw his friends do likewise. He tried to stop the screeching shriek, but now that it was loosed it would not stop. He fell to his knees and stricken with grief, glared up at the crystal ceiling, wondering what he had done to deserve this. Redemption dangled in front of him and then ripped away. Love paraded past him and then the gate cruelly locked. And now his voice betrayed him.

Another noise joined the cacophony. A rumbling and cracking sound from all around. Mareth saw a large crystal facade fall from the wall far in front of him and crash to the floor. Then Dolph was in his field of vision, a trickle of blood running down from his nose and mixing into his blond beard. An open hand swung around and slapped Mareth across the face, and he fell to his knees. His cheek stung, like he could feel the imprint of his former bodyguard's hand, but at least, he realized in relief, he was silent.

"What the fuck?" shouted Motega.

"The rock fall, it's not stopping," called Morris over an increasing number of cracks. Mareth watched his friends turn around on the spot, staring at what he had done, and he couldn't move himself to do anything. He had thought that this was going to help, that he would be able to come to terms with the horrors of the past few weeks, but it was obvious that he was truly cursed.

"It's not really a rock fall," said Kyle. He pointed to the ceiling where the first sheets of crystal had fallen. "Look. These were eggs, and they are hatching. I should have seen it earlier. These must be Ankheg."

Mareth squinted his eyes to see an insect pull itself from its crystal cocoon, wiping away ichor from its eyes and mouth with a front leg. The creature must have been at least as big as a man. There were many emerging all around the cavern.

"What do we do?" asked Trypp.

"It's not often that our people see the emergence of Ankheg. But I believe the next step is that they feed. Usually, they eat each other. I'm not sure how us being in the middle of this changes the situation."

"So...?"

"I think we should run," said Kyle earnestly.

"You heard the man," shouted Morris. "Back to the sleds. Mouse, Kyle. Get us out of here, quick. Ravens, ready your bows just in case."

The others ran back to where they had left the worms. But Mareth was dazed again. He felt like he had when he had first awakened in Unedar Halt after being rescued, and his world had crashed down around him. Perhaps being breakfast for a new born monster would be a blessing.

"I'll be able to find it again," shouted Kyle, gripping his shirt and pulling him down so they were face to face. "I can find this cavern again. When we've done what we need to do. I know how much it means to you. We can clear it out." Kyle nodded along to himself as he spoke. "I'm sure the Forger will help. But you have to go." Kyle lent over and pulled Mareth to his feet with surprising ease. He looped Mareth's arm over his shoulder and led him away. Mareth's room of light crashed down around him like the sun room in his dream, as the crawling dark appeared.

DUNDENAS 3

THE PITFALLS OF LEADERSHIP

"How can they run so fast?" called Syd. The Raven had obviously not come across goblins before, or hadn't been target of a swarm. Unfortunately, Neenahwi couldn't say the same.

In fact, it had only been around a year since the last time she had been chased by a horde of gobbos. Not a tradition she had been intending to keep.

Last time, she had the demon stone in her hand; freshly liberated from the panther demon queen. Now, she wished she had it. Why was it that whenever they ran into something underground it came with many hundreds of friends?

Why did they have such rotten luck that their path would take them right through a goblin wedding?

~

EARLIER THAT MORNING, THE DAY HAD STARTED MUCH LIKE the other days since the wonder of traveling underground had faded. Sheer monotony and intense oppression. Which meant everyone grumbled while they had breakfast, and everyone complained some more as they climbed into their sleds. Well, Mareth didn't complain. He hadn't spoken at all for the past few days since his aborted remembrance ceremony. Neenahwi felt a little sorry for him. He'd been drained, locked up in the dark, and then the love of his life had died. Officially at the hands of Lady Grey, which wasn't twisting the truth too much. After all, if it wasn't for Grey then Neenahwi would never have been in that situation, never have had to try to rescue the pair of them and then be faced with such a horrible choice. She didn't see how it would help anyone if she had to explain that she was the one who had accidentally killed Petra—it certainly did not help her mental state.

But she couldn't help but think that Mareth was milking it. Being sad was fine for a while. But people died when there was a war.

Loved ones died.

Your whole family could die and you could never see how you were going to make things right. But you had to carry on.

Sadness she understood. But she needed everyone to be angry with it. She needed them to have a fire in their belly, so they would be able to see through what needed to be done.

Whatever—specifically—that may be, she would figure out later.

But what had happened to Mareth's voice did trouble her. It was not physically possible for a human to make a noise that could burst blood vessels and shatter crystal. So that only left magic and, although she was not an expert, she'd never heard of a song weaver doing that in the past.

This is what she had been thinking of, sitting in their

sled, when there had been the tell-tale *crack* of the worm eating through stone and into a new chamber. The worm accelerated quickly, free of the obstruction, the sled sliding behind the great purple creature—gliding effortlessly on the gray effluent that the worm spewed from its rear. Most chambers they passed through were benign enough. Some of them were beautiful, rainbow shades of rock and sparkling stalagmites. Others were interesting from an academic perspective, like the one cavern that held millions of palm-sized red beetles crawling all over the walls. Apparently, an insect that Mouse said he was familiar with. Something about being good to warm beds.

This chamber, though, turned out to be part of a goblin hive. How you could drive head-first into a goblin hive was beyond her. She was sure that Kyle would have noticed somehow, or given the worm enough free reign to avoid it itself, but Mouse was the one who was driving in front today and he liked to go fast. She would have been fine to not have the crazy alchemist lead the way but he insisted on it, and as she was depending on his potions to control their transport—these worms were way past the age and size of where they typically became independent of their dwarven handlers—she thought it was best to give him some of what he wanted.

Though plowing into a chamber full of goblins who were busy drinking, cheering, singing (though it was difficult to understand), and waving around a variety of wicked looked weapons was giving her pause to reconsider her previous decision. Their worm slowed to a halt and the sled slid for a short way before stopping. She could see that Kyle's worm had entered the chamber too, but it was not slowing down. In fact, she could see Kyle sitting up in his saddle on the worm's back, waving his arms above his head.

"What are they doing?" asked Syd behind her.

"Look up there on the ledge," said Cherry. "The one that has the feathers all over them is the groom. He has to go to the surface and find birds to get the feathers. They use tar to stick them on. Apparently, the wedding night involves the bride nibbling them all off, which I imagine can take some time. That's the bride dressed in the armor and holding the sword."

"Why is she dressed like that?"

"She's warning the other goblin women that she'll fight them if they want a piece of her man." Neenahwi half listened to the exchange, surprised by Cherry's knowledge of goblin lore, though she wasn't surprised about the extent of the subject matter, as she tried to assess their situation.

"How *do* you know all of this?" asked Trypp.

"Used to have a hole near our village where a small hive would come to the surface occasionally. Young male goblins would forever be coming and plucking our chickens during the night. Not killing 'em, mind. We'd just wake up in the morning to find another bald and traumatized chuck. I guess all of their grooms looked like chickens in their hive."

"Look, this is all very bloody interesting. Seriously, I learnt something there," said Neenahwi. "But can anyone help me get the attention of our driver? I think we have been noticed."

As one, her sled-mates noticed that hundreds of the little gray creatures, with sharp claws and sharper teeth, were appraising the things that had made a new hole in the wall of their home and brought a purple worm into their entry hall. Neenahwi figured it was only the presence of the purple worm that had so far kept them from charging.

"Where's the other sled?" asked her brother.

"They didn't stop to gawk like us. Let's go after it!"

And, as one, they all finally understood the situation and called out to Mouse to get them moving.

The worm's body sections convulsed as it rippled to propel them forward. The slack disappeared on the harness connected to the chain, a lurch that caused everyone standing to stumble. And they were on their way again.

Of course, the goblins charged.

~

MOTEGA SHOT AN ARROW, TAKING DOWN ONE OF THE LEAD pursuing goblins. The Ravens—Midnight, Cherry, and Syd—all had crossbows in their hands and were shooting too, taking down a target with each shot. It was difficult to miss when there were so many. The worm seemed to be going as fast as it could and as it was following the other group, it didn't need to carve its own way through the rock. But the grey gaggle was closing on them fast. They scurried over one another and up the walls, shrieking and giggling, lobbing knives or axes that would clatter against the side of the sled. Trypp cursed as he ducked to avoid projectile launched with more precision.

Neenahwi stood behind her brother, out of the way of those who were trying to shoot, unsure what to do. She could use her silver arrows, but she was afraid they could be easily lost and there wouldn't be anywhere to replace them when they reached her home land. Of course, she wished she had the demon stone. Roast goblin would be on the menu by now if she had. As she dithered about what to do, she spotted Trypp looking at her, an eye brow raised as if he too was asking what she was going to do about this. She was almost going to shrug when she heard a shout from the front of the sled.

One hand on the railing, she pulled herself to the front of their carriage, Trypp doing likewise on the other side. Across the way, dangling from the rear of the worm, his legs twisted around the leather harness, was Mouse. He called something out but Neenahwi couldn't make out what it was so she shook her head. He tried again and much to her consternation she still didn't get it.

"Do you know what he said?" she asked Trypp.

"Look in the box?" he said. "Maybe this one?" Trypp bent over near his feet, lifting up the cage that had her brother's bird locked inside it, miserable from confinement, and opened the lid to a wooden crate. He emerged moments later with two clay balls in his hands. Trypp held them up so Mouse could see. The alchemist gave two thumbs up and then began the climb back along the worm to his saddle.

"Grenades?" asked Neenahwi, surprised. She hadn't paid any attention to the box before.

"I assume so. Let's go see if they will help scare off our goblin problem."

Trypp pushed his way past the others to the rear of the sled, hollering for them to move as he walked extra carefully, his arms outstretched above him so that someone wouldn't accidentally knock his precious cargo. He offered her one of the globes and pointed to the right. Trypp counted to three and they both lobbed the balls at the same time.

They landed a few strides in front of the pursuing horde, the clay globes shattering in a splatter of liquid that hit the front of the wave of goblins and splashed backwards down the ranks. For a second nothing happened. There was no big explosion, the disappointment on Trypp's face mirroring her own. Not even a puff of a smoke that would hopefully confuse them for a moment (but it wasn't like they were going to make a sixty-foot-long worm disappear).

But then, while she was still cursing the alchemist for false hope, the wet goblins erupted in flames—initially wherever they had been splashed, but it quickly spread across their scrawny little bodies and back to the group behind. The pursuit stopped suddenly. Shrieks of fiery pain from the goblins at the front, followed by jeers from those behind. Some of those foolishly decided to climb their tinder brethren, only to create more screams and goblin candles.

That ended the hunt.

Neenahwi turned to look at Trypp. From the look on his face she could tell he was thinking the same thing as her. "How many others are in that box and what's stopping them from breaking?"

He gulped and rushed to check.

~

"WHAT WERE YOU DOING?" CRIED KYLE AS HE STOMPED across the barren underground chamber where they had caught up with the other worm. The target of his ire was Mouse, but Neenahwi caught the daggered glares sent her direction every few words. "This is not a game! This is the Dundenas. It is dangerous here!"

Mouse slid down off the side of the worm, which was dozing after an administration of some liquid. Neenahwi went to meet the pair of them. She could imagine that certain members of her party would find a punch up between the bookish alchemist and the short dwarf to be hilarious, but she had the good sense to know that Kyle had the strength of someone who worked with stone hidden under that beard and those baggy clothes.

"I am sorry, Kyle," said Mouse. "I did not know the goblin hive was there. But it was most fascinating to watch. Did you know that was a wedding par—"

"Yes, I knew. Did you know that a goblin wedding always ends in a war party?" Mouse gulped and shook his head. "No, I thought not."

Neenahwi arrived just as Mouse bowed his head in shame. She was about to speak, her intention to try to broker some peace between the two of them, when she became Kyle's next target.

"Neenahwi. I must insist that you communicate to everyone here about the dangers we face. This is not a...a...holiday. This is dangerous." And on those words, Kyle turned on his heel, his face red with embarrassment at his admonishment of Neenahwi, and stalked off to see what had been captured for dinner, leaving her to consider how she was apparently responsible for everyone now.

~

DINNER.

Language lesson, even for her as she had hardly spoken Alfarian since arriving in Edland.

Then Motega and Kanaveen paid her a visit.

Neenahwi could tell that she wasn't going to like it by the words "we need to talk" and "let's go somewhere private."

She stopped what she was doing—which seeing as somehow she had found herself receiving a lecture from The Librarian on the breeding habits of goblins, she was quite happy about—and followed the pair back down the tunnel they had traveled earlier. She swung the The Librarian back and forth by his top knot as she walked, ignoring his pleas to put him down.

Her brother and her old guardian turned to face her.

"What's on your minds?" she asked, smiling and trying to present a façade of confidence that she wasn't exactly feeling.

Motega looked at the older man, and he nodded back. She could tell they were drawing straws to see who was going to broach the subject. Motega got the short one, simply as a result of Kanaveen having more commitment to not saying anything. "Have you looked at this group recently?" He waved his hand to encompass everyone they had moved away from. "What do you see?"

Neenahwi turned back and looked at her fellow travelers. They were sat around the cavern in various groups. The Ravens were off to one side. Alana and Fin were talking with Kyle. Trypp was polishing his knives next to Dolph. Mouse and Mareth were both off on their own. Mareth appeared to be brooding again.

She shrugged. "They look alright to me. Maybe a bit bored."

"Yes, they're bored," he said. "We're all sick to the back teeth of being underground. The problem is that everyone is sticking to their groups."

"He's right Neeni," said Kanaveen. "I have been alone too long. I didn't notice it. But we need everyone to be used to working together."

"There's time before we get home. We're probably only half way," she said.

"What is the point in sharpening a spear after you need it?" Motega and Neenahwi exchanged a look and a smile at one of Kanaveen's favorite sayings.

"You do realize that you're the leader now, don't you?" said Motega, ruining her brief moment of fun.

"Pardon? I saved everyone and told people where we need to go, but that doesn't make me the leader for everything." She heard a dry wheezing sound from close to her feet and realized that the librarian was laughing. There was no need for that. She gave him a little kick. "What about Mareth?"

"Mareth is struggling, sis. I don't know if he's going to make it through this. Even if he comes around, we're heading back to Alfaria. He isn't going to know anything about what needs to be done or how to do it."

"What about you then?" she said to her brother. "You know them all better than I do."

Motega rolled his eyes and looked back to Kanaveen. She knew he was asking for help.

"Neeni. You are my chief," said Kanaveen.

But that was the problem, she wasn't anyone's chief. She no longer knew who her real father was, and if it wasn't Sheref, then she'd have no right to be chieftain of what was left of the Wolfclaw clan. That would be Motega's right. Neenahwi tried to steady herself. The number of secrets she hid from everyone, including her brother, were mounting up; and though they didn't take a toll in the telling, their collective weight was starting to drag on her conscience.

"We're with you, sis, but you're going to need to start taking charge."

"Shit. I'm not used to working with people. You know that. How about I just tell you all what to do and you do it without complaining?"

Motega laughed. "I'm not sure that Sergeant Morris is the best example for your leadership style. What are you going to do, give us all nicknames?"

"Hah. Alright then, Shaun." Motega appeared puzzled. "Shorn? The hair? Still not funny I guess." She looked at Motega and Kanaveen, realizing that her attempts at humor were not helping. "Fine! I'll think about it and then get everyone together to talk tomorrow night. Will that do?"

"That is a good idea, Neeni. So, tell us what the plan is for when we return. The others will want to know tomorrow too."

Ah, double shit. She was dreading this moment. Or to be honest she had just been hoping that she could avoid this conversation until they arrived, and everything would fall into place, what they needed to do being suddenly apparent. "I don't know..." Kanaveen's eyebrows shot up in surprise and so she plowed on. "I don't know exactly what we're going to do. Do you? I have no idea what is going to be waiting for us when we get there. All I know is that Llewdon wants our people to help him try to become a god again. And we need to stop that from happening."

"Do you know that for a fact?"

"Well, no. He hasn't fucking told me, has he?" One challenge after another was wearing her defenses thin. "This is what I have deduced from all of my research. Let's also remember that we didn't have a whole bunch of options open to us either. Grey has a puppet on the throne in Kingshold, Ioth is a smoldering ruin, and I don't think we have any armies hidden away anywhere."

The two men exchanged looks again. Kanaveen shrugged, she hoped in acceptance. "I guess that's true. Do you know where we're going to surface?"

She shook her head. This had been bothering her too. What if they appeared right in the middle of a Pyrfew encampment? Or in the middle of a town? "No. We're dependent on Kyle. He can sense the way the land and the rock moves. He knows we're under water right now because the rock isn't that thick above us." Motega suddenly looked alarmed at the thought that an ocean could fall on his head at any moment. "He's going to tell us when we start going back up and in which direction. We definitely need to keep him safe."

"He was pretty pissed off earlier today. You should talk to Mouse. When we first grabbed him from the pirates, I thought he was a bundle of nerves. Turns out he's a little tapped," said Motega. Neenahwi nodded in agreement. She did need to get him to calm down, he couldn't take risks with all of their lives. Just another thing to add to the list. She was sure she wasn't going to enjoy the burden of leadership. "I don't know what we do when we get there either," continued her brother, "but I have something for you. Took me a little while to get it down, but our father told me about this when I was in Ioth."

Motega passed over a rolled-up piece of parchment. She opened it to see a map of the Jeweled Continent—it must have been the one he had taken from Hoxteth's house, judging by the label of Starras in the middle of it. He indicated that she should flip it over.

"It's Alfaria. He told me as much detail as he knew, which outside of the plains is not great. But still, it's a start. The east we know a bit about. The coast. The great forests and then the wall of mountains before you reach Missapik. But look here." Motega pointed to a great rent drawn on the map to the west of the grasslands and plains of her home. "He said that this is a desert, and on the other side of the desert, legend says is the place where our people first lived. That they are still there. That they welcome strangers. And they will help their people when needed."

She narrowed her eyes. "Sounds like a children's tale to me. You want to go that far and find out there's just more desert? I don't know, Motega." She shook her head skeptically. But if it was true, that could be something. Even if it wasn't true, maybe it could still be enough of an idea for them all to rally around?

"Me neither, but I wanted you to know. Might be we'll need to risk it. See what's there after all. Unless, you can do some magic and go and investigate like you did when we were in Ioth?"

Neenahwi had hoped for a moment that she had escaped any question about magic, especially seeing as she hadn't helped earlier that day with the goblins. "Er... It's not that simple."

"Yes, it is," piped up The Librarian. "Time consuming. Tiring. But simple. Or at least it should be."

"Shut up," said Neenahwi through gritted teeth.

"You should tell them," said the severed head.

Neenahwi could see Motega's head bobbing up and down as his attention shifted from her to the head of the wight and back. "What is he talking about?" asked her brother.

"It is obvious now that I think on it," said Kanaveen thoughtfully. "I should have noticed before."

Neenahwi decided to play it stupid, even though

Kanaveen wasn't usually the person to try to lay a trap. "What are you both talking about?"

"Where's the stone, Neeni?"

Shit. Stupid Kanaveen. It would have taken Motega days to figure it out on his own. She sighed. "It's gone. Grey took it from me." Motega's mouth hung open like a porthole, so she continued on with the explanation. "You heard how Grey stopped me when I was freeing Mareth and Petra. That's all true. Grimes. The knights. The dwarves coming out to save us. All of it is true." She took a deep breath, readying herself what came next. "But before we got to the Mountain gate, Grey ensorcelled me to hand over the gem. I couldn't believe what I had done once the stone was in her hand and she let the spell drop. I felt so stupid. The only way we got away is because she couldn't figure out how to use it."

Neenahwi leaned back against the tunnel wall and slid slowly to the floor, her head falling into her hands. "That's another reason why we couldn't go against her and her version of Mareth directly. I can't compete against the stone, and she's probably figured it out by now. Or just found how to do it by reading my notes in my tower. I feel so stupid, Motega! When Gawl Tegyr ambushed me last summer it was the first time I'd fought another magic user. But she was much more nuanced than he was. I still have no idea how she did that."

"I could tell you, if you were to ask," said The Librarian from where he rested on the floor next to her.

"Thank you, I guess."

"Does anyone else know?" asked Motega looking back at the group.

"No. I didn't tell anyone."

"Good. But you need to be careful. Fin is watching. That

girl has sharp eyes," warned Motega. Neenahwi looked up and tried to reset her face to something less painted with despair. "What are we going to do?"

"I really don't know. But I know we'll figure it out. Even if I can't use something like the stone as a shortcut, we'll see it out."

Motega locked her gaze with his, and for a moment she couldn't tell what he was thinking. He appeared very serious. Not like himself at all. She wondered if this is what he was like when he was 'working'. "Fine. You know I'll follow you anywhere. But this means it's even more important for you got to get this group together. We need to practice operating together. Working as a team. Do you know how much time me and Trypp and Florian used to spend getting to know each other so that we were good at what we did? It's a lot. Get started, something small to begin will be fine. Change the groups up in the sleds."

"I get it," she said as she stood up. "Tomorrow night. During dinner. Promise."

Motega smiled and hugged his sister. "Don't worry. You'll do great, and we'll all figure it out together."

~

NEENAHWI HAD RETIRED TO A QUIET PATCH OF CAVERN wall away from the main group who lay on their mats, trying to get some sleep. She'd tried to sleep the first few days of their travels but she'd found it all but impossible. The glow of their ever-lit lanterns, or the constant dull light from the bizarre mosses that grew wild here and there, made it difficult for her to still her racing thoughts and fall asleep. And when she did, she was greeted by the apparition of her guilt.

Petra.

Unspeaking, she would stare at Neenahwi—a look of deep disappointment on her face—and Neenahwi knew what she was asking: why? Why had she killed her? Why hadn't she been more careful, or done something else to get them to safety? And Neenahwi didn't like the answer. It chafed her in the long quiet moments on board the sled, as much as the demon stone necklace used to tear at her skin.

The simple answer was that she had become greedy.

She used to have such a gentle touch in how she drew the mana needed for her magics—even Jyuth remarked on it. But she'd been spoiled by the demon stone and all it offered her. Why practice restraint when you can have all you need?

Until it's gone at least.

She wondered if she should have told Motega and Kanaveen the truth. She knew they would still love her, eventually, but she was afraid to see the looks of disappointment on heir faces. And she could not ask them to keep her crime a secret from Mareth and Alana. Who would follow her if they knew the truth?

Neenahwi had intended to meditate until it was her turn to take watch. Her meditations refreshed her almost as much as sleep, and without the uncomfortable attention of her own guilt. But the conversation with Motega and Kanaveen had left her discombobulated and unready to begin. She reached over to pluck the Librarian up from where she had placed him by her satchel and put him on the ground in front of her. His eyes snapped open.

"Did you know my father well?" she asked.

"I never met him. This Wild Continent was unknown to us."

She tutted. "I meant Jyuth. Were you friends?"

The head of the wight sighed, though no air escaped his lips. "Jyuth and I were not friends. I'm afraid I found him to be rather full of himself."

In spite of her previous feelings, she chuckled. This was not surprising. "Was he a good wizard? A good man?"

"I don't know if I can judge either way. We were...very different. Your...father was very sure of himself. He would take pleasure in debating with Myank about how our abilities should be used in the wider world. I, on the other hand, was more interested in the learning and less so in the application. He was very good with certain aspects of our studies, and those with which he struggled he passed off as being less important."

Neenahwi blinked as she took in what the Librarian said. If there were aspects that Jyuth had ignored, that must mean that there were gaps in her own knowledge too. "Can you give me an example?"

"Take Tarrantha for example. Jyuth thought her weak. She could not create physical forces as powerful as your father. Or conjure energy to rival his. But she knew— sorry, she *knows*—how to delicately nudge other's thoughts through careful application of glamor. And she'd obviously learned how to disguise her own form without changing shape. These were things that Jyuth thought inconsequential."

The subject of Lady Grey, or Tarra as she now knew her to be, made Neenahwi flinch. She pictured Tarra from her Quana vision, the woman suspended and tortured by Llewdon. "Was she always evil?" she asked.

"Not in the least. She had a joyful soul, eager to learn and experience the world as it has been created. She was quite uninterested by the talk of politics that Jyuth and Myank engaged in. I must admit that it came as something of a surprise to see what she had become."

Neenahwi nodded and explained what she had witnessed of Tarra after being captured while visiting the land of the elves. The Librarian's brow crumpled during the telling of the story, and for the first time she saw a glimmer of emotion in his eyes, of anger, that was swiftly replaced by sadness.

"That would explain much, and I fear it was not the last of the foul things that the elf did to her."

"Do you know how to do the glamor magic you mentioned? Could you teach me?"

"Yes, or at least I once knew how. Could I teach you?" The Librarian's eyes narrowed as he gazed on Neenahwi. "I think the question is more should I teach you? Would you be tempted to use it on those we travel with instead of winning their support through harder, more conventional means?"

Neenahwi shot upright in shock at his words, arranging her face into an expression of outrage, hoping to mask her surprise. But she was not so lucky.

"I thought so. I think it is time for you to rest and for us to speak no more. Maybe when you are being a real leader, then we can discuss this matter again."

Neenahwi huffed as she picked up the wight and moved him back to where he had rested before. He had his eyes closed to the world before she even set the head down. At least until she knocked her satchel over to lean against his face.

Accidentally, of course.

~

TWO SLEDS DURING THE DAY. THREE GROUPS AT NIGHT AS

the Ravens got together to sit on their own. Mareth wasn't speaking. Alana and the girl assassin were inseparable. It *was* pretty obvious that something was wrong with them, and Motega and Kanaveen giving her disapproving looks as she ate her breakfast of fried dwarven bread wasn't helping. She knew she should be talking with everyone, starting to mold them into something stronger than the component parts.

Or whatever it was the Forger usually said.

She sighed and got to her feet, the familial frowning becoming too much for even her to bear, with the determined intention of...talking with them. But Varcon must have been paying attention to his world below ground and decided to spare her blushes, as she was interrupted before she even got started.

"Neenahwi!" Kyle called, as the young dwarf bustled over to her. He tilted his head forward and surveyed her under arched brows. "I have spoken to Mouse about going so fast—"

"Wonderful. Thank you, Kyle." Neenahwi was *this* close to clapping in celebration, something she had not done since a child.

"But I am not sure that he is going to listen. I think you need to speak with him. And then we need to be going. We have been here too long." Neenahwi's heart dropped, the good news snatched away as quickly as it had appeared. The dwarf didn't look happy either, his brow furrowed and his eyes darting from side to side "I am concerned *things* may come."

He waited expectantly until she said she would talk with the other worm rider. "I'll talk to him now, but you tell everyone to collect their things. Time to hitch up and roll out. They can finish their breakfast while we move." Kyle smiled and set off to work.

Well, at least one person listened to her.

She gathered her own things together and stowed them in the back of the wagon. Trypp and her brother brought their bedrolls and jammed them under the steel benches.

"Well?" asked Motega. He wasn't going to let her get away with doing nothing it seemed. Neenahwi tutted in frustration and turned to look at the group that was being corralled by Kyle. Normally she would think of talking to Mareth—he was Lord Protector after all—but he wasn't much use at the moment since he wasn't speaking. She supposed it would have to be Alana, despite the onset of guilt that she knew would be forthcoming.

Her father's former servant girl was loading up the dishes from breakfast into a metal crate as Neenahwi loomed over her.

"Alana, can I have a word?"

She looked up and Neenahwi saw that little remained of the nervous maid from last summer. She supposed that wasn't surprising after what Alana had been through in Ioth—Neenahwi knew how quickly she had grown up after the death of her own family—but while the death of Petra had crippled Mareth, Alana appeared more solid, more certain in her disposition; like she had inherited the confidence of her dead sister.

"What is it?"

"Tonight. We all need to talk. About how we can become more of a unit. I'd really appreciate your ideas, if you could think on it today."

Alana considered her words for a moment before nodding in agreement. "Makes sense. Who knows what we'll find at our destination, right? I know I'll appreciate having an idea what I should be doing."

Before Neenahwi could respond there was a call from behind her.

"Come on you slow coaches! Time to get moving,"

Mouse. Neenahwi looked back at Alana who shrugged in response. "Good. So, we'll talk later. Enjoy the mind-numbing boredom," joked Neenahwi with a forced smile. She lifted up the hem of her robe and trotted back to her worm and the metal sled that trailed behind it.

That hadn't gone too badly, she thought. *Maybe she didn't need to worry about that evening either?*

She climbed aboard the back of the wagon, Syd offering a hand to help her up as it lurched forward, and only then did she remember that she hadn't spoken to the crazed alchemist they had steering their worm.

Well, Kyle had spoken to him. *What harm could it do that she hadn't?*

WHATEVER THEY CLASSIFIED AS 'MORNING' WAS GOING A lot slower than their sled. Neenahwi wasn't in the mood for conversation and so she flipped through loose-leafed, hand-written pages she had claimed from Myank's tower. She could tell that the Librarian was looking at her disdainfully—he had been horrified to learn that the library had been sullied, and she in turn pointed out that someone had done a pretty good job of sullying the shit out of it before she had even arrived—even though she had no intention of giving him the satisfaction of confirming that by glancing where he was propped. But she wasn't really in the mood for reading either. She'd been through these pages many times before and she doubted she was going to learn much more from reading them again. Questioning the Librarian would be more fruitful, but she didn't want to speak to him after last night. The only benefit of holding the written pages was that it put anyone off from talking to her.

Unfortunately, she could still hear what others had to say.

"Aren't we going a bit quick?" asked Cherry. Neenahwi looked over the top of the essay on gods of thunder to see her clutching her knees nervously as she looked up at the roof of the tunnel flashing past.

"I thought you always liked to go fast. Isn't that right, Midnight?" The pimply boy—Neenahwi wondered if he was the mascot of the Ravens when she had met him—laughed at his innuendo and his elbow dug into the ribs of the other woman sitting next to him.

"Shut the fuck up, Syd," grunted Cherry.

"Wasn't he supposed to take it easier today?" *Shit.* Now Trypp was getting involved. Neenahwi knew where this was headed.

"Sis..."

Neenahwi sighed and slammed the papers down on the bench next to her. "Fine! I'll get him to slow down."

From the corner of her eye she could see her brother exchange a look with Trypp, the type of look where someone knows that they're walking close to the fucking edge. He wasn't wrong. "I was just going to ask if you had warned Mouse?"

"I said I'll take care of it." She pushed herself to her feet and tottered down the middle of the sled between the two banks of facing benches. The sled lurched as they started to turn a bend at speed and she had to reach over

Cherry to steady herself against the wall. They must have been traveling in an existing worm tunnel to be able to go this fast. Mouse was probably enjoying himself, the bloody lunatic. She knew the thrill of flying and traveling at speed, but she never had a death trap of a metal box on skids being towed behind her to worry about. She reached the front and stood on one of the few stowage boxes to take a look.

Ahead of her she could see the rear end of the massive worm. Its sphincter convulsed with a phosphorescent glow that illuminated the ground between her and it, even though it wasn't eating its way through the underground. She tried to see further along the body of the worm to where she knew the alchemist would be strapped chest down to the top of the creature, guiding it along with the help of his concoctions; but in the dark, she couldn't see him.

"Mouse! Slow down!" she shouted.

There was no answer. She tried again, but to no avail. *Shit!* Then the tunnel straightened and emerged into a narrow cavern, lit by glowing mosses, and she could finally make out the worm's pilot.

"Mouse!"

Mouse turned to look back just as she felt Motega at her side, his presence unmistakable. He brought his hands to his mouth and called out. "Slow! The fuck! Down!"

Motega squinted, unable to see Mouse's reaction, but she did. Briefly. Mouse cupped his ear in confusion as the worm disappeared into another tunnel and once again, they could see no further than the worm's periproct. More bodies had joined her and her brother at the wall of the sled and they were all calling out, shouting over the din of the metal skids on slick stone, unknowing if any of their efforts were reaching as far forward as the man strapped to the side of the purple worm.

Then she couldn't hear her wagon mates over the roar of rushing water. Bright orange light burst against her eyes as the dark of the tunnel receded and for a moment, she thought they had done it—got through to him—as the worm stopped ahead of them and the sled slid forwards to bounce off the back of the beast.

Her eyes widened and she gripped the edge of the sled as she realized she was wrong. The worm hadn't completely stopped. It was inching forwards ever so slowly, until the chains pulling the wagon were taught once again and they were pulled out into a vast underground chasm.

The sight was like a slap across the face. The space was massive, stretching hundreds of feet above them. From a fissure in the roof came a torrent of water, plunging down past the worm. Huge clouds of steam rose up from below them. Neenahwi struggled to make sense of where all of the water would be coming from, her mind refusing to entertain the notion of a leak in the ocean floor, as the sled lurched forward again suddenly.

And that's when she realized how much shit they were in.

The long indigo body of the worm was tensed, it's mouth gouging into the rock wall across from them. But underneath the worm was open air, the vast rent in the Dundenas continuing down some unknown distance below. And though it was trying to hold on, Neenahwi could see that it's rear was slipping toward the precipice. She turned and called for everyone to get off the wagon, pushing them toward the rear. Someone climbed over the back, falling with a grunt. The sled lurched and so did her stomach, and she tried futilely to hold onto the sled as the world spun.

The worm had lost its grip on their side of the chasm, its tail falling into the void and dragging the sled behind it. Down into the chasm. The worm swung like a pendulum to crash into the opposite wall, the sled following suit, throwing Neenahwi and the others to the rear of the now vertical wagon. She didn't have time to worry about the mass of arms and legs on top of her as the wagon smashed into the rock face, jarring them all from where they lay tumbled. Neenahwi grabbed on to someone, she wasn't sure who, and held on tight, all the while gushing forth a stream of obscenities like a spider casting out silk to arrest a fall. Thankfully, whoever she had held onto must have had a good handhold because miraculously not one of them fell out.

The wagon swung back and forth in ever decreasing arcs to thump against the rocks until eventually it came to a halt. One by one they pulled themselves to their feet to stand on the narrow strip of metal that had been the back of the sled. Her heart pounded. They weren't a mess of steel and bone and stone at the bottom of the chasm, so that was at least a positive development. She was afraid to look up and see how her luck might be changing the other way, but she did so nonetheless. The worm clung on above them, its long body stretched thin at the weight dangling from its tail. *How long would it be able to hold on?*

"Trypp, grab the line from my pack," directed Motega. "It's only about fifty feet to that ledge."

She looked down and spied the ledge her brother referred to. A small outcrop another twenty feet or so above a stretch of ground that bordered a long, slowly moving river of molten rock. In seconds the line was secured and Motega was sliding down, leaving her with the order to remember his bird. He held the rope as Cherry and Midnight descended, then Trypp. Neenahwi told Kanaveen to go on ahead, that she could float down so she should watch the line. But she was also desperately looking around for two things that she wasn't going to leave without. Per was lying against the wall of his cage stunned and the Librarian had become wedged under a bench. She ignored his lack of gratitude at the rescue.

A sound like the scraping of steel on stone came from above.

A shriek from the man strapped to the worm above.

And then she, along with the steel sled and the sixty-foot-long purple worm, fell.

NEENAHWI LEAPT FROM THE PLUMMETING METAL SLED before she'd even split her consciousness. She drew carefully at her own reserves of mana, bringing forth a cushion of air to slow her fall. She'd been worried about how she had become greedy so she'd been deliberately frugal in the thread she created to herself; so her fall might not have been quite so graceful and impressive as on other occasions.

The sled hit the rock first. Its weight throwing up a plume of shrapnel and dust, their belongings exploding out in a shower. She was slowly falling away from the impact zone, to where she now saw her sled-mates picking themselves up off the floor after they had jumped from the ledge in the nick of time. They looked up, horror etched on their faces and for a brief moment Neenahwi wondered why.

Then she realized that the worm was overtaking her.

The worm hit the ledge, its tail crumpling up as the rest of its body followed it down, a second before Neenahwi greeted the ground with a kiss; well, more accurately it gave her a smack in the mouth. The others were already scattering from the worm that was cascading from the ledge like a purple waterfall. The beast tried to latch hold of the stone with the hand sized hooks that protruded from each of its purple segments, but its weight was too great and it fell towards Neenahwi as she tried to lever herself up off her aching and skinned knees. She had to do something, and she didn't have the luxury of being subtle. Drawing once more on her own life force, she pushed out desperately at the toppling tower of worm, adjusting its fall to the side, away from herself and the others. The worm crashed down into the river of molten rock, the screams of the man still strapped to its back reverberating through the canyon. Splashes of lava flew into the air, orange one moment, a dull grey the next as they cooled in their arc of flight. There was a scream behind her as someone must have been hit but she couldn't even turn and see who it was. She was exhausted from drawing on her own strength, and she was transfixed by the great purple worm that writhed atop the molten rock. Its flesh suddenly caught alight, flames flickering up its side, and its bellows reminded her of those of the specter she'd fought for Unedar Halt.

Mouse appeared on the top of the worm's back—he must have clambered up the other side—and he set off at a run along it toward solid ground as more of the worm's length sparked into flame. He reached the head and launched himself into the air, landing in a heap not too far away from where Neenahwi was still on all fours. The worm shuddered one more time and then was still as the flames consumed it.

She got to her feet and looked back toward where the others had fled. One of the Ravens was beating another's arm with a shirt, attempting to put out a fire. Motega was already close enough to help her stand and she leaned on him in relief, taking in their surroundings.

The orange glowing river snaked through the chasm floor, illuminating rock faces that had been carved with strange beasts and shapes that she did not recognize—was this the work of the Deep People? The air was full of steam, hot and wet it clung to her hair and clothes, making them heavy.

"You fucking idiot!" screamed Trypp as he neared the fallen alchemist, a murderous look in his eyes. Neenahwi had never seen him like that before. "What were you doing?"

Mouse didn't flinch—or move at all for that matter. He lay still, though she could see that his chest still moved. Kanaveen, a shirtless Cherry, and Midnight—tears in her eyes as she clutched her smoldering arm—all approached, the steam looming large behind them.

"We'll teach him a lesson later," said Motega to his friend. He looked around nervously. "Pick him up. We need to find a way to get back to the others. And keep it down, we don't want to attract any attention."

"I think the big worm falling was already pretty loud," shrieked Midnight.

That was not a good sign. The soldier sounded manic, and they needed to be careful. Kyle's warning came back to her; that strange and dangerous things lurked in the Dundenas, when she saw the steam coalesce into a pair of floating figures, no bigger than a child, as they floated a foot of the ground. Red eyes hung in the vaguely humanoid face above an exaggeratedly pointed nose. They drifted toward them.

"Fall back," she called. She didn't know what they were, and while they didn't look imposing, experience had taught her it was always best to be careful around creatures of magic.

But Cherry either couldn't hear her or wasn't listening; of course, she wasn't used to following her orders. "Form up," she countered, and she and Midnight drew long knives that shone like shards of amber in the light of the cavern. The steam sprites floated forward, one of them blasting a cloud of steam that shot into Cherry's face. Her arm shot up instinctively to protect her eyes, and she bellowed in rage and jumped forward, knife outstretched. Midnight joined her in the attack before Neenahwi could do anything. She watched as Cherry's blade flashed toward the creature, but her eyes were drawn to a line of shadows that appeared in the bank of steam.

"Stop!" she called again, but it was too late. Cherry's knife sliced through the air where the steam sprite's head should be, the wisps of steam separating as she cut through the air. The red eyes faded and the vapor curled in on itself from all sides into a tight ball, before it exploded out into a cloud of steam that blew out with enough force to send Cherry and Midnight sprawling to the floor.

From the fog appeared the formerly shadowed creatures. They were tall and thin, walking on two legs though they were not human. Their bright red smooth skin and wide blinking eyes gave them the look of salamanders. There was more than a score, evenly spaced, and they each held long spiked spears. One of them made a sound like they were speaking and the line of salamanders spread around, encircling them. Spears held at the ready. *Shit!* She'd never seen these creatures before in the flesh, but she'd read about them while pouring through records in the Unedar Halt archives.

Those written entries had not indicated a proclivity for friendship.

"Can you do anything?" whispered Motega out of the corner of his mouth.

Neenahwi considered the question. She was too weak to even stand unaided; such had been the force required to stop the worm from landing on her. She reached out, searching for sources of mana that she could build a thread to—but this place was dead. The heat of the molten river made it inhospitable to life other than those that menaced them, and she couldn't make a connection with them as they were sentient, but it still didn't stop her from trying. It was surrender and hope for the best, or fight and more than likely die.

She found herself outside the gate to Unedar Halt once more, contemplating if that was the time when she should make a last stand, and wondering again if her time had come. But she didn't even know if she had it in her to be able to save her friends.

"No," she said finally.

She studied them intently, watching to see if there was anything they could take advantage of. One of the salamanders bent over and picked up a sword that had been thrown from the sled, inspecting it carefully with its big eyes. It turned it around in apparent wonder and clicked a few words to the one who had first spoken. She noticed now that it had a copper chain around its neck, the only adornment that any of the creatures had. "No. But maybe they don't want to kill us."

Neenahwi reached into the satchel at her waist and pulled out one of her steel arrows, holding it up in the air and letting it catch the light.

"We have more," she shouted slowly, not knowing if they could understand her but hoping that the ancient method of talking loudly and enunciating very carefully would help. The lead salamander tilted its head as it regarded the offering, its eyes narrowing through upper and lower lids that enveloped its bulbous orbs. She almost breathed out a sigh of relief as it raised its vaguely amphibious hands.

It barked an incomprehensible order and the other salamanders took two steps forward, spears lowered to point at them.

Shit. Surrender it is then.

THE SWEAT DRIPPED OFF HER FOREHEAD AND INTO HER eye. The heat was unbearable in the cavern. She hadn't thought it possible, but the steam they had left behind was actually cooler than the baking oven in which she was deposited, bound hand and foot. How she longed to be able to wipe the perspiration from her face with her sleeve, or even to take off the bloody robe and maybe cool down a little. She was shaking; the exertions of earlier coupled with the soul-sapping temperature was wreaking havoc with her body.

Neenahwi closed her eyes and tried to center herself, but her eyelids remained filled with the bright orange glow of the cave.

It was all her fault.

Kyle had told her to speak with Mouse. Motega had told her that the group wasn't used to looking to her for leadership. She'd known they were both right that morning. Why hadn't she done something about it? And how on earth was she going to go to her homeland and free her people from Llewdon's grip with little more than a handful of friends when she couldn't even get them there safely. When she didn't have her demon stone.

Her eyes opened wide, taking in her surroundings. The walls of the cave were carved straight and high, etched in relief like those of the chasm outside. The room was lit by the light from the glowing river. At one end of the chamber was a long stone table and above it, set into the wall, was a giant amber slitted eye framed with red scales. This place had the distinct feel of a temple. She knew that was probably not good news.

The others were restrained like her: with a soft red clay that had been applied to wrist and ankle that had turned hard as stone. They were scattered around the chamber, separated from each other. Her gaze skipped over to Motega as she checked to see how everyone fared, unable to avoid the accumulation of guilt at the fate that was going to befall them all because of her.

The salamanders came and went, paying little mind to their prisoners, more interested in their shiny new belongings. She closed her eyes again and said a silent prayer to her ancestors and to the Mother Tree, that their captors leave them alone long enough for her to regain her strength so she could change shape and escape. She tried to trick herself that it might only be a day or two, that she'd recovered from similar occurrences before in less time, but she knew that then she'd had sources of mana to draw on. Replenish her reserves. This place was as barren as the chasm.

She felt that she was being watched and opened her eyes again. Her little brother looked at her in disappointment and it ripped the last of her pride away. She had protected him when they had fled their home. She knew he had looked up to her, and now he saw her for the sham that she was. Not a leader. Not the chief of their clan. Just an over confident woman who wouldn't listen to advice.

Tears mingled with the sweat and her vision blurred. She mouthed "I'm sorry," to Motega though she couldn't see his reaction.

And over the altar, the giant eye blinked.

DUNDENAS 4

ESCAPE AND MUSHROOM

Thirty.

Thirty chews were the minimum needed to make the caterpillar bacon actually swallow-able. This was the latest number she had settled on; yesterday it was twenty-seven. She feared that the number was increasing every day since they left Unedar Halt.

It actually made her miss the food in Ioth, which she hadn't thought would be possible. Back before the world had turned upside down, back when it was just a problem of dealing with selfish old men, she had looked forward to getting home to Kingshold and having one of Jules' famous bacon sandwiches (smothered in Kingshold Palace sauce) with her sister before they went about their daily business.

She let the tear trickle down her cheek in silent memorial. By Arloth, it was always the littlest things that would get her thinking about Petra.

Alana felt a hand resting on her shoulder and she looked up to see Fin's concerned gaze boring into her. The assassin didn't do anything that wasn't intense, and it was reassuring to Alana that the intensity was focused on her. Fin didn't say anything and she didn't need to. She squeezed out a half smile and Fin did the same in reply.

Fin had been her constant companion since they had started their strange and bizarre journey underground—who knew that the world was like this beneath the surface? Nobody in the Narrows, that's for sure. Yesterday, it was the snarling grey goblins with their strange wedding ceremony, a sight so outrageous that she wasn't sure that anyone would believe her if she made it home to tell the tale. As she thought on this, Alana could hardly recall an hour when Fin hadn't been within sight since they had escaped Ioth.

Sergeant Morris was also someone who was keeping close to her. When they had departed the outpost of Unedar Halt, it was obvious that there should be a leader for each of the sleds. Neenahwi in the other one, and Mareth in the sled that she rode in. Morris knew the chain of command, but he'd obviously recognized that the Lord Protector was struggling now. Alana knew that she wasn't the only person to have had a harrowing experience, and Mareth in particular was fortunate that he hadn't suffered the same fate as Petra. It wasn't just the effects of captivity; the doppelgänger had left him faded and thin, the charisma of the old Mareth replaced with a weariness. And so, over the past few days, Alana had noticed that Morris was spending more time talking with her as he had done in Ioth, even providing pointers to her when she trained with Fin, or using her drills as examples for his own squad.

He had brought up a few times the question of what the plan was going to be once they eventually made it to the surface, but she couldn't answer him. She wondered if he was having second thoughts as the hours passed underground in their sled. When Neenahwi had explained her intention to travel to the Wild Continent, that they were all united in their need for revenge against Llewdon—everyone had agreed willingly, even excitedly. But now, the dark was a combination of mind-numbing monotony and—

"...danger lurks around every corner," said Kyle to no one in particular, waving his hands in the air as he walked on by. The dwarf looked flustered; although Alana did not know him that well as yet, she had been taken by his diligence, and so it was surprising to see him so agitated. Rasher of 'bacon' in hand, she got to her feet and followed him back to his pack, where he was already tinkering with glass bottles.

"Kyle, is everything alright?"

He regarded her for a moment, an appraising look as if he was wondering how much to share. "It is dangerous down here, miss. I do not like it when Mouse goes blundering through the Dundenas." He blew out his cheeks and shook his head. "Do you know that in Unedar Halt we never open a new tunnel without a cleaner crew nearby? Experienced warriors and beastie handlers, armed and ready to respond. But he just charges into the middle of goblin hives. Too much of this stuff." He shook the little glass bottle of green liquid.

"What do you mean?"

"This is the alchemy he developed to control the worms. Apparently similar to what he used to control the Draco Turtle." He crossed his arms over his broad chest. "I don't like it. I didn't want to use it. These worms are bigger than we use for digging but I still think I can get Karcan to go in roughly the right direction without it..." he trailed off, contemplating the potion in his hand for a moment.

"Have you spoken to Neenahwi about it?"

"I told him me'self! But I just told her, too. She said she's going to speak to him. But I'll be much happier if I'm leading the way today. So, let's get packing and get everyone on board."

Alana took the not so subtle hint and got to putting away the dishes from breakfast. The caterpillar bacon went into her mouth and she found herself counting chews again as she cleaned up, her mind moving to the confounding topic of Neenahwi.

The wizard had hardly spoken to her since they had begun the journey. Alana knew that she made Neenahwi uncomfortable, reminiscent of the fear of the wizard that she herself still struggled with. The guilt of not being able to save Petra hung over Neenahwi's head like a cloud. But how could she blame her for trying to rescue her sister? Though another part of her wondered, if the wizard could fight the Draco Turtle or a demon when Kingshold had been under attack, then why couldn't she have saved Petra? She knew she should talk to her about this, about what on earth they were all headed toward too. But it was not a conversation she was looking forward to.

"Alana, can I have a word?"

She looked up and as if in answer to her own unconscious summons there was Neenahwi, looking as imposing as ever, though Alana was thankful to see that the Librarian's unnervingly disembodied head was not dangling from her belt.

"What is it?"

"Tonight. I think we all need to talk. About how we," Neenahwi eyes flickered to encompass those around them, "can become more of a unit. I'd really appreciate your ideas if you could think on it today."

Alana wondered what was driving this thought, even though she couldn't disagree. Neenahwi had seemed quite happy to have her own private time on this journey; in fact, many of them were keeping to themselves. "Makes sense," she said, before seeing this as an opportunity for a broader conversation and casting a line, "Who knows what we'll find at our destination right?"

Before Neenahwi could respond there was a voice from behind her.

"Time to get moving," urged Mouse excitedly as he moved from one group to another. She could see his eagerness to be away. From the corner of her eye she could see Kyle visibly wince. Raising your voice in the Dundenas was one of his no-nos.

Neenahwi made to head back to her crew. "Good, so we'll talk later. Enjoy the mind-numbing boredom." She lifted up the hem of her robe and trotted away. Alana quickly finished off cleaning the plates with sand and got back in the sled as Kyle called time to leave.

They all took their seats on the metal benches, closed up the rear door, and braced themselves as the sled lurched into life. From where she sat at the rear of the giant purple worm, she could never see where they were going, but from the absence of the other worm behind them she was certain that Kyle had not had his wish and been the first to leave.

The morning passed slowly. She found herself thinking again of the remembered bacon sandwich, and how it represented her banishment from her own home, the chances of ever having another again looking slim. She was jarred from her thoughts as the sled slid to a halt unexpectedly and Morris stood up to look ahead of them.

"Something's wrong," she heard Kyle shout back to them. "She doesn't want to go on."

Alana squeezed past Mareth and Forest to get to the front of the sled, eager to see what was happening. She held her sheathed rapier in one hand and Fin's grasp in the other. They were in a cavern that looked much like many others they had passed through. She couldn't tell whether it was made by the earth itself, a confluence of worm tunnels, or some other creature's crafting— but what made it different was the billowing cloud of steam escaping from the tunnel mouth ahead of them.

Kyle slid down from the worm so Alana and the others leapt from the rear of the sled. Flanked by Sergeant Morris on one side and Fin on the other, Alana walked to where Kyle stood still, watching the venting tunnel, concern writ large on his face. She stopped behind the dwarf. There was only one person experienced in the Dundenas and if he was worried, then she was too.

"I don't like it," muttered Kyle. "I think something is coming. Sergeant, crossbows if you please."

"Already ahead of you," said Morris, as the catch unlocked on his and the other two Ravens' bows.

Alana could see a shadow moving from side to side in the steam now. She held her breath as Morris calmly called for the aim. Her mind was already conjuring a variety of horrors that was going to appear, when the mist parted and there was Syd, the youngest of the Ravens. His eyes were wide, and his cheek scraped bloody as he stumbled toward them.

"They...they've all gone."

It took a few minutes for Morris and Dolph to calm Syd down enough to realize that, first of all, they weren't in any imminent danger and secondly, to understand what he'd meant by "they've all gone".

As the young man explained how the worm had plummeted off the top of a ledge down to the fire and fury of the underworld below, and he was the only one to escape, Kyle trudged around muttering and kicking at loose bits of gravel. Eventually, Syd had said all he had to say, his words spluttering to an end though his mouth kept on flapping, and she felt her brain doing similarly, struggling to process. It was Dolph who got things moving again, turning to look at her and the dwarf.

"So, what's the plan?"

Alana was not sure on specifics, but she was refusing to accept that they were dead. At least until she saw the bodies. If that was really true then whatever ruined fragment of her world that still stood would come toppling down. Thankfully, Kyle took charge.

"Let's go take a look. I have a feeling they are as tough as a hulk's hide."

Kyle led the way through the steam, all of them keeping close together, a sword or a crossbow in hand. Even Mareth looked alert at the apparent danger, armed and tensed, though he still would not speak.

The tunnel itself was short, taking a dog leg after thirty strides or so, opening into a rent in the earth so massive that it could have housed ten Palazio Confluens. The heat that hit her made her stagger back, and then the sight of the great cascade of water falling from the ceiling and down into the abyss made her take another step back. It was only Fin's reassuring grip that pulled her forwards.

Kyle and Morris were already at the edge of the chasm, peering down. Alana and Fin joined them while the others watched their backs.

"I can't see a thing. Too much steam," grumbled Morris.

"Too much steam is good. That means it's not too far down," said Kyle as he squinted under his bushy eye brows. "Focus and be patient. Let your eyes adjust."

Alana wasn't sure about that—the steam rising straight up into her face was hot enough to scald after a few seconds, and she wasn't sure it was doing much for her eyes either.

"Look, there," said Fin, pointing. "Doesn't that look like one of the sleds on its side?"

Kyle nodded, sniffing and wiping at his eye from the stinging heat. "Aye. And there's the molten rock that's causing all this steam. Across it there's Rannak, the poor worm. He's...he's burning."

Alana sucked in her breath in shock. She cared about the plight of the great creature, but her first thought was her friends befalling the same fiery fate.

"I can't see our lot," said Kyle, answering her thoughts.

"Let's get the ropes," suggested Morris. "We need to go and see if they are down there."

"No! There are other creatures roaming. On two legs. They would see you, and you would be a sitting mushroom."

"Are they goblins? Like yesterday?" asked Alana.

"No. Come, we have seen enough." Kyle moved away from the ledge and quickly back down the passage to where they had left Karcan. Alana, her hand shaking in Fin's reassuring grip, and the others stepping urgently behind.

Kyle was waiting for them, his eyes closed and breathing deeply in and out. He didn't respond as they all lined up before him.

"Kyle? Are you alright?" asked Alana tentatively.

"I. Am. Rather. Angry," he said evenly, between exhalations. His eyes flicked open. "I warned Neenahwi!"

"What are we going to do?" asked Dolph of Mareth, still looking to him for direction.

"What are we going to do?" answered Kyle instead. "Well, we have to go and find Neenahwi. The others too. The way down they took is too abrupt. So, we must dig. Quickly, on board the sled and hopefully this endeavor will help me forget the terrible fate of Rannak."

Unsurprisingly, it was slower going eating through rock then traveling along already formed passages. And more time in the back of the sled to think about what was happening was not what Alana needed right then. She clutched her knees so tightly that her knuckles were white and her mind couldn't decide which situation was worse—Neenahwi and the others were dead at the bottom of a long fiery drop, or they were going to have to fight some unknown creatures to rescue them.

She was painfully aware that she had killed before. Some nights she could see the faces of the men and women that she had stabbed with her rapier in the thick of the action in Ioth, those Pyrfew soldiers who in her dreams had pitiful expressions instead of the cold regard that she remembered in the waking light. She knew she should be able to do it again, but there was a difference in having all the time in the world to think about it, instead of it happening in the moment, when it was live by the sword or die by the sword. It made her realize how she couldn't possibly bear to imagine what it must be like for soldiers on the eve of battle.

They were heading down, and at a steeper angle than they had previously negotiated. She could tell, because they were all sliding down the metal bench against each other to the front of the sled. And the sled in turn would slide down into the rear of the rock-eating worm ahead of it, only for it to be flicked away, the sled lurching and its inhabitants being coated in stone-grey sludge from the worm's tail. They were heading down and away from the chasm, which seemed nonsensical to her at first when Kyle had told her of his intention. "Can't go straight down; need to come at it from an angle!" he'd shouted.

She assumed he knew what he was doing.

The grinding from up ahead suddenly ceased, replaced with the sound of a rock fall. The worm moved faster, free of obstruction and into another cavern that resembled the inside of a vast whale's ribcage. Dolph and Morris shifted in their seats to the back of the sled, sword in hand for the former and crossbow armed for the latter. She felt Fin's hand gently touch hers and she noticed that her friend had drawn one of her long sai. It was only then that she realized that now might be the moment—that for all she knew, they could be about to face whatever had taken her friends.

Alana picked up her rapier from where it was wedged under the bench beneath her and got to her feet. She peered over the side as the worm-pulled sled slowly slid to a halt. Checking in front, and then behind, her breath held tight the whole time, she searched for danger.

But there was nothing. Not trusting her eyes, in case she was missing something, it was a moment before she relaxed enough to exhale and voice that she couldn't see anything.

But the worm had come to a definite stop and Kyle was climbing down.

"What is it?" she whispered as loud as she dared.

The dwarf pointed to the end of the chamber where the ceiling sparkled with a twinkling light, like the clear night sky had got lost early one morning and found itself trapped underground. Beneath the entrancing canopy was a forest of abnormally large mushrooms, tall stems and caps a rainbow of colors. "Just want to take a quick look," he said.

Was he hungry? Or was it something about the stone in the ceiling that called out to his dwarven mind? She didn't know, but it hardly seemed the right moment to be distracted.

"Is now the best time?" she called after him as he tentatively crept forward. She looked around to find Mareth standing next to her. She raised her eyebrows quizzically but he just shrugged, his eyes sorrowful; he always looked like he was on the verge of tears these days. "I guess, we better follow him."

The back of the sled was lowered with barely a clang and they all stealth-ran after Kyle, each of them keeping an eye on the shadows. Alana caught up to him just as he reached the fungi forest. She was about to ask him what on earth he was doing, but the sight of the dwarf looking at the mushrooms open mouthed, made her stop and take it all in too.

Each of the mushrooms was the size of a child and would probably have weighed as much as most of the scrawny specimens you would find in the Narrows. Just one of these mushrooms could feed a family for a month! Her mind instantly wanted to think about how she could grow these to be able to feed the poor of Kingshold; that would surely be a bit of good news even old Eldrida could get behind. But no, she wasn't able to go home anymore, much less to her old position.

She blew out a deep breath to steady herself. That wasn't the way to think about it. They were going back. The journey may not be straight, but she was certain they would reclaim Kingshold. They had to. And in the meantime, she'd see more of the world than she ever imagined.

She reached out a hand to touch one of the caps.

"Careful, Alana. Could be poisonous," warned Dolph.

"No. Definitely not poisonous," interjected Kyle. "But I still wouldn't try to pet them."

Pet them? Why would anyone pet a mushroom?

And then they moved.

The red-capped mushroom in front of her spun around, the cap tilting back to reveal two beady black slits that must have been its eyes. All around her the other mushrooms were doing the same, facing the shocked, armed and non-fungal group. From the stem of the mushroom two things, that she could only describe as arms, emerged, though there were no hands at the end—just fluffy tendrils. There was a poof of air and a cloud of spores shot forward to envelop her.

"Cut them down!" called Morris as the spores tickled her eyes and slipped up into her nose.

"No! Stop," screamed Kyle, as he grabbed hold of Dolph's arms with a tight grip.

No harm.

Red Cap now glowed with a comfortingly gentle yellow light. Weirdly, it hadn't spoken. And she hadn't really heard any words either. It was more of a feeling...

Welcome.

It was the feeling of an old woolen blanket that her dad would drape over her shoulders when the winter nights crept in. She looked back at her friends and saw smiles paired with creased brows. "Do you feel that too?"

"Aye," said Morris. "A roaring fire in the hearth at The Battered Shield."

"A clean wall ready for scribing," said Kyle.

"Mummy... ahem, I mean..." said Dolph attempting to correct himself before giving in. "Arloth's balls. Who am I kidding? Mummy."

She looked at Mareth and could guess what he was feeling, the first smile that she had seen on his face since she had left for Ioth. But Fin looked implacable; she wondered what it was that made her feel welcome.

The mushrooms ahead parted and Red Cap beckoned with one frilly appendage, and Alana remembered trailing behind the baker's cart, the smell of the fresh baked bread pulling her along.

Follow.

Red Cap led the way, another mushroom falling alongside —Green Cap—as Alana and Kyle and the others passed through the forest of mushrooms that turned as they passed. Upon closer inspection, Alana noticed that it wasn't just the color of the Mushrooms that differentiated them. Some were taller than Dolph but looked so skinny that she wondered how they held up their flat caps. Others were short and wide, their caps festooned with glowing nodules.

Red Cap and Green Cap slowed to a halt as the forest stopped parting, their guides swept to either side revealing a spherical fungus about chest height on her. Thousands of short tendrils covered its surface, delicately swaying too-and-fro, though they were strong enough to hold the fungus off the ground. She could not see any eyes—if that was what they were on the other mushrooms—but the tendrils flicked at the air like an insect's antenna or like a thousand roving eyes.

The tendrils stiffened and pointed at the group, and with a soft woosh of air, a cloud of spores burst out and enveloped them.

You are a long way from home.

Definitely words this time. Not just a feeling. She wondered whether anyone else could hear it when Kyle answered that question.

"Only for some of us. I was born beneath the earth, and will always live beneath the earth. I am of the Deep People."

I know you are searching. Your thoughts are clear. Friends lost with the lizards of flame.

A vision appeared in the air of a goblin war party facing a few score of tall lizard type creatures, frozen in time. And then the image moved, the opposing groups launching into each other, spear and swords swinging.

The grey ones you saw yesterday. The salamanders live by the river of fire. They are at war. Death saddens us. We will stop this waste.

What about our friends? Another voice penetrated her mind and she turned in surprise as it sounded like Mareth, but he hadn't spoken since the incident. She then realized that he still hadn't spoken.

The mushrooms turned towards Mareth too, and she could have sworn that they sagged.

You are very sad, Singer. I feel your pain. Let us help.

Red Cap and Green Cap stepped forward to flank Mareth, each of them raising a mushroom arm and then gently stroking the Lord Protector from shoulder down to his waist. Puffs of spores covered him with each caress, leaving him coated in a white powder. In unison, Red Cap and Green Cap stepped back from Mareth, apparently pleased with their work. A smile crept across his face as tears filled his eyes.

Mareth cleared his throat and spoke. "Thank you. Thank you, truly. But what about our friends?"

Your lost ones will soon be sacrificed by the lizards of flame to bring fortune before they attack the grey ones.

We will stop it.

The Myconids march.

~

"KYLE?"

"Yes, Alana...?"

"Can you see where we are going?"

"Not really, I must admit."

Suddenly, ovals of varying sizes around them began to glow with a subdued light, enough for her to see her feet and the floor upon which she walked—the phosphorescent caps illuminating the more than two score mushrooms who were accompanying them.

She felt the shame of a young girl caught trying to slip her Wintertide copper coin into her father's empty purse. The mushrooms were saying sorry. Or, she supposed, she should call them Myconids.

"Thank you."

Now came the remembrance of a church helper asking her to shush as she sat next to her mother and sister as a child.

Alana guessed she was being advised to be quiet.

She looked around at their escort, one of two groups of Myconids she had seen earlier. The other had headed back the way they had come yesterday; she assumed they were destined for the goblins. Alana wasn't sure if this was a war party (they didn't have any weapons) or a peace delegation, but being surrounded by the Funghuys (a joke Mareth had made before they had set out) reassured her.

It must have been an hour or more through tunnels twisting left and right, sloping up and down, by the time she felt the air become hotter and damper. The air became misty, the light of the mushrooms reflecting back at them, illuminating the Myconid's tiny legs that kept a rapid pace as they stepped out of the passage and into the space that was at the bottom of the chasm. There was the mangled sled, crumpled and upturned on a rock across the red river from them. She looked all around, searching for signs of Motega, or Trypp, or even Neenahwi, hoping not to see their bodies lying broken on the ground, and as she did so, she saw a creature leaning inattentively against the wall. It was like a giant, orange, stretched frog, though with a tail and a wicked-looking barbed spear in its hand.

"Salamander," hissed Kyle, obviously recognizing it. Alana felt Fin leave her side, knowing without looking that she had her sai in her hands.

But the Myconid closest to the reptile was faster.

It was no taller than the smooth waist of the salamander, and Alana's eyes widened in concern as the mushroom's arm rose to point to the creature's face. There was the now familiar poof as a cloud of spores was released. *Did they mean to talk to these salamanders?* The lids around the bulbous eyes of the red skinned creature closed gracefully and it cascaded to the floor. *That was handy*.

As one, the Myconids nodded their caps at a job well done, like a wave of multicolored hats, and proceeded into the cavern. They moved soundlessly, and Alana tried very hard to be as quiet as possible—though it seemed as if her breathing was louder than Fin's footsteps. They passed over a shallow-arched stone bridge that stretched over the river of hot molten rock, and from that vantage she could see the entrance to a tunnel in the far wall. Red Cap and Green Cap led the way, and the two of them, along with two smaller Myconids, bustled off ahead, moving even faster than she would have expected. They moved in different directions but as she traced their paths, she discovered that they were in fact making their way toward silhouetted figures in the mist. A few moments passed and the shadows disappeared, the Myconids returning shortly after. Alana was struck by the memory of Petra holding her hand and guiding her out to the street some summers ago to see a broad rainbow that arced across Kingshold to Mount Tiston. She guessed that they meant it was safe to follow.

She saw the crumpled and ruined form of the sled first, teetering on the edge of a rocky outcropping, the rear gate swinging open below it. Canvas bags and crates lay on the floor below, the belongings of her friends thrown out in the impact. She looked back expectantly toward Mareth and Sergeant Morris, and they both nodded in wordless agreement. Alana moved quickly forwards, eager to see what clues might be waiting for them, Mareth close behind as she heard Morris giving silent orders for the rest to fan out and secure a perimeter. The jettisoned equipment had been rifled through; belongings pulled from bags and tossed back on the floor, perhaps not worthwhile to whomever was doing the searching. But there were no bodies. She didn't know if that was a good thing or not.

"There's the bird," whispered Mareth as he stepped over

a sack of dwarven bread toward an iron cage. It was tilted, leaning against the rock wall and Alana could see that Per, while alive, did not look best pleased. She felt sorry for the bird having to be caged, knowing that Motega felt likewise, having little opportunity to take wing except for when they rested in the largest caverns they found.

"Ahem. What about me?" came a voice. Alana turned, trying to see where the voice came from without initial success. "Down here."

Alana looked again at the sack of hard brown loaves, apparently nonperishable though not particularly tasty, and did a double take as she saw an eye looking back at her. She crouched down, and gritting her teeth, pulled from the loaves the disgruntled head that Neenahwi had previously, dismissively, introduced as The Librarian.

"Are you alright?" she asked, wondering momentarily what else could be worse than already not having a body.

"You mean besides falling ignominiously hundreds of feet, bouncing off stone walls like a child's ball and wondering if I would spend eternity alone at the bottom of a hole without so much as a good book to read?" Alana nodded uncertainly, a trifle uneasy at holding a severed head in her hands, even if it was in some ways alive. "Well, then yes. I suppose so."

"What happened to everyone else?"

"I believe they were taken that way." His eyes flicked toward the tunnel entrance she had seen before.

"By the Salamanders?"

"If that is what the orange creatures are called then yes, I do believe so. They and the steam imps."

"Steam imps?" asked Mareth as he joined her, holding Per's cage. "What are they?"

"Creatures of magic and air, coalesced steam. Quite vile. There is one now."

Alana turned to see three feet of vaguely humanoid steam separate itself from the bank of mist between them and the tunnel entrance. Two more similar forms followed closely behind it. A tall, thin brown mushroom placed itself in front of the creatures and puffed a cloud of spores, but they did not fall into a sleep like the Salamanders had done. Mareth put the cage down and drew the sword at his waist.

"That's not good. Get behind me, Alana."

Behind the imps came a dozen Salamanders, long wicked looking spears levelled at her and her friends. No, it didn't look good. Alana supposed that there would be fighting now, just when she'd hoped that they'd be able to walk in behind the mushrooms and rescue their friends. She put the head of The Librarian down gently and reached for her own rapier. Mareth hadn't seen her in a while. She had changed, and she wasn't going to hide.

A BLAST OF STEAM CAME FROM THE IMP'S MOUTH, enveloping the Myconid that had faced it. Its mushroom arms raised in the air, as Alana suddenly relived the day she grabbed the kettle from the hearth floor when she was a child. She saw similar winces of anguish on Mareth's and Morris' faces as Syd and Forest rushed forward swords drawn. The latter's bastard sword, flashed through the imp's body, cleaving the steam in two. Alana saw a Salamander move in behind it and push its spear straight out, skewering the scolded Myconid's arm. Then the imp exploded in a blast of hot air, knocking Forest on to his arse and sending the Salamander stumbling back.

And all of this happened before Alana could even have her rapier fully drawn from its scabbard.

She heard the twang of a crossbow and a Salamander took a bolt in the chest. Morris threw down his crossbow and pulled his blade free. A red lizard came from the flank to intercept Mareth, the Lord Protector fending off the long probing stabs as he inched back to where she stood. Forest writhed on the floor, clutching his eyes and Syd, seeing the fate of his squad mate, thought twice about meeting the imp he had been stalking toward. But Alana saw that Fin had no such fear.

As the Myconids fanned out to block the Salamanders' approach, Fin leapt forward to strike at another imp, moving with the grace and speed of a shark on the hunt, slipping past it before the creature could explode. Alana couldn't help but smile in entranced amazement at Fin's exploits. *How was she so brave? So precise?*

"You might want to help," came the voice of the Librarian from the floor, as Mareth's foot bumped back into hers as he continued to retreat. Snapping her attention back to the imminent danger, she moved to the side of the bard, presenting a second target for the Salamander. Now it wasn't sure which person with a blade it was supposed to fight, and Alana was thankful that the Myconids must have been preventing their foe from getting any reinforcements. It stabbed at her and Alana flicked out her rapier to knock the attack aside. Mareth moved right, attempting to flank the creature, but a warning thrust stopped his movement. Alana feinted, pretending to rush in, and the Salamander snapped its attention, and its spear, back to her. The red lizard's thrust narrowly missed her shoulder, and she found herself wishing for a shield like she had used in Ioth.

But Mareth saw the opportunity. Instead of attacking the Salamander, as the spear whistled past Alana's arm, Mareth sidestepped and brought his broadsword down with a clang onto the haft of the weapon. It didn't snap—the spear was all metal—but it bent and ricocheted down to strike the floor. Alana held her breath, pushed off on her strongest leg and moved as quickly as she could to get in close. The bulbous eyes of the Salamander opened wide as she approached, her arm back—rapier parallel to the floor, she thought Florian would be proud of her form—as she pushed forward with all of her strength. She drove the sharp thin blade through the ribs of the creature, its mouth opening and forked tongue lolling as the sword slid easily, almost to the hilt. The Salamander collapsed, dragging the rapier from Alana's hand as it fell.

Not good. No weapon.

She risked a glance over her shoulder as she reached for her blade, looking to see if there was more trouble on the way. But the fight was over as the final imp exploded, Dolph finishing his charge with a turn and a flourish in order to escape the radius of the blast. The other Salamanders were down; a few in pools of a bright scarlet blood, others lay by the feet of Myconids, most likely sound asleep. Alana pulled the rapier free, unsure of what to wipe it on before putting it back in its scabbard, so she kept it in her hand. She looked up to see Mareth regarding her.

"Surprised? Florian and Dolph told you I was better than you with this thing." She let herself forget that she had killed again and basked momentarily in Mareth's surprise. "Looks like you got a sword that you're more comfortable with?"

Mareth nodded. "Shame it's not Bertha, but it's better for me than one of those skewers. I guess you had to use that in Ioth?"

"Yes. Eight times I killed someone. I'm not sure I'll ever forget them."

"I'm sorry, I didn't ask before. I knew it was tough, but I didn't mean for this to happen to you," he said with a tinge of sadness in his voice, but still he sounded better than he had done in some while.

"It's not your fault. How are you doing?"

"I feel...alright. At least since they..." he pointed to the mushrooms that were closing ranks ahead of them, all pointed to the tunnel she had seen at the apex of the bridge, "Since they helped me. Speaking of them, it looks like they are moving out. We should catch up."

The Myconids were lining up in a long, arrow formation. Red Cap was at the tip, and the other humans, along with Kyle, were in the rearguard. Forest was back on his feet, his skin red from the steam explosion, but he gritted his teeth as he waited in position. Alana and Mareth found a safe place to stow the Librarian and Per. Probably a lot safer than she would be.

Red Cap turned around to look at the ranks of mushrooms, all different sizes and colors, along with Alana and her friends. The mushroom raised his arms in the air and Alana found herself suddenly remembering the steps of the Sanctum in Ioth, Florian whispering to her to be ready to run. There was a lump in her throat as she recalled the horror of that night, he and Morris rushing off ahead of her, into the cathedral to warn the boy saint.

The mushroom's arms dropped and it turned, running at a pace she did not expect down the tunnel, the other mushrooms following silently behind. Alana felt a slight nudge in her back, and after turning she was reassured to see Dolph behind her, he gave her a brief nod, urging her to follow, his confidence in her calming the worms in her stomach. The tunnel was long, the light from the floor of the chasm fading until a new light gradually infiltrated the darkness. There was a sound, a harmony of voices she couldn't understand, that bounced off the tunnel walls and warred with her own footfalls and heartbeat for her attention.

The tunnel opened into a long, carved chamber. The Myconids were already amongst rows of Salamanders who were all on one knee, heads bowed, facing the end of the room where a sole Salamander, a chain around its neck, had been leading the crowd. Puffs of spores came from the Myconids' arms as they moved amongst the red lizards who were scrambling to their feet; any caught in the fine powder gracefully fell to the floor in a slumber. She scanned the room, thankfully safe from the action, looking for Neenahwi and Motega. She was more grateful than she realized when she saw a purple-robed figure slumped against a stone plinth set before an image of a great reptilian eye on the wall—the whole situation looked rather too much like an altar for her taste.

The chained Salamander at the front called out what must have been a series of orders by the gestures that went along with it. The far ranks of the Salamanders that had not been put to sleep yet were already on their feet and running to the walls to obtain spears that rested there neatly. They organized into small groups and advanced on the stretched-out Myconid wedge formation. Morris, Forest, Syd and Kyle armed their crossbows to fire at the ranks of Salamanders—the red lizards towered over almost all of the Myconids so

Alana imagined it to be a relatively easy shot, though what did she know, she'd never used any bow before. Maybe she should learn how, if only to avoid running headlong into trouble every time. Much like Mareth, Fin and Dolph were doing right then. She briefly considered running to join them but she noticed a passage clear of Salamanders by the side of the chamber that lead all the way to the front and where Neenahwi was. Maybe if she could get up there and free her, then she could help too?

Alana took in a deep breath. Fight or rescue? She knew she couldn't waste any more time deciding so set off at a run toward the captured wizard, all the while watching in concern as the Salamanders, mushrooms and humans met. She saw Mareth and Dolph chopping alongside Myconids, but Fin moved in and out almost too fast for her to see. Alana wasn't sure how she would manage against someone armed with a spear, but she knew she could look after herself.

As she was halfway to the altar, she noticed that Red Cap had been isolated at the front of the wedge, enclosed on three sides by Salamanders and their spears. The red lizards fell with each puff of spores but many got a thrust in first, puncturing Red Cap, though it did not seem to slow it down. A spear sliced from the side, and Alana didn't know whether it was through the luck of the wielder or their skill, but the cap of Red Cap was sliced from the stalk, spinning through the air before falling out of sight. An anguished shriek pierced the cavern and Green Cap was running to where Red Cap had just been. As it ran, the entirety of the mushroom turned black in splotches, at first giving it the look of a spotted dog before any other color or tone was eliminated and all that remained was the black. Now it looked like a

Myconid version of Fin, but she supposed it would be less murderous...

The black mushroom reached the Salamanders who had decapitated Red Cap and exploded. A cloud of black spores burst forth and hung in the air around the red lizards. They must have breathed no more than once before they each in turn clutched their throats, mouths open, and fell. Alana was getting close to Neenahwi as they went down, probably a score or so at once, but the black spores clouded the air. What if they moved to where she was heading? She had a hand on her sleeve, about to rip it from her shirt and wrap it around her nose and mouth to maybe stop her from being poisoned when a pair of mushrooms stepped forward from their tasks and, sucked in the foul dust through the gills under the caps. The pair got punctured a couple of times for the trouble of saving their stabbers from death.

Running once more, rapier in hand, Alana was thankful to see that the Salamander with a chain around his neck was no longer by the altar—just Neenahwi, slumped against the wall nearby. She skidded to a stop and saw that the wizard's eyes were closed, even with the noise of battle. She was bound at wrists and ankles by a hard clay like substance. Alana grabbed her by the shoulder and shook, Neenahwi's eyes opening wearily and looking up at her. "Alana?" she asked weakly.

Alana tried to saw at the clay around her wrists with her rapier but it was hardly a blade for cutting, and the blade's length made it difficult to get the right angle for leverage.

"Use the dagger," breathed Neenahwi. "At my belt."

Alana saw what the wizard referred to and she pulled free a long broad-bladed knife, the steel looking strangely blue. Not giving it any further thought, she cut at the clay and the right tool did the job, the manacles falling away easily. She freed Neenahwi's feet and helped her to stand, taking her weight on her own shoulder. A movement of red caught her eye, and she looked up to see the chained Salamander glowering at her, gesturing and barking orders that Alana could only assume had something to do with leaving its sacrifice alone. It too had a knife in hand, a tool for what it had been intending to do to Neenahwi. Alana didn't know what to do. She couldn't fight and hold up Neenahwi, and it didn't look like the wizard was going to be much help. Alana tensed, ready to push Neenahwi away from her, hopeful that the lizard would focus its attention on her.

But suddenly the eyes of the lizard rolled up into the top of its head and it fell, face first to the floor, a shadow lurking behind it.

Fin.

The hilt of one of her sai still held high from where she had used the pommel to strike.

"You didn't kill it?" was all Alana could think to say.

"They asked me to stop killing them," said Fin as she pointed back to the mushrooms. There were very few Salamanders left on their feet now, and the ones that were threw down their weapons in surrender. Without a sound the Myconids subdued them all to a slumber.

~

THEY FOUND THE OTHERS ON THE OTHER SIDE OF THE altar, similarly bound but largely unhurt except for cuts and bruises. Alana found it strangely easy to cut through their bonds with Neenahwi's dagger, even easier than Dolph or Morris but she said nothing of it. Once she was done, she tucked the blade into her belt. The hairs on the back of her neck prickled, as if someone was watching her. Kyle, his eyes narrowed, looked her up and down intently. She smiled weakly back.

There were brief embraces of thanks and relief, along with further glowers from Kyle directed at Mouse. The alchemist had the good sense to hang his head in shame. They'd find out the full story later, but he had been the pilot and he had been the one to lead the group down a bloody big chasm, so she knew he must be at least partially to blame.

All the time that Alana and her friends had been freeing their comrades, the Myconids had wandered around the fallen Salamanders, sprinkling more spores over their sleeping bodies; a fine pink dust in the air that quickly disappeared as it settled. They picked up the pieces of Red Cap carefully, gently holding the fallen mushroom as they waited to leave. Now was not the time to talk or to get answers to the many questions that Alana had, and thankfully everyone else recognized the same thing.

Trudging after the parade of mushrooms, they left the chamber by the tunnel they had entered and back out to where the Librarian and Per had been left. Motega lifted the cage carefully, reaching a finger inside to stroke the bird and receiving a nip in return. Neenahwi tied the severed head to her belt once more as if in a daze, ignoring the verbal peck she received as a reunion gift. They spent a few nervous minutes amongst the other sleeping Salamanders to retrieve whatever equipment was still in good enough condition to be useful whilst the mushrooms sprinkled more of the pink spores. Mouse was particularly happy that one steel chest seemed unharmed, and he cajoled Cherry and Syd into carry it for him. Alana found herself watching Kyle as the poor dwarf glared in equal measure at the clearly giddy alchemist and the charred form of the other purple worm that partially emerged from the river of molten rock. She hadn't noticed it before, and though she had seen the broken wreckage of the sled, only now did it hit her that they would all be crammed in the one conveyance now. It would make the Narrows look positively salubrious.

Alana picked up the dwarven bread and swept it back into the sack it had spilled from—she couldn't imagine a bit of dirt and grit was going to make it taste much worse, in fact she wouldn't be surprised if that was what it was made of. Supplies gathered, they tramped wordlessly after the Myconids as they led the way back to the glittering cavern of the mushroom forest.

It was slower going on the return than the way there, which seemed to be against the normal way that journeys went, but given their injuries and the additional loads they all carried it was not surprising. Alana caught the look of wonder on Trypp's face as they arrived at the forest—by the number of mushrooms waiting for them she surmised that the other party that had left earlier was already back—and she shot him a smile of shared recognition. Dropping their things in a pile, they all fell exhausted to the floor, and no one said anything for a blissful few moments.

"Thanks," said Motega, finally breaking the silence. "I thought we were done for. What are these? Can they understand us?"

A small brown mushroom broke away from the circle that surrounded them, spraying the newcomers with spores and Alana remembered her mother handing her a shiny red apple, all to herself, and the gratitude she felt at that sweet prize. "You're welcome," her mother said.

Alana smiled ruefully at Motega's surprise, and not for the first time wondered what memories the Myconids stirred in those around her. She explained what she knew of the strange silent mushrooms that had helped them. When she had finished, it was Kyle's turn to speak.

"There are many of us Deep People who have a temper, nurturing it like the fire of our smiths. They say that passion is essential for their craft. But I am a Chiseler. That requires patience, a steady hand, and so while I am not usually one of them, let me tell you, I am angry." The cheeks above his short beard and his forehead flushed. "Rannak is dead. Your sled is destroyed. By Varcon, what happened?"

Mouse looked down at the ground as he mumbled a response. "I must have got my measurements wrong and used too much potion. We were going too fast. I couldn't stop her in time when I saw the gap..."

"I knew it!" exclaimed Kyle. "I knew your potions were not the way to manage these creatures. And you, Neenahwi," Kyle pointed a stubby finger in her direction, the anger in his voice now awash with disappointment, "you said you would speak to him."

Neenahwi slowly lifted her head to wearily the meet the eyes of the rest of the party, slowly blinking away her apparent exhaustion. "I'm sorry, Kyle. I'm sorry all of you."

Alana gawped at the sight of Jyuth's daughter, the whirlwind of Kingshold that had entranced her and scared her all at the same time, looking so weak and forlorn. "What's wrong with you?" she blurted out. Neenahwi slowly turned to regard to her. "I mean, I've never seen you like this before."

"The fall. I was the last to climb to safety but I ran out of time. I had to use magic to arrest my descent."

"But..." she let the thought trail off unsaid.

Neenahwi raised an eyebrow. "What? Spit it out, Alana. I think it is best that we be much more open with each other from now on."

"Why did it weaken you? That never seemed to happen before..." Then it hit her. Neenahwi looked different. No longer did she have the amulet around her neck. The realization on her face must have been clear.

"She's figured you out, girl," rasped the Librarian from where he rested on the ground in front of Neenahwi. "Time to talk."

Motega, sitting by his sister's side, nodded in agreement. He must have known already.

"The magic I used to fight the Draco turtle, to fight that demon in Kingshold. I used a demon stone as the source of that power. But... I lost it."

"We can go back and look for it," said Kyle, his anger gone. "I know how much finding that thing meant to you. I know how to get back to those lizards. We can all search."

"No. It wasn't here. I lost it to Grey..." Neenahwi placed a hand on Motega's shoulder and used him to lever herself to her feet. She looked around at those that traveled with them. "I lost the stone to Grey and only just escaped with Mareth before she could figure out how to use it. I... I couldn't save Petra, though I tried. That was one of the reasons why we cannot retake Kingshold. Grey will have unlocked the stone by now and I won't be able to beat her. So, we go to the Wild Continent to stop Llewdon from using my people. And to find an army to retake our home."

Alana had heard the last part of this before, when the news of her sister was still a fresh wound. She'd wanted revenge then. Wanted to be able to make the emperor of Pyrfew pay for what his agents had taken away from her. But now, there in the dark, away from the surface for who knew how many weeks, and after learning what had been omitted, it all sounded hollow.

"But when we get there—*if* we get there—I don't know what we should do..." Neenahwi trailed off and, for a moment, Alana was not sure whether the woman was crying. Neenahwi sucked in a deep breath and calmed her body. "I don't know for certain what we shall do. I can't tell you I have a master plan. But I know we will work it out. Motega had a vision. Our father told him of a place where my people came from, where they will help. We shall travel there and free those we find along the way."

Alana looked around the circle of faces that buried Neenahwi under the pressure of their attention. Morris' brow was furrowed. Mareth's jaw hung open. Fin's arms were crossed stiffly across her body and Trypp was shaking his head. She knew how hard that must have been for Neenahwi to put all of that out there, to be honest with them all, but she could also see that Neenahwi was about to lose them all. Why would they follow someone who didn't look like she believed in herself?

Alana stood, her feet knowing what she needed to do even before she had fully thought it through, and she took the few short steps to stand with Neenahwi.

"You're right. We'll figure it out," she said. She glanced over her shoulder at Mareth and raised her eyebrows. His mouth clamped shut and he too rose and joined them.

"We have to figure it out. Together." Mareth's voice cracked as he spoke, like the words were hard to force out, though he put a reassuring hand on her arm. "No one expects you to have all of the answers."

"Oh, fuck it," said Trypp as he joined them. Motega, still

sitting cross-legged on the floor, looked up in surprise, though he had a smile on his face. "I don't have anywhere better to be. Actually, that's a lie, but I don't have anyone better to be with. And I know someone who would be cursing me from the afterlife if we didn't stop that elvish bastard. We'll take it one step at a time."

And that did it. Trypp, the sensible one, the one who more than once had questioned why he was in the middle of this mess—he was the one who stopped things from falling apart. The others got up and joined them, trying their best to laugh and realize there was joy in just being alive and together. All except Fin. Alana saw her still standing with arms crossed, apart from the group. Everyone else melted away from Alana's perspective, it was just her and Fin alone in the Dundenas, and she knew then that she needed her. She mouthed 'please' and Fin's resistance wilted. Alana welcomed her into her arms, Fin's scent filling her head.

Something dug into her ribs and when they separated, Alana saw that she still had Neenahwi's dagger tucked into her belt. She pulled it out and offered it back to the wizard hilt first.

Neenahwi held up a hand and shook her head. "You keep it. You'll have more use than me."

"But the Forger gave you that—" began Kyle.

"And it is mine to give as I please, Kyle. Do you doubt that?" The dwarf reluctantly shook his head, the exchange rather passing Alana by.

The mushrooms around them parted and the great round fungus rolled forward slowly, propelled by its tiny tentacles. Dust motes sparkled in the air as the leader of the Myconids sprayed them with spores once more.

Your path is free if you leave now. The red lizards sleep. Your worm will find the way.

"What did you do today? Why did you help us?"

We stopped a war. The lizards believe they killed the goblins. The goblins will similarly awake to the memory of wiping out the lizards. Peace. At least for a while. Before you leave, we have a gift. For the singer.

A Myconid stepped forward carrying what looked like a large serving dish, though Alana thought it was likely to have been the cap of a Myconid in a past life. Other mushrooms shook their arms over the top of the dish, sprinkling spores into it until there was a heap of white powder. The mushroom handed it to Mareth and bowed.

This will help with your sadness for a time. But you must find the true answer within.

Mareth bowed in thanks and took the dish, putting it down on the ground beside the steel chest they had reclaimed. From it he pulled a stone jar, carefully transferring the powder inside. Once he was done, he tipped the dish over his head and let the spores fall. He breathed deeply before thanking the Myconids, and she felt a small beginning of hope for him deep inside her, his voice back to normal once more. They all packed up their things and trudged over to where the purple worm still rested.

"At least we don't need to worry about us all not spending enough time together," said Motega to his sister.

She laughed. "Everybody in. Don't hog too much space. It's going to be a tight fit and we have a long way to go."

Mouse put the bag he carried on the back of the sled and then turned around, his eyes bright with mischief. "Can I drive?"

"No!" shouted everyone and Kyle ran to take up his position in the saddle.

DUNDENAS 5

BLUE SKY, GREEN FOREST, RED PLANS

Motega had chosen the wrong place to sit and Trypp was finding it hilarious. They had been going uphill for most of the day, and it had the effect of everyone in the only remaining sled sliding down the metal bench to the rear. Motega and Trypp had been the last to get on the sled, and so they sat opposite each other, both squeezing in next to the rear flap, but while he had Forest sliding into him and squishing against the rear wall, Trypp was getting cozy with Midnight.

Bastard. Why was he always so lucky?

It had been slower going today than other days. They weren't racing through the tunnels that he had been surprised to learn existed below the earth like Andovian cheese. Their worm was eating a new path, its body giving off an intense heat; which only added to the sweltering and stifling conditions of the metal sled. Sweat dripped off his brow into his eyes and he'd given up elbowing the big Raven on his left to try and create some breathing room. This would be how he would die—suffocated by a half-giant soldier in a worm oven.

So it took a moment for him to see the sliver of light that caused someone at the breathing end of the sled to exclaim. In fact, he didn't even hear what they said.

He smelled it.

The barest whiff of fresh air, of grass, of rain, of the world outside the dark. A place free of goblins, salamanders, mind-reading mushrooms, explosive clouds, umber hulks (who knew how dangerous a mother umber hulk guarding her eggs could be) or bloody gnomes. It smelled of home.

The sled lurched forward and everyone slid in the same direction in their seats as the dark of the tunnel above them was replaced by a broad expanse of blue sky, the worm breaking free of the earth and sliding down a grassy hill before coming to a stop. Motega stood, staring up into the air, arms out wide as he took a deep breath. Oh, how he had missed the open. They'd done missions or taken jobs that required going underground before, but spending a few days in a dungeon or catacomb was nothing compared to what must have been months underground. But they'd made it. At last he could finally show his oldest friends where he had come from...

He paused and looked at Trypp, who had his eyes closed and was filling his lungs too. The emptiness was palpable where he had, for just a moment, expected to see Florian.

"Get down! Quickly!" called Kyle, the extremely sensible dwarf who had done what he had promised and led through the Dundenas. He looked quite agitated as he ran toward them, fumbling with a pair of rose-tinted goggles.

"What's wrong?" called Motega.

"We have to unhitch from the worm. Now. She doesn't like the light and she'll pull us underground again."

That was enough to get everyone moving, even though Mouse was muttering to himself "the worm would stay put if I could use my potions." But everyone ignored him. Motega and Trypp led the charge off the back of the sled and they ran around either side to the front where the long chains were attached to the harness around the worm. In the agonizing light of day—his eyes still dealing with change from below to above ground by sending sharp daggers into his brain—he could see how the harness had chafed against the worm's purple skin, causing long red marks that stretched across her body. Trypp was starting to disconnect the chains from the sled.

"Leave that," called Motega, as he pulled a knife and moved to the worm's side. "Just cut the harness free." Trypp nodded and followed his lead. Within moments, they were all cutting away the leather straps that wound around the length of the worm.

Kyle patted him on the back. "Thank you, Motega. Well done."

The leather was tough but soon the bindings fell to the ground and the worm was free. The beast reared its head, twisting back to look in Motega's direction; he couldn't tear his eyes away from the yawning maw of razor-sharp teeth, arranged in concentric circles and perfect for eating rock. The worm roared and Motega took a step back at the roar power of the creature.

Kyle, however, waved.

"Goodbye friend," murmured the dwarf, a smile at odds with the melancholy visible in his eyes.

The purple worm rippled away—the hand-length hooks

across its body digging into the soft earth—back down the hole from which they had appeared. They all stood there in silence for a moment, watching their transportation disappear. Motega was home and there was nowhere to go but onward.

"So, this is outside," said Kyle. "It's a bit...big."

Motega laughed and clapped him on the shoulder. "Nothing bigger."

Trypp lay down on the flattened grass where the worm had been. "Finally. Sun!" A few of the Ravens collapsed to the ground as well, enjoying their liberation.

"What do you think you're doing, you lazy bastards," roared Morris. "Perimeter! Now! Let's make sure it's safe before we make camp. They don't call it the Wild Continent for nothing."

"Let's call it by its proper name as we are here, Sergeant. Alfaria!" chided his sister, gently. "...But it is dangerous, so that's probably a good idea," she conceded.

"Whatever you say. Midnight, up the hill and take a look around. Cherry, Syd, circle clockwise. Forest, you go the other way. Run and then holler if you see trouble." The Ravens got up with a grumble as they followed Morris' orders. "And keep a look out for fresh water. I'm sick of that dank piss."

~

WHILE THE RAVENS TRAIPSED OFF, MOTEGA WENT BACK to the sled, pulling from it the brass cage that had housed Per for too long. The bird gave him an evil look and Motega couldn't blame him. He unfastened the door, opened it wide, and set the cage on the ground. Per jumped out, stretching his wings tentatively.

"Sorry about that. But look, we're home." Per shot him another look and leapt into the air, flapping his wings again and again to gain height. The falcon flew higher and higher, and further and further away, until Motega couldn't see him anymore. He was sure that Per would come back. Pretty sure.

Motega looked around at what to do next. Trypp had disappeared somewhere, and Neenahwi was a little distance away talking earnestly with Morris, Mareth, and Kanaveen. The others had gone up the hill where Midnight had been sent, and as he was not feeling like talking about serious matters with his sister, he set off up the slope after them.

He thought it had been hot and clammy when they were underground, but it had nothing on the humid air they now found themselves in. Motega's shirt was already sticking to his back. The hill was grassy, dotted with patches of fern. As he gained in elevation, he felt a breeze and smelled the salty sea. There at the top was Midnight, a spy glass in her hand, diligently following orders. Alana, Fin, Dolph, and Mouse were sitting on a rocky outcropping. Motega stood behind them and while they looked out to the ocean, he gazed out across Alfaria.

He really had no idea where they were—who knew where Kyle had led the worm? —but the sight before him was familiar. Forest, as far as the eye could see, an unbroken strand of green stretching out before him. No fields. No towns or cities. Just the world as it had been created. Forest that only ended here, near the ocean where it became scrub and bush, and further to the west where it met the great border mountains. Seeing it gave him mixed emotions; a hint of completeness at being once again in the land he was born, but also apprehension and fear as he remembered what it had been like to flee through that forest when he was a child. What they had endured and encountered. He turned on the spot, his eye casting out to the similarly unending ocean that led back east, only interrupted by a few islands to the southeast.

"How are you folks doing?" he asked the four that were sitting in silence; Alana and Fin shoulder to shoulder and leaning against each other, while Mouse and Dolph were slightly apart.

Alana turned around and smiled up at him. "Thought I heard someone."

"I knew you were there," said Fin, surprising him with her words. She had hardly been talkative in the broader group for the whole journey. He assumed that her and Alana spoke when they were alone but he couldn't be certain.

"If I didn't want you to hear me, you wouldn't have heard me," said Motega, winking at Alana.

"I'm not so sure about that," said Fin. Alana laughed but Motega wasn't sure it was a joke.

"I think we're all glad to be out in the open again," said Alana. "And I was just thinking about..."

"Home," finished Motega. "Yeah. Me too."

"You are home, though. Right?" said Dolph.

"I guess so. I mean, yes. But Edland and the lands around the Sapphire Sea, that's been home for a long time too..."

Alana nodded and Motega knew she understood that it was as much about the people who were left behind back there across the ocean as any particular place. Special people that wouldn't be going anywhere.

"I wonder what's been happening at home," said Alana. There was no answer.

"See that island over there?" said Mouse, pointing to a place with twin sharp peaks in the distance. "I think I've been there."

Motega didn't know what to make of that statement, or even of the alchemist. When he and Florian had first met Mouse, on the back of the Draco Turtle, he'd taken him for a coward. A fiddler of potions and flasks, hidden away from the action. But as he'd seen more of him since they left Unedar Halt, Motega had observed a wild side to the skinny man, a streak of insanity that perhaps explained the crazy ideas.

"Bollocks," said Dolph. "When have you been out here?"

Mouse looked at him, puzzled, as if the answer should have been obvious. "With Kolsen, of course. The pirate king."

There was a cracking laugh behind Motega and he turned to see Mareth striding up the hill to join them. "We need to talk more about your time with that bastard, Mouse. I'm sure there are plenty of stories you haven't told yet," croaked the Lord Protector. Mareth's brows furrowed at the sound of his own voice. He dug gently into a small leather pouch with two fingers, extracting a grey dust and sniffing it up his nose. He cleared his throat and his voice returned to normal. "But for now, you have all been summoned."

Motega followed Mareth back down the hill, and spotted Trypp walking alongside Morris toward the same destination. Motega jogged over to join him.

His friend gifted him a wistful smile. "Well, we made it. I said I would come," said Trypp.

"Yes, thank you, my friend. If only we weren't—"

"—one short. Yeah, I know. He would have liked it."

Motega nodded. Not trusting himself to speak for a second. Instead, just imagining Florian's excitement at somewhere new to explore. Not to mention a grand mission to free an entire continent. Good natured idiot. His ideals would probably still get them all killed even though he was gone. They walked in silence for a moment until Trypp spoke again.

"Any idea what's going on?"

"Well, we're here to free my people and poke Llewdon in the eye. We need an army to retake Edland. This is the biggest job we've ever had. You know what that means?"

Trypp nodded. "We need a plan."

~

"IT FEELS SO GOOD TO FLY AGAIN!" SQUAWKED NEENAHWI.

They were soaring high above the green carpet of the forest below, Motega inhabiting Per's mind, and his sister flying alongside. She had taken the form of a peregrine falcon so they could communicate more easily on the wing. Motega always found it difficult to understand other kinds of bird because of their strange accent. *And it was true*, he thought as much himself.

"I, too, agree," came another voice in his head. One that was not Per. He flinched at the sound.

"What the fuck?" he screeched. Neenahwi looked over at him concerned, but continued on their northerly course.

"Sorry, nephew," came the voice again. *"I did not mean to startle you."*

Who is that? he thought.

"I was Nanichita, chief of the Wolfclaw long ago." The voice

paused as if in thought. *"You do know that spirit animals are called so because they have the spirit of an ancestor?"*

I guess so. But you haven't spoken before. I didn't know how it actually worked.

"The distance from the Jeweled Continent to our home was too great for us to converse. But now you are here and so we can talk. I know the others can't wait to speak with you too."

Motega knew what that meant. Another visit from the old wolves in his dreams. He wasn't sure he was looking forward to it. *Great. Me too. Can I ask a question? Are you there all the time?*

"Only slightly. You can call me by name and I will come. A piece of me gives Per his abilities to bond with you. But I have little interest in being a bird all of the time."

Good, he thought, relieved that he didn't have to share Per's head with another. He enjoyed the avian mind's presence and wasn't sure he could handle another passenger. It was difficult enough to fly at times. But then he realized that his thought had probably been heard and he didn't want to get off on the wrong foot with the dead people as soon as he'd got home. *I mean, that's reassuring. Can we talk more later, I'm kind of in the middle of something.*

"Of course," came the reply and Motega sensed the presence had gone.

"What's wrong?" asked Neenahwi.

"Nothing. I'll tell you later," he answered, wanting to push the new discovery to one side. He wondered what else would be different now that they were home. For now, though, he needed to focus on what they were doing.

They flew north, keeping the coast to their right and the dipping sun on their left. They were searching for signs of life, signs of the Alfjarun towns of those who lived by the ocean. The kind like those who had sold he and his sister to Llewdon when they were children, but that was a memory he had to push away, after all, he was there as liberator not as someone seeking vengeance. It was just that Alfaria was a huge place, as big as the Jeweled Continent, and they lacked intelligence about what had been happening there in the years since he and his sister had been taken. They needed to find Alfjarun, and hopefully Pyrfew too.

But the whole afternoon had almost passed and they hadn't seen anything but trees, cliffs, and beaches.

The land east of the great boundary mountains was foreign to Motega, he couldn't remember any landmarks from when they had traveled through it before. There were few great forests left in the Jeweled Continent, except in Pyrfew and Wespar, and he hadn't had much reason to go to either of those places in the last ten years. He'd never flown over the plains of the Missapik, which was to the west of the mountains, but he was sure there would be more for his huge falcon eyes to see than the impenetrable canopy of trees.

The light was dimming and the window of time when he could rely on Per's superior sight was closing. Neenahwi could change form into an owl if she wanted to carry on, but they had agreed before leaving that they would find a place to roost and resume at first light. Motega nudged Per to dip his wings and slowly glide down to the upper-most branches below them. He landed, spotting a barb-tailed lizard on the branch opposite which made Per think of dinner. *Soon.*

Neenahwi landed beside him. "I'll see you tomorrow," he shrieked. "Be safe."

"Of course," she said in reply, and he released his hold on Per.

His eyes opened and he was back at their camp, near

where they had made surface. A fire had been built before him and six rabbits roasted away on spits. Definitely better than lizard. The others were all seated around the fire, except for a couple of the Ravens that he assumed had claimed an early watch and were acting as sentries. Trypp was sitting on one side of him, leaning back against his pack like a pillow, and Mareth was sat on the other, scribbling away in a journal.

"You're back," said Trypp, idly. "See anything?"

"Nope. Maybe tomorrow."

"At least we can start dinner now. Mouse, let's get to eating."

"Mouse is cooking? Are you sure that's a good idea?"

"Don't worry. We all helped with preparing the hares. There's no funny seasoning involved. But he likes staring at the fire, so..." Trypp shrugged.

Dinner turned out to be heavenly. The supplies they had brough from Unedar Halt, and what had been available to hunt or capture underground, had required an acquired taste. And he didn't have it. Whilst you'll eventually eat anything if you're hungry enough, having real meat was something that he had missed. He licked his fingers and wiped at his beard with the back of his hand after he threw the leg bone in the fire. They'd eaten in silence, apparently his sentiment shared by all except Kyle, who was eying his food warily. Motega chuckled to himself.

He looked over at Mareth, who had not finished his helping. The Lord Protector needed to eat. Or failing that, his food needed eating.

"Are you going to finish that?"

It took a moment before Mareth realized that someone

was talking, blinking his eyes as he pulled his gaze away from the fire. "Oh, no. You can have it."

Motega took the offered plate and set to work. He understood that Mareth was struggling. By Marlth, sometimes he was the same. But Motega had also not had his soul sucked out by some faceless creature and his voice turned into a weapon. He worried about the Lord Protector.

"So, really. How are you doing?"

Mareth looked at him and shrugged. "It depends. When it's quiet, it's worse. When there is nothing else to think of, I can still see her. At least I can talk now." Mareth forced a laugh.

"How much of the mushroom stuff have you got left?" he asked. Motega knew that it helped. But what happened when it ran out? He didn't think they were going to run into any more of the strange creatures above ground.

"Don't worry. It will be fine. I can ration it," said Mareth, pointedly not answering the questions he was asked. Motega didn't want to push it, so merely nodded. "I should probably get some sleep so I'll be rested for my watch."

"Aye."

Mareth pushed himself up from his seat with a grunt and went to his bedroll. Motega turned to face Trypp. His eyebrows arched; he'd obviously listened to the whole exchange. Now it was Motega's turn to shrug.

"I think he's got the right idea of it. Time for some kip. It's been a long day."

~

THE ROCK BENEATH HIS BUTTOCKS WAS FAMILIAR, AND though he had been expecting it after the visit he had received mid-flight, he would much rather have been dreaming about Cherry or Midnight than having family time. The circle was empty, and the long yellow grasses that bordered it waved gently in the breeze. The sky was green, which was peculiar, but it lacked the menace of times before. The land of the dead almost seemed...peaceful.

The absence of howling wolves or scowling grandfathers definitely helped. He sat still for a moment, while searching the sky for Per—but he could see no sign. Motega was just about to get up and walk around when the grasses moved.

For the first time he was not greeted by wolves. Men and women, some old, some in the prime of their lives, strode forward through the grasses, seemingly unaware of their nakedness, weapons of spear or axe or hammer or sword held in their hands, all following behind a woman of advanced years. She was clearly old, there was no other way of describing it; her skin was mottled and wrinkled, and areas of her body—elbows, breasts, belly, knees—were seeing who could get to the ground first. But she too held a spear in a strong hand, bones and feathers and teeth hanging from near the stone head. Behind her was his father and great grandfather, and others that he recognized from his visits; but Motega did not remember having seen her before.

"Ho!" she called in a strong voice.

"Ho, Motega!" came the refrain from the others.

"Welcome home, boy," she added. Motega wasn't sure about being referred to as a boy, even though it was something his great grandfather did, but he let it pass.

"Thank you," he said, bowing his head. "We have not spoken before..."

The lady cackled. "We talked today, foolish boy. I am Nanichita."

Motega gulped, now having the image of the soul that inhabited his spirit animal firmly lodged in his mind, droopy bits and all. He bowed again and added, "Well met ancestor. I am sorry I didn't know you."

She laughed again. "Not what you were expecting, eh? This is how I looked close to when I died, having seen one hundred and forty-six summers. I was chief for all but thirty of those years and let me tell you that I fought off my challengers myself." Nanichita lifted her spear into the air with one arm and then began to rapidly spin the weapon, passing it from one hand to another. The shaft of the spear slapped against her open palm as she stepped forward, the tip hovering just a couple of feet away from Motega's chest. "But if this form is unpleasant to you, maybe you'd prefer my appearance to be from when I was a similar age to you?"

The wrinkles on Nanichita's face smoothed and her back straightened, the grey disappeared from her long hair and her body became taught and tight and lean. Watching her in her nakedness, Motega suddenly felt very uncomfortable. He was sure it was not appropriate for him to find a dead ancestor attractive but his body was not cooperating. "I'm not sure that's any better," he mumbled.

Nanichita laughed again and Motega suddenly thought that he might have preferred his grandfather shouting at him.

"You'll get used to it," she said. "Now to matters of more importance. You and Neenahwi are finally here and we want revenge." The smile disappeared from her face and was replaced with a steely resolve. "Find the green men. Find Pyrfew and cast them from our lands. All of our lands." Motega knew she wasn't just talking about Wolfclaw territory; it had to be everything, all of the Wild Continent.

"Bring the life back to Alfaria with their blood. See our weapons, see our strength, and know that we will always be behind you."

Motega beat his chest with his fist and looked her in the eye. "We are here, with friends, and we have travelled under the great ocean, through the dark for many moons. We have no way of leaving. We must stop Pyrfew, as Llewdon has even more evil planned for our people."

"That is good, son." Sharef, finally stepped forward to speak, his father's jaw jutted forward proudly and Motega could see a kind of peace in his eyes. "And speaking of friends, we know of Florian. We are saddened, too. Know that if you ever find his spirit, he would be welcome in our hunting grounds."

A lump formed in Motega's throat at the thought. He was about to ask if that was really possible, but Nanichita had other thoughts.

"Do not be maudlin. Florian was a fine warrior and he would have been a good champion. But champions die. That is the way of the world. Let us instead tell stories." She beckoned the others closer and they sat around Motega. "Tell us about the underground and the tunnels of Rabbit. These are things we do not know." Nanichita sat down cross-legged before him too.

"I'm not sure the tunnels were dug by a rabbit, more a worm bigger than a longhouse, but..." and Motega settled into his rock and told his ancestors of their journey in what the dwarves called the Dundenas.

~

THE CRISP AIR AT ALTITUDE WAS PLEASANTLY COOLER THAN

the humidity where he had left his body behind. The wind also had the added benefit of cleansing away some of the feeling that he had woken up with that morning. It had taken him a while to tell the story to the gathered crowd, but time passed in that dream world much differently, so unfortunately, he had still time for other dreams before waking.

One of *those* kinds, involving the young Nanichita.

But he was trying very hard not to think about it in case he accidentally called her to share Per's body. He wasn't sure if a bird could blush, but he had no intention of finding out.

Neenahwi was in no mind for conversation, which was fine as far as he was concerned. He wondered what was going through her mind now that they were home after so long, but it would have to wait until later for him to talk to her. He should probably tell her about the dream too. He'd hoped that once she was back in Alfaria, she would be dragged before the ancestors too. After all, wasn't she supposed to be chief? Maybe they had spoken to her separately last night?

Their reconnaissance continued in much the same way as the previous day until after the sun was past its zenith, and two trails of smoke could be seen ahead. One by the coast, and another out into the forest. Neenahwi had spotted them too and she took the lead.

Eventually they reached a town, reminiscent of the place he remembered from his childhood, but it wasn't the same. This one was built next to a long beach that reached out to the sea, canoes resting on the sand. He wasn't trying to do an exact count, but he would have guessed there were roughly a hundred or so houses, all built of a white timber from the nearby forest and constructed above ground. There was no real organization to the placement of the homes, no defined streets to speak of, like a city in the Jeweled Continent.

Locals walked the town or sat huddled in groups, mending nets or preparing dinner.

They glided slowly over the habitation, Motega taking time to utilize Per's sharp eyes and look for things out of the ordinary. He needn't have tried so hard, as when they got to the north end of town, the activity and make-up of the place began to change. Large barns had been constructed and arranged in perfect squares, a stone smithy nearby, and Alfjarun townspeople moved with purpose to and from the only two-story building in the town.

There was the glint of metallic green and Motega spied a pair of Pyrfew soldiers standing guard outside the two-story building. Behind the building stretched a yard with a score, or four hands from the Pyrfew perspective, of troops going through drills.

The thermal on which he and his sister soared took them past the town and over furrowed fields of vegetables and wheat that was emerging from the ground. Alfjarun dressed in grey tended the fields, a handful of soldiers standing around talking nearby.

In the center of the fields was another wooden construction, little more than a long roof over dirty ground without walls. Rough blankets lay crumpled underneath the shelter. *Is that where those working in the fields sleep?* Separate from the town, and overseen night and day by Pyrfew. What had happened to his people? How could some continue their lives as usual when others were treated in such a way?

Neenahwi banked left and headed out toward the forest. A gravel road threaded its way through the fields from the town and out into the darkness of the trees, so it was that they followed. It snaked through the forest for many miles until the location of the other source of smoke was revealed, a scar in the center of the woods where the earth itself had been torn apart. Rough buildings lined one side of the clearing, next to which was a long shallow hole that had been dug. Rock of varying colors was exposed, and the hole was worked mainly by men. They were stripped to the waist, tools in hand, as they gouged away at the ground. Nearby, other Alfjarun, whips in their clutches instead of tools, watched over the work crew with evil intent.

There was not a Pyrfew soldier in sight.

His stomach heaved. Motega had seen slaves before. He'd seen the petty-minded people that lorded it over slaves, too. He just never expected to see it in Alfaria, even though Vakaka had alluded to it when Motega had questioned him in Ioth. He guessed that the grey clothed field workers had a similar state of freedom.

"Let's go back," squawked Neenahwi. "We've seen enough. We know what we have to do."

"Yes. I'll go ahead."

Motega released his hold on Per's mind and his eyes opened. He was sitting cross legged by the remains of the fire from the night before. His buttocks were sore and he realized that one of his legs was numb. Trypp lounged nearby, picking at a finger nail with a knife. He looked up.

"Are you back, or just having a seizure? I hope it's not the latter because I'd have to get up and I'm really quite comfortable."

Motega smiled and stretched out his legs, rubbing the life back into them. He'd learnt his lesson in the past—trying to get up too fast after one of those long spells of sitting and ending up falling on his face when he couldn't feel his feet. It was embarrassing enough, and painful enough, for him to slow down for a change.

“Yep, I'm back. Where is everyone?”

Trypp waved a hand all around. “Doing stuff, I guess. Being productive. I took responsibility for watching you.” Motega laughed, but inside he appreciated the thought. “You find something I assume?”

He thought back to what he had seen. A score of Pyrfew soldiers and maybe a few unseen administrators with hundreds of Alfjarun in thrall. He wasn't worried about the soldiers; they could handle them. It was his own people that was concerning. Heartbreaking even. How they had fallen to such depths he couldn’t understand. Now he understood his father’s warning back in Ioth that he wouldn’t be able to escape fighting his own people.

“We found our first destination. The first place we can make a difference. We know what we've got to do and where we've got to do it. Now we've just got to figure out how...”

THE FURTHER ADVENTURES OF AN OLD MAN AND HIS PYXIE

The wind whipped through his long hair, the breeze a welcome respite from the late summer heat that had decided to make a permanent home in his room below deck. From the railing of the ship he could see the small town of Colvin, little more than a handful of wooden buildings congregated around the crude harbor. Capital city of Wespar? Hah, it paled in comparison to Kingshold. But then he supposed that Serenus never did care about those things. And she had another place to call home, where visitors were less welcome. He flexed his shoulders, stretching out some of the kinks, and marveled once again at the strength of this new form. Yes, he had declared that he would not use magic again, and he really had cut down—but one did not simply expect someone such as he to go unnoticed when traveling.

After all, everyone knew of Jyuth the Terrible.

The boat was tied off against the harbor and within minutes. Jyuth walked alone down the gangplank—his occasional companion having disappeared again—the pockets inside his cloak bulging with gems. After he had left Kingshold his first port of call had been Danteth, where he called in multiple favors to get his hoard exchanged for something a little more portable. He'd spent a few weeks there, had started to get into the retirement mindset. Much of that involved drinking, studying his new book, and attempting to put some of it into practice.

On the day he left Danteth he had been somewhat surprised to see Eden stepping off a boat onto the dock. He really did not like that odious prick—he had to admit that he had rather enjoyed stripping him of his lands and title—but what he did now was none of his concern. He was sure the news would get back to Mareth all too soon.

There were a few Colvin locals who had come out to greet the boat; all humans. There were none of Wespar's most famous inhabitants who would call a town like this home, but he gave their greetings and exultations regarding their fine giant-wrought goods little more than a dismissive wave as he breezed through the town and headed north following the cart track.

He could have afforded a horse to make the journey faster, but for the first time in centuries he wasn't in a rush. Why not enjoy the countryside and feel the road beneath his feet?

It took five days through unkept meadow punctuated by fields of crops and lonely farm houses until he saw the edge of the forest. He slept under the stars every night, staring up at the thousands of pin pricks of light and marveling at how the stars were probably the only thing that had not changed in his long life. He smoked pipe weed by the campfire and for the first time since he was a boy, since before Myank had plucked him from obscurity, he almost felt free. There were just a few loose ends that he had to tie up responsibly, and then he could feel truly liberated.

Grey clouds harboring thunderous intention were blowing in from the west when he reached the edge of the forest. It was called Ihlathyim Fihlokya, a very long name for something that, in giant, basically meant 'home in the trees.' Long, long ago, this had been a fearsome place, somewhere that even heroes avoided, mindful of the creatures that lurked beneath the ancient and spectacularly high canopy. And that was without even considering the man-eating giants that ruled.

That reputation still held, keeping out all but the bravest of adventurers, even though Serenus had done much to change the giants. Where once they had eaten human flesh, now they were vegetarian.

Jyuth was immediately aware of when he had entered Ihlathyim Fihlokya; he instantly felt his muscles twitching and a clicking of joints as his new younger form—wide shouldered, muscular and quite attractive to the ladies judging from recent experience—expanded to his usual portly self. He still didn't know how she did it, but no magic was possible in Wespar that was not the Matron's.

It smelt of cinnamon, like the fresh pastries he used to buy off the White Road, wafting in waves as he walked along the forest path. When would he ever get to have one of those sticky buns he had grown to love from Mrs. Butterbowl? He stopped suddenly. No, she must be dead by now. Well, whichever descendant was running the business now he hadn't noticed any diminishment in quality. Quite why the forest smelled of cinnamon, he was not sure. Maybe it was that these great trees, many paces around and hundreds of feet tall, were related to cinnamon trees but he didn't know.

He had asked to study them once but Serenus had refused. She sure did like to say no to him.

Jyuth noticed eyes in the fern covered ground watching him as he walked. Maybe badger, or lynx, or sprite. Either way he was sure that his imminent arrival would be expected.

He was not disappointed. As he turned a tree-lined corner and the heart of Ihlathyim Fihlokya came into sight, he knew there was a welcome party. Ihlathyim Fihlokya was both the forest and the giants' home, the two inseparable. Instead of constructing homes and shelter from earth or wood, the giants lived *in* the trees. Another secret that Serenus wouldn't share; how they coaxed the trees to grow in such a way to create these homes that rose up the side of the sturdiest trunks or dangled from the greatest branches like fruit, with vines and other branch-created pathways in the sky sturdy enough for a giant's weight connecting it all. And it appeared, that in his honor, every giant had come out of those wondrous homes to line the path.

For those not used to the giants' ways, this would be a terrifying sight. Male or female they stood naked; tits dangling, members hanging down to the knees, their bodies covered in thick quilts of furry pubes. Their hair styles were fascinating, for giants took great pleasure in using a strange substance drawn from the sap of the trees to mold their long hair into a variety of shapes that Jyuth wondered if they were supposed to mimic the trees. No longer were they daubed in dried blood as when he had first met them, but still, all this coupled with the fact that the smallest of them was twice as large as the average human man would send all but the most stupid or brave running for the meadowland. Jyuth walked between the opposing ranks unconcerned, tossing "hello"s along with the odd "good morning", only to be answered by a nod of the head of the receiving giant.

It had not gone unnoticed that the honor guard was funneling him directly to the Matron. Or that there was no turning back seeing as the twin lines of giants merged to parade behind him once he had passed. No matter. For his business was with the Matron; there was no one else he would wish to speak with here. For while giants were big and fearsome in battle—he remembered that time, a few hundred years ago, he had convinced the giants to fight against Llewdon's northern push and what a sight it had been—and he knew that they were not dumb, their immense size did mean that they operated on a slightly different frequency than he did. And he was not known for his patience.

His procession ended at a great yew tree that branched out huge limbs from the base in all directions, wooden tendrils curling in gnarled twists up into the forest canopy. The trunk of the yew tree was bigger around than many of the tallest towers of the palace of Kingshold, and at its base was a v-shaped entrance. The home of the Matron. Serenus. His old classmate.

Jyuth stopped on the threshold, turned and bowed, thanking the forest of giants for his escort, before stepping inside.

Within was much as he remembered from his last visit with Neenahwi. The inside of the tree was covered in bark too, testament to the space not being carved, nor the bare wood of a dead tree, but because it had been willed to grow in such a way. And while the bark outside was a deep chestnut, inside it shone with silver, reflecting the light that drifted in from the top somewhere. The ground beneath his feet was soft with moss, which stretched to a large mound ahead. Reclining on the mound was a giant, chin propped up by a hand as she watched him enter. Her pendulous breasts and expansive stomach reached for the ground. On a stump nearby rested a bowl of red fruit and another container that emitted a gentle whisper of smoke. It smelled of lavender but it was probably anything but.

"Jyuth. I would say what a surprise to see you. But of course, I knew you were coming."

Serenus, or the Matron as she now preferred, was a seer. Jyuth had never known anyone to have as accurate and as vivid premonitions as her. And the fact that she could relive those visions with another had made her extremely useful in the past. He had expected that she expected him.

"Serenus, my dear." Though he knew she preferred the moniker of the Matron, he refused to go along with other people's petty egotism. He quite enjoyed being a cantankerous old sod. No wonder he didn't have many friends left. "You look ravishing."

"And you look as ugly as ever." She paused, eyes narrowing. "Some of your purpose I know, but always the mist surrounds you, old man. Always there are secrets I cannot pierce."

"I wouldn't have it any other way. I might lose my allure if all of my truth was evident."

"There is war coming. I have sent an envoy to Edland to see your Singer-King and bring him back to me so he may see what is to happen. Know that the giants will not fight for you again. Too many great souls were lost the last time. We harm no one unless they threaten our home."

This always happened. Every time he saw her, she would bring up the last time the giants had fought for the people of the Sapphire Sea. In the Green Desert they were nearly wiped out, and Jyuth knew that they would not have prevailed that day without the giant's help. Serenus had cried for twenty years when the few score of survivors made it home. His guilt was real, but then there were many things he felt guilty for.

"I understand. I too miss their presence. It makes my heart glad to see that the giants are strong once more. But I should make it clear to you, the one you call the Singer-King is not mine. He was chosen by the people of Edland. I am... done." *Done*. Such a simple four-letter word, but the hardest thing he had ever set his mind to.

"Done?"

"I go to the east to retirement. As you said, I am an old man, and I am eager to live out my remaining years in some form of happiness. I just have a few things to take care of first."

"My vision showed me that you wanted to put something you treasure into a hole of mine. Is that true?"

Jyuth grinned. "Why, yes. As a matter of fact, it is."

THERE WAS MUCH GRUNTING, SQUELCHING, AND SWEATING as Jyuth thrust into the Matron. Their rotund bellies squished together, Jyuth's head nestled between her breasts making it somewhat difficult to breathe, and her great hands clasped on his buttocks driving the tempo. He realized he probably didn't have to do anything other than stay alive and stay hard. With a shudder it was over and Jyuth lay panting against her like a beached walrus.

A moment passed and she flipped him onto the moss bed beside her, his magically enlarged member flopping against his chest bone, altogether too close to his face for comfort.

"Fuck, Serenus. It's been a long time..."

She didn't respond to his statement. Her attention was focused elsewhere. "It seems we have an audience. He's been there for some time."

Jyuth followed where she was looking, only to see the wrinkled pink form of Basharaat hovering in the air and looking at the pair of them open mouthed, sharp teeth revealed, eyes reveling in delight at the show, hand doing something unmentionable to his usually smooth nether regions. The pyxie cackled and disappeared in a puff of sulfurous smoke.

"Yes, he keeps doing that."

The Matron rolled on to her side to look at the wizard. "Keeps doing that? There have been others?"

"Hah. Don't tell me you haven't been keeping the boys outside busy." She shrugged in reply. "I've got a few centuries to catch up on."

"You were always too obsessed," said Serenus. "When we were in the tower, it was with Tarra. Then after she had gone, it was with Llewdon. You should have just fucked them both and been done with it."

"Well I have been trying to fuck that elf over for quite a while. And I'm sure he had something to do with her disappearance. You were the one who told me she was going to Pyrfew to talk to those pointy eared arse wipes. Then she didn't come back!"

"Maybe she didn't want to come back," murmured Serenus sadly.

"Aye. Maybe you're right." He thought about the things he'd said to Tarra after Myank left. Not something he was proud of either. It made him wonder how different things might have been. "Seems like I've been a shit for a long time."

She nodded. "That you have. But I'll miss you all the same."

Jyuth felt a lump in his throat. By Marlth, he hated goodbyes. First Neenahwi and now his oldest living friend. "Me too, you crazy old hag. But you need to do something about this first." He waved toward his donkey-like penis flopping flaccid against his gut.

Serenus laughed and his cock returned to normal.

"Now, about that vision of yours," said Jyuth. "Not to say I didn't enjoy the sex, but I do want to put something else safely away in a hole in your tree..."

FREE OF THE EASTERN EDGE OF THE FOREST, JYUTH HAD A bounce in his step. Well, he hadn't done *that* with Serenus in a few centuries, and he felt his burden becoming lighter. The sun was peeking up over the horizon, filtering through some early morning cloud and the air was thick with dew.

There was a pop to his right and the little pink pervert appeared. It scowled at him; arms crossed.

"Morning, Basharaat."

"Why did you do that?"

"Did the sight of our coupling vex you? It seemed like you were enjoying yourself."

The pyxie shook his shiny head. "Not that. Why you leave the muluwaza in that tree?"

"Basharaat. I told you I was retiring. That means no more wizarding. I'm done, and I don't need these damn stones anymore. They are a temptation that I don't know how long I can resist."

The pyxie king narrowed his eyes, clearly distrustful of what he was hearing.

"I mean it," said Jyuth. "Instead of just watching me fornicate, how about you help me? I need to put the stones away in safe places."

"Why would you want me to know where they are hidden?" growled Basharaat.

"What if I said I trust you?" The pyxie barked a laugh. "Fine, just help me so I can move onto the next stage of my life. Maybe I'll be able to help you before I do?" Jyuth stuck out his hand and waited.

Basharaat eyed the offered deal warily, but eventually brought his own taloned hand up to his mouth, spat a bright green blob of phlegm into his palm and, before Jyuth could move, shook the wizard's hand. "Deal."

Jyuth flicked the mucus from his hand once they had sealed the arrangement, wiping it off on the side of his soiled robe for good measure.

"Well, let's get started then."

~

"THIS IS THE PLACE," SAID BASHARAAT PROUDLY. "NO ONE here no more. Stunted ones long gone."

"Stunted ones?" asked Jyuth eying the stone archway that stood proudly in the side of the mountain. "You mean Dwarves? Isn't that a little rich considering they are about four times the size of you?"

"I was not referring to height!" the pyxie replied haughtily, puffing himself up.

Jyuth decided not to engage in a debate but instead wanted to see what the pyxie had found for him. They had spent the past two weeks walking slowly across Skaria until they reached the mountain range in the north, and another three days climbing which had played havoc with the old man's knees (though he wasn't likely to let the little demon notice). From the outside it looked good, an abandoned dwarven mine—and as he thought about it, he may have paid them a visit once more than six or seven hundred years ago, it all ran together when you were his age—another perfect dark hole.

The entrance led to a long passageway ending in a large pair of locked doors. The doors were little problem, just one more *final* time to use magic. Beyond was another tunnel, leading to a metal cage hanging above a pit from a chain and a long set of stairs that circled the side of the shaft. The thought of the chain holding the cage made his head swim. Who knew if the mechanism or the metal links were still reliable? He decided to take the stairs.

Any light from the outside disappeared quickly, so Jyuth conjured a fist-sized ball of light that hovered an arm's distance away from him. The descent was long and monotonous; round and round it went without ever seeming like the shaft had an end.

Until it did. Opening out onto a circular landing of flat carved stone, tunnels branching out in six different directions. Scattered across the ground were bones; broken or gnawed upon.

"Does something live here?" Jyuth asked the pyxie.

Basharaat nodded eagerly. "Oh yes. Many things. Things that like the dark."

Jyuth clapped his hands together with glee. "Excellent. They shall act as a deterrent."

Picking a tunnel at random he strode off, the pyxie floating along behind. It soon became clear what was living there. A family of unusually-large rodents, know by those who studied them as ratchen, had taken up residence in a series of storage rooms. They walked on two legs, which could give you the impression that they were intelligent enough to reason with, but those who made that mistake usually ended up studying their sharp claws and puncturing front teeth a little too closely for anyone's long term health.

Not that he had made that mistake before.

Or at least he wasn't going to admit it out loud.

Splitting his consciousness, gathering a thread of power from the green demon stone he wore on his left ring finger, he created a block of force around their feet before they could move. The ratchen mother and her children hissed in anger at their confinement, scratching at the air as they tried to reach the wizard. Others came to help at the cries of their family but befell the same fate.

Jyuth stepped warily past the ratchen, pressing himself to the wall of the corridor to stay out of range of one who was in their path. Basharaat took great pleasure in hovering in front of the creatures and blowing raspberries and spittle in their faces.

Beyond the ratchen family Jyuth was happy to be led past sabre-centipedes, gas-shrooms, a particularly talented mimic moss that had taken the shape of a pool of clear still water to capture its prey, and an extremely ugly proto-slug. Each beast he avoided or incapacitated before moving on. He didn't want to harm them when they would serve his purpose later.

He found himself whistling a little ditty as he went about his business.

Just when he was starting to wonder if he was going to find a suitable place to stow his treasure, or the exit again, he came across a room unlike all of the others. It still had its door intact.

He looked for the handle, but there was none visible, nor had there ever been. He gave it a push and it wouldn't move. It was only when he had the floating ball of light hover before the door and turn from a soft yellow to a bright blue light, did he see the inscription. He traced the letters with his finger and the door popped open silently. He gave a chuckle of appreciation; a dwarven lock. He hadn't seen one of those in quite some time. He pushed it open and looked on to see what he had found.

A long stone altar was at the far end of the room, metal benches arrayed in rows before it. A shrine to Varcon—these Dwarves must have been particularly devout to worship so close to where they worked. But no matter, it was the perfect place for his needs.

Still sitting atop the shrine was a purple pillow of silk, miniature silver bellows resting on top. He picked up the ceremonial object and tossed it into the corner of the room, pulling a blue ring from his left hand and setting it down on the cushion in its place.

"There. That should do it," he said, as he stood with his hands on his hips. He turned around on the spot, considering what he had passed on the way there. *But what if the other direction was easier?* He didn't want to go and secure all the passages, that sounded like too much hard work, and his use of magic was already starting to make his stomach hurt. *Damn ulcer.*

He pushed on the amulet that hung around his neck, driving the pin on its back into his flesh. The power from the yellow stone seeped into his body like an old friend, and forming the image in his mind, he suddenly snapped out an arm. It disappeared in midair up to the elbow for a second or two before he violently yanked it back out again, his hand dragging a snarling big cat. He was extremely careful to keep the poisonous fangs pointed in any direction other than at him. Jyuth pulled on another invisible thread from the amulet, winding it around the tiger's head and linking it to the ring that rested on the altar. Instantly, the beast fell into a magical sleep.

"Now, that should do it." He nodded to the pyxie who had been watching the proceedings intently. "And with that, your royal highness, we should leave."

~

THEY HAD DECIDED TO CELEBRATE THEIR HARD WORK IN A town they found in the foothills, a day's walk back from the dwarven mine, home to a dozen decent sized farms and the few hundred homes that they supported. There were three inns but Jyuth and Basharaat had shown little concern as to which to frequent first; they had every intention of hitting them all that evening.

And so it was that they started their evening in the Voluptuous Pear (the sign hanging outside the door of a shapely orchard fruit), so named by the landlady, a former whore made good from Carlburg. Jyuth liked it as soon as he walked in through the door. The no-nonsense woman behind the bar. The sawdust on the floor and roaring hearths at either end of the common room. There had been a moment when the locals had wondered what Basharaat was, but Jyuth had waved their concerns away with a "he's with me." Once he and the pyxie were comfortable, had ordered and then been presented with oversized tankards of ale and a heaping plate of sausages (with no vegetables), he was in love and willing to live out the rest of his days there. Or at least stay through Wintertide.

The only problem was, that it was a little quiet.

"Drink up, Bash, we have to celebrate a job well done. And we're going to have to make our own party." Jyuth knew he was being a little unreasonable on two counts. First, the great tankards of ale were bigger than the little pyxie was tall, but he knew that the creature was able to put away his booze better than most regular humans. Secondly, it was only six o'clock in the evening, and so there might be time for things to liven up. But he had no intention of being sober enough to leave it to chance.

"Party?" The demon lifted his head out of the tankard from where he'd been submersed, and shook it like a dog coming in from the rain. "This no party."

"Exactly. That's what I said."

"Hmmm." Basharaat rubbed his pointy chin thoughtfully. "Wait. I get party." The demon disappeared and the ale sloshed in the cup where it had been moments before.

Jyuth busied himself with getting another drink, taking it as a chance to get to know the landlady. There was something about friendly efficiency, combined with experience, especially given her former employment, that piqued his interest. He tried flirting a little, even though he knew he was terrible at it. She recognized his clumsy conversations for what he had been attempting and so did her best to keep her customer happy without making him feel bad. Jyuth was grateful for this and his interest only increased.

Then the party arrived.

First was Basharaat, appearing on the bar beside him and pulling his sleeve to attract his attention. His face was plastered with a wicked grin as he pointed to the far side of the room. Jyuth turned to follow his tiny finger, eager to see what might happen next.

There appeared a gathering of musical instruments, all carried or pushed out of the ether by pyxies wearing tan colored long coats. There was a harpsichord, a double bass, a few different brass horns as he had seen before in Ioth, and a handful of drums and cymbals. The brown-coated pyxies placed the instruments where they were happy with them, all the while watched silently by the few locals who were trying to enjoy their drinks. Jyuth marveled at the ability of country folk to just go along with whatever was happening; there was nary a word of complaint as the same pyxies started to move the tables and chairs away from the impromptu stage. Even when those that were occupied were lifted into the air.

Jyuth grinned as he watched burly men, their confusion plain on their faces, as they were carried aside by little pink critters, one lifting each chair leg. The furniture was suitably organized and then it was time to begin.

Basharaat clapped once and everyone turned to look at him. "Let the party begin!"

Ten pyxies appeared wearing dark trousers, waist coats, and things over their eyes that looked awfully like the protective lenses that dwarves wore when above ground, and they set to work on the instruments. The instruments were all of a typical size for a human, so it took more than one to play anything but a drum.

Two pyxies jumped around from key to key on the harpsichord, occasionally bumping chests in midair or playing games of leapfrog as they jumped from one side of the keyboard to the other. One pyxie manned the top of the bass and the other floated around the bridge plucking strings. For each horn there was a pyxie to hold it up and another to take unexpectedly deep breaths and blow with all of their might.

And surprisingly, even though he wasn't sure that any of them were playing a traditional tune, or at least not the same one, it sounded good. Before he knew it, Jyuth's head bobbed and his foot tapped in much the same way as all of the other punters.

"What do you call this music?" He shouted to Basharaat who appeared very full of himself.

"Jyuzz."

Taken aback for a moment, Jyuth nodded his head for want of something better to do. "What an...honor..."

Jyuth gestured for the landlady to come over and talk to him again. He fished a diamond the size of a walnut out of a pouch and held it up for her to see. Her jaw dropped.

"Yes, it's what you think it is. And it's yours. Drinks are on me, all night. For everyone. We good?"

She plucked the gem from his hand, gave him a wink that made his heart skip assured him it would be a *night to remember*.

The drinks flowed and word got around town. The plan to go to the other two bars went out of the window as all of their customers (and staff) appeared at the Voluptuous Pear. Tables were cleared to the side of the room and the dancing commenced. The pyxie band was tireless; Jyuth wasn't even sure they stopped in between tunes. Everyone in town came to thank him for the evening, a succession of hugs and welcomes. Basharaat hopped from person to person, occasionally 'accidentally' slipping so he could fall into the cleavage of well-endowed ladies like a cliff diver. At one point, Jyuth convinced the landlady to dance with him even though she protested she was too busy. He moved in for a kiss with his eyes closed only to find that she had moved on. He turned in merry befuddlement, looking to see where she had gone, only to come face-to-face with a straw-haired haystack of a man, large welcoming eyes staring deeply into his. He grabbed Jyuth around the head and brought the wizards lips to his. He momentarily thought that this man looked like Duncan, but then he realized he must have been dead many centuries. So, he lost himself in the kiss.

The man broke away first. He smiled and leaned forward to whisper in his ear, "Do you have a room here?"

Jyuth considered the situation, and the situation was good. "I do now. Let's get a key."

THE WINTERTIDE BUNTING AND DECORATIONS WENT UP. The pheasants were roasted. Mulled wine was consumed by the vat. Parades were had and then the decorations came down. And every night was a party in the Voluptuous Pear. On the evening of the Blessing of the Children, Jyuth finally got the landlady into his bed. As they lay there afterward, he'd asked her how it was. The "fine" he got in reply had him retreat back to his copy of the Sexomnicon to address the damage to his ego in the only way he knew how. Study.

But eventually it had got to the point where Jyuth realized he was going to need to keep moving and get out of town before he cavorted himself into the grave. Basharaat had wanted to leave even less than the wizard but one morning, the ground dusted with a light snow, they finally left, the whole town waving goodbye to the most interesting visitors they had ever had.

The route took them northeast, skirting the Kolsavan mountains on the caravan road to Kolsvick. They bypassed that city, Jyuth fearful of distractions from his course, for this was a destination he had in mind for a long time. They hugged the coastal road before they came across the river of Eragorn and followed it to the south, staying close to the river where they could. It was a peaceful journey, because unlike most waterways in the Jeweled Continent they saw no sign of people, for where they were going no humans lived.

The river eventually disappeared underground as the land rose steeply to a series of hills sandwiched between two mountain ranges. Jyuth trudged upward, the pyxie sitting on his shoulder, complaining of boredom but also unwilling to leave him the fuck alone. He crested the hill and looked down on the valley below.

The river emerged from under the hills far below, winding through one of the most beautiful sights he had ever seen. It was a verdant green, lush meadows and broad trees at the floor of the valley, a natural bowl protected from the elements. Herds of creatures, tiny from this distance, ran to and fro. Flocks of birds circled in the air, and the sun peaked through the clouds to send a shaft of light shining down onto this little piece of paradise. And there was not a shred of evidence that anywhere within lay the most pervasive pest in the world; humans.

"Here we are. The Vale of Estaya."

"Waste of time," said the Pyxie dismissively. "Look, nothing to do here."

Jyuth turned his head to look at the little demon, and with him perched on his shoulder, he had to hide the involuntary shiver from seeing the pyxie up so close. "Humans can't enter here, so it's no surprise there aren't any pubs." He reached out theatrically to push on a solid wall of invisible air. "In any case, there is more to life you know."

The pyxie shrugged. "If no humans, why you here?"

"Lest you not forget, your majesty. I do have other means."

He unbuckled his belt and lay it next to his backpack before pulling his purple robes over his head; the pyxie leaping to safety before being enveloped in the ball of stinky cloth. Jyuth stood there naked, letting the chill wind blow away the cobwebs. He pulled on a thread from his amulet and the form of Jyuth shimmered and warped. In moments the fat wizard was replaced with the strong form of a white stallion, a medallion around its neck. The horse picked up the belt and its attached pouches with his teeth and methodically plodded down the steep incline to the valley floor, leaving the little demon behind.

Halfway down Basharaat appeared out of the air, landing on Jyuth's back. He flicked an ear at the annoyance but the pyxie laughed, grabbed hold of his mane and kicked his little heels into his back. Jyuth momentarily thought about trying to buck him off but he knew the little shit would only think it was a game and get right back on. He'd been to this valley only once before, a millennia ago on a field trip with Myank and the other students. He'd been awestruck by the beauty even then, and it had been one of the reasons why he'd come to love taking an animal form so much. He'd always intended to come back, but as he'd been consumed by thoughts of power and politics, and the constant game of cat and mouse with Llewdon, he'd never made the time for a place that he saw as a frivolity.

The air smelled of a mixture of grass and honey as he cantered along the valley floor, elated to find that the Vale had not changed. Herds of wild horses and antelope ran in the distance. He passed a pair of great horned lions tending to their cubs, a giant bear reaching high into the bows of a tree to reach a bee's nest and a long-nosed elephant stripping leaves from the branches of an elm as he headed toward his destination.

In the center of the Vale was a lake, fed by streams that ran off the mountain ranges nearby and dammed at the far end by flat-tailed beavers, where the river ran away. Jyuth's hooves stepped through the muddy shallows and long reeds, the lake shimmering like a perfect plane of glass before him. Gliding across the surface like ladies on a dance floor were a dozen brilliant white swans, bigger than any he had ever seen anywhere else, and in the center of the group was a black one. Jyuth stared at the black swan, hoping that the magnificent form he had chosen would catch its eye; but when it did not look, he whinnied loudly and stamped his hoof to splash in the water.

The black swan glided over, the others falling into formation behind it.

The voice that appeared in his mind was that of a benevolent queen, regal but not unkind. "You are not from here."

"No, I am not. Though I did meet you once before, long, long ago. I come to ask for your help."

The black swan cocked her head as she eyed him. "And what can *I* do to help *you*?"

"There is magic that must be hidden from the world of men. Would you safeguard it?"

"Why should I care about the world of men?"

"Others can change shape too," he said, not unaware that he was making it sound more commonplace than it strictly was. "They can penetrate your protections. With this magic you could be more secure."

The white swans behind her ruffled their feathers and honked, disagreeing with what he was asking. The black swan turned her long neck and hissed them into submission.

"Show me."

"Basharaat?" tested Jyuth, unsure whether the pyxie was included in this conversation, and even though the demon didn't answer he felt him stand on his back. "The second pouch if you please."

The pyxie scrambled down the horse's face and rummaged in the belt, eventually pulling free a black stone that was as big as the pyxie's fist. Basharaat's face shone with ill intent and Jyuth momentarily wondered if he had made a mistake, but the black swan glided over and the demon presented the gem for her to see.

"I accept," said the swan and then her head snapped forward to pluck the stone from Basharaat's grasp with her beak, her neck straightening into the air afterwards as she swallowed it. "Now you must leave our home, never to return."

Jyuth nodded and turned to leave, but before he did so he remembered the sight of the horses running free when he entered. "Please, may I stay one night?"

The black swan regarded him once more before bobbing her head in silent acquiescence, and then turning to swim away.

She'd accepted. That was a relief. He didn't know of a better place to store the one stone that even he did not like to use. He splashed out of the lake and then set off in the direction of where he had seen the horses earlier. Eventually he found them, thirty in all, with heads bowed as they grazed. They didn't bolt at his approach and he joined them, enjoying the feel of family, even a borrowed one, around him. There was one brave filly who took a shine to him, maybe it was his white coat, maybe it was because he was new, but that night he mounted her.

And for once Basharaat did not stick around to watch.

~

THE REFLECTION OF THE MOON FRACTURED ON THE WAVES as their small boat bobbed up and down on the Namaxan Sea. Though it was an inland sea, the strong winds that came down from the mountains of Skaria made it treacherous, especially so at night and when close to the shore and the submerged rocks. Jyuth wasn't particularly keen to be out there in those circumstances, but Basharaat said that he had a good location to hide the penultimate demon stone. The wizard leaned forward in his seat to pull on the oars and send the boat forwards, while Basharaat stood on the seat opposite him, pink skin wet with sea spray and pointing in the direction of where to go.

"There," growled the demon.

Jyuth secured the oars and turned in his seat to see where Basharaat was pointing. "Where? I don't see a cave."

"Told you. It floods with tide. It only visible twice a year in moonlight. Tonight one of those nights. You'll see."

Jyuth focused his attention on the shadows, holding his hand near his eyes to keep the whipped rain from blurring his vision. Gradually, he thought he saw the outline of a dark place. Between them and the cave was a series of sharp, angular, pillars of rock. He did not like the idea of trying to navigate the boat any closer.

"So how are we supposed to get in?"

"Fly," said the Pyxie. "Or swim."

He'd used magic each time he had hidden a stone so far, even though he was supposed to be weaning himself off it. He knew he'd still be calling on the power of the amulet before the night was out, so really, he should swim.

Five minutes of hard flapping through the rain and an eagle disappeared into the dark of the cave, a grinning naked baby-like creature floating along just behind. Jyuth regained his natural form and conjured a ball of light so he could see where on earth he had landed, his bare feet feeling soft damp sand. Out of the wind, the cave was warmer than he expected, a welcome development as he'd left his clothes behind on the boat. All he'd brought was his amulet and a very specific pouch. Where he stood, on a small sand bank beside a patch of rocks, was almost the only patch of dry ground in the cave. Beyond the bank of rocks was a still pool of sea water, the surface like glass, and in the center of the pool was a tall but tiny outcrop of rocks that created the most perfunctory of islands. All of this under a low, broad ceiling, ribbed so it made him think that he had been swallowed by some enormous fish.

"Over there," said Basharaat, pointing to the small island. Jyuth sighed—he supposed he was going to swim after all.

The water was warm and he was almost enjoying himself until he felt something slippery slide past his feet. He hoped it was just an eel. And a normal eel, not a shark eel. Then he felt something pass through his legs, tickling his tackle. Jyuth squealed and set to swimming a lot faster.

The pyxie was waiting for him as he clambered up on to the rocks, relieved nothing had nibbled on him. He had to admit, it was a good spot. Hard to find, hard to get to. Even when the tide was in, it looked like the top of the island remained dry from its lack of sea weed and lichen. It just needed a little bit of protection. Jyuth reached into the pouch that he had been carrying and pulled out a green gem that he nestled in a crack between two rocks.

"Just one left," said Basharaat, and Jyuth could see him hungrily eying the stone in his amulet. He wasn't surprised. After all, that was the stone that was tied to the pyxie, the reason why he always kept coming back. "I have idea for last place."

"Yes, just the one left old friend. But I know where the last place is to be."

"Where we go then?"

"I'm afraid *we* won't be going there together." Jyuth looked pityingly on the pyxie, like he was passing on news to a child that their beloved pet had come to a sticky end. "You were right. It's much too dangerous for you to know where all of the stones are hidden. So, you will be staying here to protect this one."

Basharaat's face went purple with anger; Jyuth would not have been surprised if steam had come out of the creature's ears. "You bastard. You are liar."

"Unfortunately, that is true. And unfortunately, this is one last thing you must do for me." Jyuth held the amulet in his hand, the meaning apparent to the little demon. "You will guard the stone and not let anyone take it unless they can answer your trickiest riddle. Understand? And once someone does, then you are free."

The pyxie ground his needle-sharp teeth together, the

noise audible in the otherwise silent cave. Jyuth reached out to pat him on the head in goodbye, but the demon flinched away. Not a particularly surprising response.

"Goodbye, Basharaat, king of pyxies. I will miss you."

"Oh, fuck off."

So he did.

The eagle flew over the still water toward the cave mouth, leaving the demon to the dark.

~

HIS ARMS ACHED. HIS BACK WAS SORE. BUT HE KEPT THE strokes constant, the manual labor a pittance of a penance for the guilt he carried. And by comparison to all he'd done over the preceding thousand years, abandoning Basharaat was merely a drop in this sea he was navigating. Though he was only a demon, he'd also been something akin to a friend over the years, and they'd definitely had a good time together since he'd left Kingshold.

The sun was beginning to come up over the eastern shore of the Namaxan sea. The row boat was no kind of vessel to get out of sight of land so he hugged the coast. It would take some time to make it to Kalomat, and he'd probably need to sleep for a week once he made it, but the 'gateway to the east' was a good place to start the next phase of his retirement.

He felt the chain that held the famous amulet of Jyuth drag on the back of his neck. Just one stone left...

He'd hidden four, surely, he could keep one? Who knew if he might need it?

He had fully intended to part with them all, he really had.

But now it just seemed...unnecessary. He was certain he wouldn't use magic, unless he absolutely had to.

And so Jyuth, his only possessions a demon stone, a few bags of gems, and a sex education book, rowed off into the early morning light and whatever adventures would await him.

THE WANDERER

A glorious day.

The early morning sun shone down on Yamaagh as the smoke from the hearths of home came into view, the twisting grey ribbons rising into the sky. He pushed through the last of the long grasses as they gave way to the tilled earth where the vines of squash grew. There weren't any farmers in the field which was disappointing. He'd anticipated their looks of surprise and awe at his return, already practicing his own look of smug self-satisfaction that he was destined for greater things than tending *vegetables*.

Yamaagh was a man now. A dozen days in the wild, naked and unarmed, exposed to the plains, his body and soul open for the gods to judge.

And he had been found worthy!

You will be the greatest living warrior of the Tigereye clan.

And for the first time in three generations, the Tigereye clan had a spirit animal, the Great Plains tiger that padded behind him. He smiled and his chest puffed with pride as he looked back at the cat, its sandy-colored coat shimmering in the golden sun. Its shoulder was chest high to Yamaagh, longer than he was tall, and the long teeth that poked out past its lower feline lip nagged at the boyhood fear that lurked inside.

He was special.

So why hadn't anyone come out to greet him? To celebrate him?

The longhouse was the village center, a series of homes built around it in familial clusters. Outside the dug-out homes, signs of industry—tools, animal hides, drying grasses—were on display, but where was the clan?

A familiar face emerged up the steps from a home near his own hut, moving with haste. It was Mosi, his grandmother's niece's son, and the person who was closest to being his own brother. Mosi glanced over his shoulder as he made to sprint toward the longhouse, double taking and then stopping.

"Yamaagh! You're back..." Mosi trailed off as he noticed the tiger trailing behind, sniffing the air of the village.

"Yes, I am. And you are too, my friend." Yamaagh embraced him, slapping his back. It wasn't often that children didn't come back from the Quana, but it happened and he was happy that Mosi was a man now too.

"Is that...?" Mosi was having problems getting his words out.

"Our ancestors have blessed me, Mosi. I knew I was destined to be special."

"Ha. Special indeed. But I will always remember when you cried when you first saw the butchered Bhiferg." Yamaagh scowled at the story that Mosi always brought up from his childhood when he was jealous of Yamaagh's prowess with the spear or axe. Mosi noticed the reaction. "I am happy for you. Happy for the clan. Truly. But come, there is a meeting called in the longhouse. Important news that we must hear."

Yamaagh nodded and set off behind his friend at a jog, the tiger trotting along behind. The longhouse was of a similar construction to the other buildings of the village—dug out of the ground with a v shaped roof of reeds and then thatched with hay—but much bigger, large enough to house the family of the chief and her champion, and for the entire village to meet as the need arose.

It was stifling hot as he went down the stairs and saw the throng of people. The tiger thankfully stopped at the top of the steps; Yamaagh was still not sure how to communicate with the animal, and didn't want to be embarrassed by that knowledge becoming evident to all. Mosi pushed through the mothers and fathers tending to the small children at the rear of the room and Yamaagh followed him until he could see Tiva, the chief of the Tigereye clan.

"...they are gone. All of them." Tiva was finishing speaking as Yamaagh found a place to squat. From the looks of the people around him, there'd been some unnerving news.

"How can this be?" asked one of the elders.

Tiva gestured to Chitto, the clan's champion, to step forward. He was the warrior that Yamaagh looked up to most of all; he wasn't the biggest man of the clan, but he was the quickest and the keenest of eye, precise with the spear. Qualities of the tiger.

"We went to raid in Wolfclaw territory," piped Chitto, his voice singsong and unlike what warriors from other clans expected from a champion, almost universally to their cost. "No matter where we traveled, we came across no one. We slowly moved to their seat, but still there was no challenge." He paused, the whole clan listening with rapt attention. "Though there were only two claws of us, we approached the clan seat and there we witnessed the destruction of the Wolfclaw. All of their homes were burned to their pits. Bodies, ravaged by whatever attacked them and by vultures and coyotes, lay untended on the ground. Warriors. Elders. Children. All dead."

"Who would have done this?" asked the same elder as before.

Chitto shrugged. "We have no idea. All the bodies were Wolfclaw. Maybe their attackers left with their dead. It took a while for us to find trails of heavy feet that had come and then left to the east, as it must have been some moons ago."

Yamaagh had been quiet and focused on Chitto, but as he now took in the reaction of others in the clan, it seemed at odds with the joy he felt in the destruction of their enemy. "Surely this is a time for celebration. Our enemy gone. The hunting grounds solely ours," he called out.

Tiva shook her head. "We do not celebrate this destruction. Children and elders are sacred to all but the scorned. Fire is the weapon of demons. We enjoy the fight, but without our enemies to test ourselves against, how do we know that the Tigereye are superior? Think of them as the Bhiferg, we don't hunt them all in order that they will come again another season."

Yamaagh blushed in embarrassment at the dressing down.

"We will find who did this. We must know if they are a danger to us. Do not worry brave tigers, we will not suffer the same fate," reassured Tiva. She turned her attention back to Yamaagh. "It is good to see you have returned. You are the last. Tonight, we shall feast our new men and women of the clan."

He smiled, stood, and puffed himself up again. "We should make it a grand celebration for I have wonderful news." He put two fingers in his mouth and whistled, praying that he wouldn't be embarrassed again.

From the doorway came a roar and then the shrieks of the children at the back of the room. The head of the great tiger blinked a hello to the rest of the clan.

HE STEPPED THROUGH THE EMPTY SHELL OF THE VILLAGE, feeling the howls of outrage of the ancestors of the clan that had called it home. He didn't know who they had been, or how long they had called it home, but now it was nothing but a home for ghosts. There were no bodies, but the scattered remains of their belongings lay littered on the ground. They left fast, whether they fled or were taken by the green men, he didn't know for certain; but given the usefulness of what had been discarded he would be surprised if it wasn't the latter. He'd lost count of the similar places he had found.

Dark clouds had been following him all day and by the initial spits of rain on his face knew that the Thunderbird would be there soon. He didn't like to spend time in these haunted places, but it seemed unwise to pass up shelter when a storm like that would leave him damp for days, so he picked a house at random and descended into the dark. It smelled stale, like the memory of people, but a fire in the hearth would burn that away. There was a pile of dried dung in the corner for fuel.

From a hide bag across his shoulder he took a flint and

dry tinder and sparked a fire before freeing the small round tubers he had pulled the day before and set to cleaning them, waiting for the hearth to glow before nuzzling them against the warm stones for his dinner.

"Cat! Get in here out of the rain," he called.

The tiger stepped warily down the stairs. She disliked these places even more than he did, preferring the open and the hunt.

There would be hunting soon enough. Green men to find and teach a lesson.

Once the Eagle had come and blown away this storm.

YAMAAGH SAT ON THE LEFT OF TIVA, A FAVORED PLACE AS the spirit warrior of the clan, though Chitto was still her champion and sat on her right. The longhouse was full, though the children had been left in the care of Gama, parents, elders and of-age youngsters hugged the edges of the room, leaving the space in front of the chief and a corridor to the doorway clear. Clear for their guests.

There were five in total. Four men who shimmered in green armor of overlapping leaves, metal swords hanging at their waists. Yamaagh had never seen this grey metal before, or as much of any metal all in one place before. The Tigereye clan didn't have the fire or the ore, but there was bronze in the village that had been traded from the eastern clans close to the mountains. Bronze was good for tools to tend the fields with, and Chitto himself wielded the only bronze blade weapon in the clan. Something that Yamaagh was not afraid to covet; one day, when the warrior was too old to beat him, he knew he would take his place.

The other guest wore no clothes of metal nor carried weapons. He wore a fine wool-spun robe that went down to his knees, and a gold chain hung around his neck of such intricate work that Yamaagh had to force his gaze away so as not to appear rude and covetous. The man held before him what Yamaagh had initially thought was a rolled-up piece of hide, but it was almost translucent in the light and he could see strange dark markings inscribed on the other side. The man spoke their language with a strangled accent, looking at the hide as he spoke.

"By the order of Llewdon, god-emperor of Pyrfew and bringer of light to the world, we bring you greetings and salvation. Long have you toiled in depravity and baselessness, worshiping false gods and struggling to survive. But no more. Llewdon and Pyrfew have claimed all of this land, from the ocean to the far end of the plains, and you are now under his protection. We bring technology and education. We bring food and medication. And we bring with us the opportunity to worship our lord and to one day join him in paradise. Obey and you will be favored. Resistance is futile."

The man rolled up the hide and tucked it under his arm, looking up at the chief of the Tigereye who sat placidly on her stool.

Chitto was not so stoic.

"How dare you come here and threaten us? You walk into the tiger's den—"

Tiva held her hand up for him to stop and he did so, abruptly and with a scowl.

"And if we obey, what would happen then?" There were gasps around the longhouse at the question.

"Once the message has been delivered, I will return with those who will help with your education. We will bring iron and seeds so that your fields may flourish. Your children will leave you for a while so they may truly learn the glory of our lord, but they will return after a few moons."

Yamaagh seethed inside. Who were these people to come and order them around so?

"Are you responsible for what happened to the Wolfclaw clan?" asked Tiva, her eyes not leaving the weak face of the man who spoke.

He didn't flinch. "Yes. Consider it an example."

Tiva rubbed her chin as she thought. Yamaagh found himself holding his breath like the rest of the clan, awaiting the words of refusal from his chief. Eventually, she spoke again. "We accept your terms. Leave here so you might hurry back with what you have promised." There were cries of indignation all around, but Tiva hushed them with a look and a raised hand.

"Your sensibility pleases the empire." The foreigner bowed, turned, and left the longhouse, the warriors that had accompanied him following behind. In their wake they left a silent confusion, a sense of bristling anger that Yamaagh expected to be resolved in a challenge to Tiva's leadership.

Hotak, a grizzled warrior sitting in the front row with aspirations that went beyond being champion, stood and glared. "How can you do this? We are proud. Tigereye should not surrender."

"Hush, Hotak. Today is not the day that you will challenge me. And today is not the day that we will surrender to these invaders. But I am not foolish enough to do a battle with a guest in my own home."

"Then, what is your plan?" snarled Hotak.

"These men of Pyrfew have a long journey back across a wilderness that is dangerous to those who do not know its ways. Hunters roam the plains. Tigers are lurking." She paused before throwing up her arms into the air, casting her voice loudly across the room. "Go, Tigereye warriors. Show the invaders that we will not bow down and that we will not go so easily as the Wolfclaw. Butcher them. Drink their blood and take their strength. Leave no trace of them."

Yamaagh stood, as one with the other warriors of the clan, and bellowed a ululating cry. It was time to hunt.

HE ROLLED WITH THE GAIT OF CAT AS THEY PASSED through the long grasses, the sky wide and blue above him, the winds from Eagle's wings taking the storm of the previous day and sending it on its way. His mind was still foggy with the memories that the dream tubers he ate the day before had conjured during the night. He knew he could avoid the feelings that the tubers brought on if he ate them more sparingly, if he supplemented his diet with game from the land, but he could not stand the smell of meat cooking anymore. Nor would he kill another living thing that belonged to Missapik; enough harm had been done to her. The focus of his hunt was just one people, one species that fouled the land—and until they had gone, he had sworn to do nothing to increase the pain that Missapik, the vast plains, felt.

Ever south and east he went, and for the first time he could see the mountains of the sleeping Wolf. The border of the plains. Green crept up the side of the great peaks like moss up a rock, trees taller and stronger than those you would find on the plains. His sharp eyes could make out a scar on the Wolf's side, where the trees had been cut away, smoke rising into the air from nearby. Signs of life. Signs of destruction. Signs of the invaders doing their evil work.

This would be a good place to hunt.

FIVE SEASONS HAD PASSED SINCE THE VISITOR HAD COME and demanded the surrender of the Tigereye clan. Five seasons since Yamaagh and his tiger, along with the other warriors of the clan, had hunted them down, stripping them of their metal and leaving them staked out in the plains for Missapik itself to show what it thought of invaders.

And now the green men were back. They had been there for three days, camped within sight of Yamaagh's village.

He had thought that these green men would know when their people did not come back that they had met their match, but Tiva was not surprised when word came that a force more than two hundred strong had entered their lands. Word had gone out to the more distant members of the clan to return to the seat, to help defend against the inevitable attack.

They had expected an attack during the night after the first day of their arrival within sight of the village; a bright full moon shone down and would have been perfect conditions for one of their own raids on a rival clan. But nothing had come. They had laughed it off as the invaders being weak, needing to rest after traveling through a land hostile to them, but they did not attack the next day either. Three days passed, without the green invaders wanting to talk or wanting to fight. Finally, Chitto convinced Tiva that they needed to eject the foreigners from their lands.

It was time for the whole of the clan to roar. For the foreigners to lose their bowels in fear and flee.

More than five hundred clans people strode out with Yamaagh that day. Mothers, fathers, sisters and brothers—everyone of age in the clan wanted to protect their home. He rolled his shoulders, the weight of the metal armor that he wore, previously green, but scratched back to a shiny silver was uncomfortable. There had been four sets of armor and four silver-metal swords that had been won when they killed the Pyrfew delegation. Tiva took ownership of all on behalf of the clan, but then passed on a set to Chitto and Yamaagh. Surprisingly, she also gave one to Hotak, primarily to build an alliance with him. The sword hung around Yamaagh's waist on the same strip of leather that its previous owner had used; and although he had tested its strength and sharpness, it was not the same as his spears, so he was not planning on using the length of metal.

He walked at the fore, with Tiva and Chitto, the rest of the clan in family groups behind them. They stopped two arrow lengths away from the green invaders, who were quickly assembling into a straight line.

His chief cupped her hands around her mouth and called out. "Leave our lands. You are outnumbered. Flee with your lives."

No response. And no movement to leave. Not that they had expected them to have the sense to run. Besides, if they did run, they were still going to attack anyway and kill them as they fell from exhaustion.

"Be ready," called Tiva to the clan. Yamaagh threw two of his three stone-tipped spears, to the ground before resting the third in the shoulder of the atlatl.

"We fight!"

Yamaagh ran forward ten steps and, twisting his body as he flung his shoulder forward, he launched the spear from the atlatl and out toward the green men, thirty or so others doing the same. He picked up his other spears and watched as his missile sailed through the air, the other clan members rushing past him, bows held at the ready. Yamaagh had judged the distance perfectly and his spear fell down upon the foreigners. But instead of skewering the warrior who was staring at death from above, he lifted his shield above his head and the spear clattered to the ground. Yamaagh swore. He'd seen shields before, other tribes used ones made of stretched hide that offered some protection from poorly shot arrows, but they would never have been able to stop a spear. The ones these green men had must be metal too.

Seeing that his spear's progress had been halted, he ran after his clan, who had now stopped within arrow reach of the invaders. They loosed a flight of flint tipped arrows. Yamaagh knew what the result was going to be before he even saw the arrows bounce off the shields. He pushed himself back to the front of the clan alongside Chitto.

"We need to be close enough to bite."

The champion of the clan nodded and he drew the silver sword that had once belonged to the green men. Chitto nodded once more to Tiva and she saluted him in return. She would fight, but it was Chitto who would lead them from the front.

Chitto shouted and charged. Yamaagh followed, momentarily wondering if he had done the right thing by leaving the tiger to guard the children.

His moccasined feet pounded into the earth as they closed the gap, a war cry rising in his throat, his spear thrust out before him. Chitto had the silver sword raised high above his head, like he was about to chop wood. On Yamaagh's other side was Mosi, a spear gripped as tight as his face, his fear plain to see.

"Mosi!" he called to his friend. "We are strong! We are tigers and they are our dinner!"

Others behind him heard his call and they cheered. Mosi smiled and faced the enemy with renewed strength. *Listen to how they follow me,* he thought. He knew that one day he would be a fine champion. Maybe this would be the day when he would prove himself over Chitto and Tiva would smile her favor on him.

The line of green men huddled behind their shields. Fools. Staying close together would mean that Tigereye would hit with every blow.

And then, when they were thirty strides away, the front line of invaders dropped to one knee, revealing those behind all holding objects that Yamaagh had never seen before. That was when the angry wasps came. There was a buzzing noise, and a streak of pain across his temple as one of them must have stung him, blood dripping into his eye.

Then Chitto was stung, the force of it catching his shoulder and sending him spinning before another wasp hit him in the side of the head, his eyes rolling as he fell to the ground in front of Yamaagh, the fletching of an arrow protruding from near his eye. *What are these strange bows that these invaders have?*

He had no time to think further, or to stop and tend to their champion. He heard the cries of others behind him but would not turn to see. All he focused on was the man behind the shield just steps away from him. He aimed his spear at the man's chest and the shield moved to stop it.

Yamaagh tilted the shaft upwards and the spear slid up

over the top of the metal shield emblazoned with a tree and into the neck of the man. He gurgled and Yamaagh laughed, pulling the point free as he pushed over the dying warrior and stepped into the space he left. Yamaagh pulled the haft of the spear back across his body, smashing it into the green warrior in the line next to him, a clang as it hit the metal protecting his head. It knocked the invader forwards and a seasoned woman named Sakhyo hit him in the face with her axe.

But she had no one watching her side and the next green warrior in line cleaved down with his sword, slicing through her arm at the elbow, her lifeblood spurting into the air as she looked down aghast at the wound. Yamaagh tried to move to help her, thrusting forward with the tip of his spear. It hit the side of one green man but didn't penetrate the metal leaf shirt, just skidding off against his back. Yamaagh was pushed back, a shield slamming into his side and trapping the shaft of his spear before it was wrenched from his hand.

He lost his balance and stumbled backward, tripping over a woman and falling, the face of Kaya staring at him. Kaya had been the first person that Yamaagh had kissed who was not his mother and father. He remembered those lips, so warm and soft, and for a moment he couldn't wrench his eyes away from how they had gone so pale.

A scream brought Yamaagh back. Mosi was fighting like a mad man, but his spear had broken and now he wielded nothing more than a club. Mosi batted away jabs from the swords of the green men, but one blade sank into his friend's thigh, sending him to his knees. Yamaagh stood, spearless, and watched as his friend's head left his shoulders and struck the ground.

All around him the people of the Tigereye were falling. Tiva screeched as she fought for her clan. He drew the silver sword and pushed through his own people to reach her side. He chopped and stabbed, more blows striking shield than finding man. With his free hand he pushed away at one shield and then stabbed down at the foot below another. More green men stepped forward into the gap, standing on their own fallen to keep their line whole. Another sword probed forward at him, punching him in the gut—but the metal shirt he wore stopped it from freeing the worms in his middle. He grabbed the blade with his free hand, howling in pain as the edge, sharper than any weapon they had, sliced into his fingers. But he pulled on the blade anyway, pulling the man holding it toward him and Yamaagh's sword chopped down onto the man's head, crushing the metal that surrounded it and sending blood shooting out the green man's nostrils.

His ear popped. His left eye went black and the world tilted as pain blossomed in Yamaagh's head. The earth of the Missapik welcomed him, his neck jerking as his head struck the ground. He tried to move but his legs didn't want to respond and a weight pinned him down as someone landed on top of him. Looking up he could see Tiva, fighting with ever less clans' people around her, and all he could think of was that he was supposed to have been the greatest living warrior of his clan. How could these heathens have taken away his destiny?

Yamaagh saw the sword coming at her long before she did. Tiva was focused on the invaders to her right and so didn't see the man coming from the left, not until the blade pushed into her armpit and out past her collar bone. She fell and the line of green men stepped forward in unison, so close to him that he could have spat on their shiny leather shoes if only his mouth was not full of the taste of blood. He tried again to move, to roll free and help his people that still fought. But the green men stepped forward once more, a booted foot kicking at the obstacle in its way.

He felt the thud in his head but there could be no more pain. Through his half-closed eye he saw an ever-increasing shadow descending on him as another fallen friend landed on top of him. He could feel the flesh of whoever it was on his open mouth, someone he would have shared meals with, hunted with, but he could not move. It was so hot; there was no air and he was unable to push himself free. Yamaagh felt the pain of his body slowly drifting away as lights danced in the edge of his vision.

And then black.

HE WEAVED THE ROD THROUGH THE FRAME HE HAD constructed, taking care to give it solidity though the weave was not tight and wouldn't have made his grandmother proud. He spent many hours with his grandma after his parents' deaths, remembering the comfort he'd felt from her embraces when he felt alone. Even after he came of age, he loved to spend time sitting with her as she worked, weaving by touch alone as her eyesight failed her.

But this wasn't a basket anyway. This was a trap.

The wicker construct finished, he attached it to the ramshackle body that he'd finished earlier. From his pack, he pulled a hooded long shirt and trousers, clean but torn and cut in places from when the previous owner had suffered their fate. He dressed the scarecrow, pulling the hood up over the wooden head, and moved it into position next to the other construct around the unlit campfire he had built.

Stepping around the shallow ditch he had dug, he set to putting up the simple hide-covered shelter that his people used when traveling, all the while humming a song that his grandma used to sing when he missed his parents and the tears had flowed.

~

His vision returned to see the open mouth of a tiger descending on him, the breath hot on his face. The beast's teeth gripped the metal leaves of the shirt and pulled. He felt the bare earth on the back of his head as he was dragged along the ground, feeling lighter as he was freed of the weight that had laid on him. Slowly he felt himself rising up off the ground, his arms and legs dangling down like a rag doll.

Yamaagh's head lolled and bounced as the tiger trotted away. In the distance, he could see flames rising from his home, dark shapes moving between the houses. And he knew then that all hope was lost, the Tigereye were no morc.

He drifted in and out of consciousness as the tiger took him away from his village, eventually resting him gently on the ground by a burbling stream. The tiger licked his wounds, and after some time he was able to drag himself to the stream to take a crisp sip of clean water. The tiger disappeared, leaving him by the water's edge. He tried to rise, but fell in an uncomfortable heap. Yamaagh grew worried that his spirit animal had abandoned him—obviously he was a failure, and his ancestor had been mistaken in saying that he was chosen —but as the sun dipped on the horizon the tiger returned. The cat used her nose and pushed Yamaagh forcefully onto his back, giving him a disapproving look. Her muzzle was red, and he was concerned that maybe she was injured but she walked off before he could inspect her. A few moments later she trotted back with pieces of deer meat torn from a nearby carcass.

It must have been at least a week of blinding headaches, lapses of unconsciousness, and the ministrations of the tiger; but eventually he was able to stand with the help of a hand gripping the sandy coat of the big cat. For the first time since his Quana, he embraced the tiger, weeping into her fur, both in thanks for her help and for what he had to do next.

It took three days for him to hobble back to what was once his village and was now just a series of smoldering pits. Coyotes and ravens, the carrion creatures of the plains, those that clean the messes of the world away, had been busy. Yamaagh stumbled through what had once been avenues between the homes where children played and elders sat and smoked their pipes, his gaze turning from one ravaged body after another.

Out of the village he went, to where the battle had taken place, and his people awaited him. In silence. In piles and pieces. In glaring, terrifyingly judgmental faces they wanted to know why he still walked.

And so did he.

He found the place where Tiva had fallen, her carcass stripped of the metal leaf shirt. Chitto the same, the thick short arrows still pinning a thatch of hair and skin to a skull scored with teeth marks.

He could take no more. He bent over and ejected the contents of his stomach onto the ground. Yamaagh sat on his behind with a thud, right in the center of his people, and stared at his hands. Flies occasionally buzzed around him, but there were greater prizes nearby so they generally left him alone. Collapsing onto his back, staring up at the stars, exhaustion overtook him.

Yamaagh felt shamed the next day. Shamed by his inability to protect his clan, or even to show them proper respect. But he resolved that would no longer be the case. Cradling each body, he carried them to the burnt shell of the longhouse and lay them down side by side. In his state it took days to ferry them all from the battlefield and he refused to drag a single corpse, or choose a closer location. Each person, though he could not always tell who was who, was treated with reverence. And then he saw Mosi, or at least he recognized his friend by the beaded necklace he wore, one that Yamaagh had made with his own hands. He lay him down with a kiss to the man's ravaged head.

As he worked, Missapik was quiet, mournful of what had happened in its great expanse. The green men did not come back, and why would they? All those who had resisted were gone.

Once the bodies were lain, he gathered wood from all around, building the pyre above his village. It was late one evening, the sunlight all but gone and the moon shining down from overhead when he had finished. Exhaustion wore at his bones and he stumbled as he sifted through the wreckage of his grandmother's old home, looking for a flint. With his prize in hand he lit a length of tinder, walking around the outside of the longhouse and setting light to the tall dry grasses he had packed under the branches, all the while humming a tune his grandmother had sung for him though his voice cracked with pain. The fire caught and he stood back, the flames launching high into the air, carrying the souls of his people into the beyond. The smell of roasting flesh made his stomach churn. He let the tears come, honoring the dead, and with a sooty hand he reached out to pet the tiger that he knew was beside him.

But his hand met empty air.

Looking down he saw the great tiger lying on her paws, her ears tucked back. And Yamaagh felt the presence behind him.

He spun on his heel, raising his hands to fight but cursing himself for not having fashioned a weapon with which to defend himself.

"I bring you no harm." The voice was deep like the canyon and it came from a man, massive with broad shoulders and thick chest. Tight curly hair wove up his breast and neck to the head of a buffalo. The flames of the village pyre reflected in the black eyes of the man as he looked down on Yamaagh. Yamaagh took a step back.

"You are the greatest living warrior of the Tigereye clan. How does it feel?"

Yamaagh burned with indignation. That wasn't what he had wanted. He had wanted what was good for his clan. Though a voice inside him disagreed and reminded him that he had not been so selfless.

"There is no Tigereye," he spat. "You see what is left. Fire and ashes!"

"I see," he boomed. "I see someone who can get vengeance, or someone who can move on with his life." The buffalo man bent at the waist to bring his face close to Yamaagh's, his breath hot. "Which it will be, is up to you."

The buffalo man half turned and began to walk away, out of the light of the fire and into the darkness.

"Whatever you choose, it is a long path you will wander."

ONCE THE HIDE WAS SECURED, THE TENT WAS DONE. HE looked around the campsite; the fire was ready to be lit, the two scarecrows were in position, and the hole dug. Taking his grandmother's flint from a pouch, he bent and struck it against a stone until a spark lit the twined dry grasses. He fed it into the stacked fuel, blowing gently until the fire caught the kindling and the larger lengths of wood. He stood back as the green grass began to smolder, sending a thick plume of smoke into the air.

It would be visible for miles on a clear day like this.

Cat was by his side. He leaned over until his forehead touched that of the tiger, idly scratching behind her ear.

"Let us once again show them whose land this is," he whispered, before pulling aside the flap of the tent so that Cat could enter.

He pulled the long metal knife from his belt and gazed at the edge. 'Steel' they called it. He didn't know how it was made or where it came from, but he'd learned that it was sharper than any stone blade he'd had before. And so had the woman he had wrestled it from. He climbed into the hole, squatting down on his haunches so that his head didn't peak over the top, and he pulled a thick blanket over, the world going dark. These still times, these times when the dark was all around and the lights danced around his eyes like he was screwing them up tight, that was when he saw the ghosts most of all. His parents. His grandma. The people of his village and all the other homes that he had seen abandoned or destroyed. All of them—dancing on the corpses of the green despoilers and those who had sided with them, those that he had killed.

His legs ached with cramp. He wished to stretch or run. Run headlong into the fight. But that wasn't the way to hunt. That was the way to die.

Who would come? he wondered. Would there be more than he and Cat could take, even with the element of surprise? He doubted it. There were always five. But would there be Alfjarun with them too? If there was, they would be the first to die. Traitors to the land and their people, he could not understand how any Alfjarun could ally themselves with the green men. The ghosts danced on their bones too.

Hours passed. He chewed on a raw tuber, the taste acrid and bitter, and he washed it down with water from his skin, wondering if his lure was going to work.

And then a call.

"Ho there, travelers. Have you come to join us and hear the true word of god?" The voice was accented but not unfriendly.

He said nothing. The scarecrows were quiet, too. A few moments passed and he pictured his prey walking closer, confident in their numbers and steel.

"Are you deaf?" the voice was more urgent, angry. "Know that all of this land is Pyrfew. Throw out your weapons."

He clutched the knife in his hand and gritted his teeth. The voice changed tack when the scarecrows didn't surrender their arms.

"Lie down. Get on the floor, now. Or we'll shoot."

He didn't lie down. A Tigereye doesn't lie down.

And neither do their scarecrows.

He counted his breaths, reaching twenty before he heard the twang and the soft thud as the arrows hit the woven forms of the scarecrows. More tears in the clothes. He heard the sound of one of the scarecrows toppling from its seated position to the floor. Then footsteps. Closer. Someone said something in a language he couldn't understand. Then there was the crack of twigs as if someone had kicked a bush and more of the foreign words. He closed his eyes.

The sound of the tent flap being pulled aside.

A mangled scream and the crunch of bone as Cat moved as quick as lightning.

And the wanderer leapt from his hole, steel blade glistening in the sunlight, to begin his work.

STRAYS

Click

Noises like that were generally not good in their line of business. Crossbow knocked. Locked door opening. Traps arming...

"Nobody move. That fucking cat stood on the pressure plate."

Trypp froze in place, hoping that Motega and Florian were doing likewise behind him. The cat, black and with a disgustingly smug little face—it knew what it was doing—stared back at him. He'd noticed the pressure plate in the vault as soon as they had made it inside, the eight different locks securing the door having not given him too much trouble. He'd noticed the cat too, back in the banking hall, curled up on a long oaken counter where customers were served during the day. He just hadn't expected the cat to follow them and mess everything up.

Who keeps a cat in a bank anyway? A guard dog he could understand, but a cat?

If he could just get to the bloody thing before it moved,

maybe he could keep the pressure plate depressed while one of his friends found something else heavy enough to weigh it down. There were plenty of other heavy things in this particular vault, most of them worth a small fortune to the right buyer. But there was no need to concern himself with that right now. His focus was on the gold bust of some long dead Iothan that rested on the plinth.

He dug his finger nails into his palm, frustrated with himself. His focus was supposed to be on the cat, not the shiny objects. Trypp took one small step forward, quiet as a mouse, his soft leather soles hushed against the marble floor. The cat tilted its head. Another step, and then a third. He was halfway to the cat when it rose onto all fours, its tail straight in the air behind it. He exhaled through his nose. *It's going to run. It's going to run.*

Trypp dashed forward. The cat shrieked and bolted past him, but he wasn't concerned about that. It was the pressure plate that mattered. His foot stamped down on it barely a heartbeat after the cat had ran. He put his whole weight on it, held his breath and waited for the inevitable.

There was silence.

No poison darts. No noxious gas. Trypp looked back at Motega and Florian and winked.

Then the ceiling fell in.

Or more accurately, it swung open like a pair of doors, and reminiscent of one of those old stories of how Mother Marlth would send storms of insects on the faithless, a cascade of a thousand of spiders tumbled down.

They landed in Trypp's close-cut hair, fell down his face and tumbled onto his shoulders. Some of them hung down from the ceiling on silken strands, dangling in front of him, their legs twitching. There were ones as small as a finger nail crawling up and down his arms and others as big as Florian's hand scuttling across the floor.

Somebody shrieked. *Big girl.* Then he realized it was him. Florian shouted "gerroff!" and one of the big bastards sailed through the air and smacked into the wall opposite. Motega was annoyingly cool about the whole thing, though Trypp, between shivers and swats to the spiders crawling on him, could see that a bunch of the arachnids were nestling into Motega's long hair. He'd be finding them weeks from now.

Then it started. The sharp flares of pain all over his body, under his clothes, in his breeches, as the spiders started to bite. *Please let them not be venomous.*

"Time to go." Trypp grabbed the golden bust, and he staggered as he felt the weight. He hadn't expected it to be solid gold. He lugged it across the room and shoved it into Florian's midriff. "Here, you take it." The big man grabbed it with one arm as he smacked at the spiders crawling over him with the flat of his hand. Then Trypp heard it, the ringing of a bell, muffled, like it was coming from a room or two away.

"Shit! It's really time go. There was another trap. Alarms."

Motega led the way out the vault and back into the long banking hall. It was officious and grave, even without any of the stuffed shirts being present. Trypp was sure they were all tucked up in their nice comfortable beds, what with it being two bells past midnight. It was the kind of place that would not ever consider letting Trypp or his friends inside, even though they'd have plenty of coin once this job was done. Well, maybe Florian would at least get the haughty attention of a teller, but for the likes of Trypp and Motega—the non-white types—they wouldn't get past the guards at the door.

The guards who Trypp could clearly hear running toward them at that very moment.

A rope dangled from the very expensive, very impressive and not actually that secure, glass ceiling that they had used to gain entry. Motega hauled himself up it without a moment's hesitation. Florian got to the bottom of the rope and stopped. He looked up, and then down at the bust tucked under his arm, a quizzical expression on his face.

"No way I can climb and carry this thing."

"Mot," called Trypp. "Another line."

A second rope unspooled as it fell to the ground. "Go," he urged Florian, who hesitated for a moment before pulling himself up arm over arm. Trypp tied a noose in the end of the second rope and flipped it over the head of the golden bust to nestle under its chin—judging by the other rich bastards he'd met, Trypp was certain he probably deserved it. He pulled the loop tight and gave the signal for Motega to haul it up.

The door behind the bank counter burst open and an assortment of a half dozen overweight or aging soldiers skidded into the room, some of them still wearing city watch uniform, obviously too lazy to switch garb for their night-time moonlighting. They gawped at Trypp and he glared back, assessing.

They didn't have crossbows. That was good. They were only about fifteen feet away, which was bad. But the steel bars above the counter would at least stop them from jumping over. The guards must have finished their own similar thought process as they made a run for the cage door, just as Trypp jumped up to grab the rope, quickly climbing with hands and feet to the sky light above.

He felt the rope tense below him as Motega offered a

hand to help him to the roof. There was cry and a grunt as whichever imbecile had thought it would be a good idea to follow him made his acquaintance with the stone floor once Florian had cut the line.

Trypp looked around, taking in the crisp, early winter night, Carlburg arrayed before them. The capital city of Skaria was quiet except for the odd drunk wandering home singing, the tiled roofs of the nearby shops and inns giving way to thatch as the residences began. They were now definitely in Plan B territory. Plan A had been to climb down the rope at the rear of the bank that they had used to get up there in the first place. That was off the table now, the bank guards would be out on the street any moment. Plan B was Motega's plan.

It was not a good plan.

He was really going to have to talk to him about that.

"Ready for Plan B?" asked Motega, as he looked over the edge of the building to the street fifty feet below.

"Do I still have to carry this fucking thing?" asked Florian, holding out the bust in one outstretched mitt like he was strangling a disembodied dwarf.

"Yes!" said Trypp and Motega in unison.

Florian swore under his breath before muttering, "we should really bring a bag next time."

Trypp ignored him and resumed his attention to Plan B. The rooftops of the buildings surrounding the bank were all a good twenty feet drop from where they were, and there was a street in the way. Doable, but also plenty of chance of doing yourself a broken leg.

Trypp blew out his cheeks and nodded. "Let's do it."

They ran to the edge and leapt out into the dark.

Feet on the table. A roaring fire. Beer in hand. The boys off playing somewhere. Trypp was a happy man.

Atarah's Hearth was always one of his favorite hostelries, and there was nothing like the glow of getting paid to go with the glow of a warm fire. Giofre had been happy with their work, and their fixer was certain his employer was going to be happy too. Trypp drained his beer and returned the tankard to the table. Another appeared beside it, froth spilling over the top, and Isabel the bar maid gave him a wink. Customer service, that's what it was all about; whether you ran a bar, or did 'other' jobs.

Granted this job had proven to be slightly less lucrative than they had originally expected—the cost of the antidote to that spider poison had been significant. He was just glad that Motega had for some reason been immune to the effects; he and Florian had collapsed when they'd made it back to their safe house, those last few yards an agony as fire lanced up his limbs with every step. As the apothecary who had administered the cure said after Trypp had regained consciousness, "What price would you put on your life?" Their more modest profit was much preferable to the alternative.

It was at quiet times like these that he had the opportunity to be grateful for what he had, given where he had started out from. He had no idea who his parents were, whether they were dead or merely absent, his earliest memories being those of the orphanage where he fought for food, clothes and warmth with a couple score of other children, all the while trying to avoid the attention of Master Levin. Unfortunately, trouble was his shadow even back then. And so something would happen, a fight with another boy, or something was stolen and he would get the blame; so then he'd run away and live on the streets of Kingshold, before eventually getting caught again. If he'd have stayed at that orphanage, he had no doubt that he would be living in some hovel in Bottom Run or Randall's Addition, struggling to stay alive.

Instead, he had a full belly, a jangling purse, and a partnership in a thriving business. Trypp granted himself a smile and he looked around to see what the boys were doing. Motega, smile flashing, was chatting up a couple of unaccompanied women, not whores by the look of them—the landlady of the Hearth liked to keep the kind of business out of her establishment. Maybe they worked in one of the stores local to this part of Ioth. Florian, meanwhile, was sitting with a group of men, Edlanders by their accents, regaling them with stories of his army days and generally laughing it up. Motega and Florian were like brothers to him, the family he never thought he would have or need. He didn't mind being left alone; he respected that they all needed a little bit of space after spending the past week cooped up in a modest berth on a ship from Carlburg to Ioth.

It wasn't a bad life, this adventuring lark. Trypp chuckled to himself. *Adventuring*. That's what Mot and Florian called it, and it's definitely what they had left Kingshold to pursue. Sure, they did the odd job that could be considered recompensed public service; but Trypp had no illusions or qualms that most of their income came from being high class thieves. *Extractors.* As long as there was enough excitement to stop Motega from getting bored, and they minimized the unnecessary casualties to keep Florian's conscience content, his friends went along with it. And it was six-shits better than his other two career opportunities after getting out of the orphanage; an assassin with the Hollow Syndicate or a burglar for the Twilight Exiles.

He also took pride knowing that they were good at it too. Probably the best, and no one other than a few fixers knew who they were. Anonymity combined with enough coin not to worry about a good meal and better room to sleep in. Not a bad life at all. If he could keep the boys at this for a few more years, keep squirreling away a chunk of their pay without them noticing, then he'd be able to surprise them with a nest egg to set up wherever they like; maybe marry, get fat, and watch each other's kids get into trouble instead of them.

Trypp felt a blast of the winter air rush through the room, reaching through to his place by the titular hearth and he looked up to see the door to the street open. The door closed again, but from his slouched position he didn't see anyone enter, just the parting of the crowds as something made their way through. A boy, dirty from the streets, appeared from around the wide form of Florian and made a bee line over to Trypp. Trypp resumed looking at his feet, hoping that he was wrong and the kid wasn't seeking him out.

"Excuse me," came a piping voice, surprisingly well-mannered for a street boy. "I have a message for you."

Trypp turned to regard the boy. He could see the familial relationship now. Lai Giofre must have sent one of his sons; the smell of pipe weed hanging over the boy evidence that his father had him working in the pipe shop that fronted his under-the-counter activities. Motega and Florian loomed behind the kid.

"You sure you got the right person?"

The boy gulped and nodded. “Papa told me you’d be the only black man in the Hearth.” Trypp looked around. He was not wrong.

“Spit it out then.”

“Papa says you need to get to the shop. There’s a special pipe you’ll be interested in, but if you’re not there soon he’ll find someone else who is interested.”

Trypp sighed. So much for a relaxing evening. But that was the price you had to pay in their line of work if you wanted to keep your customers happy.

“LET ME BUY YOU ANOTHER ONE.” TRYPP RAISED HIS HAND to attract the bar maid’s attention.

The man opposite him half-heartedly waved his offer away. “I should be going. Nice meeting you and all, but I got to get back to the wife.”

“Ah, Luniki, you’re a family man. That’s good. I understand, and I would hate to keep you away from them.” Trypp pulled his arm down but he winked over to the bar maid who had already seen his call. “I’m in the business of helping families myself. I know what’s most important in life.”

“What does that mean?”

“It can mean different things.” Trypp leaned in and lowered his voice. “Sometimes I help people make sure that the members of their families are safe. Other times I help the families of those who help me. Do you know what I mean?”

Luniki, a broad-shouldered man who Trypp had observed delivering supplies to the villa of Este Palombi earlier that day, did not seem to be fully understanding what Trypp was saying, though his eyes had brightened with greed at what appeared to be an opportunity to make some additional coin.

"What do you mean?" asked Luniki again, as another cup of wine appeared before him. He eyed it pensively, while the barmaid cleared away the other two empty cups. His indecision lasted only a moment before he brought the wine to his lips. "I don't do anything to get me into trouble with the Pula."

Trypp looked around, making a show of ensuring no one was close enough to overhear. "You don't need to worry about the watch. I have been hired..." he began, "by a concerned father, to check on the wellbeing of his daughter. A daughter who is in the employ of one of your customers and who he fears may have been taken advantage of. And forced into an... unplanned situation." Trypp raised his eyebrows, hoping that Luniki's imagination would fill in what he was leaving unsaid.

He knew it wasn't the best story, but it was the best he had come up with on short notice when it looked like Luniki might actually leave.

It was, of course, all hogwash.

But Trypp was confident that telling Luniki that actually he was trying to work out how to break into the villa of Palombi, so he could steal back a solid gold bust of some dead guy that he had only handed off to Este via a series of intermediaries just a couple of days before, was not going to help his cause.

Luniki took a sip of his wine, his eyes narrowing suspiciously. "Which customer?" Trypp whispered the councilor's name and Luniki coughed in reply. He took a big gulp of his drink. "That's quite an in important person." Trypp nodded seriously. "What kind of help are you looking for?"

"I just need a look around the place. Hopefully I can just see the girl, make sure she is fine, and give the father some peace of mind. I know he would be very grateful." Trypp paused significantly. "And I know I would be too."

There was a *thunk* as the cup, drained once more, rested on the table. Luniki looked down at it expectantly and Trypp waved for the bar maid's attention once more. Not for the first time, Trypp considered how often the information they needed for a job was bought with a few drinks. If he ever actually paid taxes, he'd need to track his bar bills as a business expense.

Luniki blew out his cheeks as he made up his mind. "Just how grateful?"

THE RISING SUN FILTERED BETWEEN THE BUILDINGS OF THE old city of Ioth as Trypp sat at the prow of the gondola, gliding along the narrow canals. Palombi's villa sat proudly on the grand canal, with a majestic entrance way for family and guests that led straight into the center of the complex. But Trypp knew that he wouldn't be able to walk in that way. There were few people of color in Ioth, and those that were struggled to make a living through jobs much more modest than the merchants that were the heartbeat of the city. To attempt to play as a merchant, looking to make a deal or a connection with Palombi, that would be far too conspicuous.

But a manual worker—that would go unnoticed.

So he sat quietly as Luniki poled the boat through the narrow canal behind the villa, stopping at the landing for the entrance to the kitchens, and he followed Luniki's order without complaint to pick up the baskets of fish fresh from the market. Luniki himself hauled a crate of vegetables on to the narrow stone landing and then knocked on the door. It was opened by a spotty teenager who looked like he was playing dress up as a soldier—a chain mail shirt too big for him almost slipped off his shoulder in the style of a whore prowling for business, and his hand rested untrained on the pommel of his sword at his hip. The scowl that he had probably learned from some elder guard was momentarily displaced at the sight of the delivery man, before his brows knotted again at the sight of Trypp.

"Who's he?"

"Fredo's sick. Had to get some other help," said Luniki coolly, though Trypp caught his shifty glance. *He better not blow this.* Luniki grabbed an apple from the crate and tossed it to the boy, who caught it eagerly. The boy's prize won, he stepped aside to let them enter, laden with food for the household's day. Trypp followed his master for the morning into a short passageway that opened out into the center of the villa; a courtyard of marble and potted plants enclosed by four open air passageways. He stopped and quickly took in all he could; the grand entrance opposite, the three stories rising above to tiled roofs, and not missing the other four armored and more mature figures. They stood guard outside closed doors that led inside the building.

"Stop gawping and follow me," ordered Luniki, maybe enjoying his role a little too much for Trypp's tastes. He let it slide, though he had a mind to help him a little less when this was all said and done. Trypp followed him down one of the open-air passageways to an archway that led into the kitchen. It was bright and airy, with high ceilings, but it still felt scorching inside from the heat emanating from the great stone fireplace. The smell of baking bread filled his nostrils and made Trypp wish he had risen a little earlier to have breakfast. He knew that right about then, Motega and Florian were probably tucking into heaping plates of eggs, crusty loaves and cups of weak beer. Bastards. They never realized the sacrifices he made for them.

Luniki placed his crate of vegetables on the long table in the middle of the kitchen. The cook, a plump, golden brown woman with a welcoming smile and dusted in flour—a loaf of bread made flesh—looked up from where she was cutting a huge slab of butter into chunks with a knife that would have made Psycho Silas proud. He meandered over to the table as he took in the others in the room. A boy at the sink scrubbing dishes. Another woman of middling years who was stirring a large pot of something on the stove, giving some unheard instructions to a younger cook. And a girl, probably not much younger than him, just turned twenty and dressed in a maid's robes, who stared at him wide eyed. She was an attractive sort, the kind of girl that he usually found to be friendly and warm hearted. The kind of girl that he imagined Florian settling down with in his visions of their retirement. Not exactly his type; he usually preferred a little more danger, a little something out of the ordinary. But then again, he wasn't there to meet his future wife. This was work.

Trypp flashed the maid a smile and when he saw the corners of her mouth turn up in return, he gave her a wink.

His winks were legendary—or at least, Motega always said so. That they could cause a woman to swoon at twenty paces. Trypp knew it took more than that though.

He went to put the basket of bream and shrimp onto the table alongside Luniki's crate, but he stopped a few inches short at the tut that came from the bread lady.

"Not on the clean table, thank you! Just cleaned that and

don't want it smelling of fish when we've got sweet breads to make. Luniki, show him where the cold room is."

The delivery man grabbed Trypp by the arm, making a show of scolding him, and guided him away from the table and towards a door opposite the range. He looked back at the maid and rolled his eyes. She stifled a laugh behind a cough. They entered into a long passageway, storerooms to either side, that led to a room encased in sheets of metal, sides of beef and pork hanging from the ceiling on hooks, bowls of offal stored for later and a deep open hole in front of him where he would bet that the ice was stored. Once the fish was safely deposited, Luniki nudged Trypp out ahead of him and back down the passageway. As they reached the kitchen, Trypp, looking over his shoulder to give Luniki the evil eye, bumped into someone.

He stayed his hand from automatically reaching for the small knife tucked away in his pocket, an involuntary reaction developed for his own self-preservation while being a thief with the Exiles, as he realized that he had bumped into the maid. She took a step back from the impact and he reached out to hold her arm and steady her.

"Hello," he said.

"Hello…" she returned, rather shyly.

"Oi. No flirting. She's got jobs to do." The cook seemed a lot less welcoming now—this bread had a tough crust that could probably knock a few teeth out, not to mention that big blade she was waving around as she spoke. "As I am sure you two have as well. Be off with you."

Luniki apologized and gave Trypp a shove in the back to push him toward the door, but before Trypp left he gave the maid a deep bow. She laughed, not a titter but a large full-throated laugh, and as Trypp was ushered back out to the rear exit, he could hear the cook audibly telling the maid to beware of tall dark strangers.

TRYPP HAD NOT BEEN HAPPY ABOUT HAVING TO CONTINUE making deliveries after going to Palombi's villa. Luniki had laughed at first and told him he needed to keep up appearances. But after the second residence, Trypp had told him he was going to have to charge him for his labor out of his 'contribution'.

Luniki let him off at the next street, the delivery man a few gold coins richer. Trypp was not sure how much of that would make it home to his family, given the greedy look in Luniki's eye.

He'd learned a little from the errand, gaining an understanding of at least what lay behind that front door onto the grand canal and what level of security existed, and all before breakfast. But he hadn't seen the bust proudly on display to impress any visitors as soon as they entered. No one ever made life easy for him. Not since the night he'd been given the job to steal from Neenahwi's tower. Who gives a job of stealing from the daughter of the wizard of Edland to a lanky teenager? He'd often wondered about that. Wondered if Silas had been setting him up for a fall. Maybe the father of the Twilight Exiles had found out about some of his extra curriculars. The bastard had been positively gleeful when giving the order to run him out of town after Trypp had the gall to survive getting caught.

You live and learn. And what Trypp had learnt was you don't rush into a job without having a full understanding of whatever situation you might be getting into. That, and also that Motega and Florian were two souls so bored that they would run off with a thief they just met for as yet undefined adventures, rather than stay in their gilded cage. It was funny how sometimes the worst situations led to the discovery of unlikely treasures.

So he spent the day wandering the narrow streets across the narrow canal behind Palombi's villa, hoping that he could turn the little nuggets of information he had discovered earlier that morning into a real horde. He occasionally caught glimpses of Motega and Florian going about their own reconnaissance on their tod—as they generally preferred in these instances—but he stayed out of sight.

It was midafternoon by the time the early morning staff at the villa left for the day. Eight servants, trudging back to their homes, but it was one in particular that he had his eye on. The laughing maid. Following at a safe distance, so not to be observed by anyone who might have seen him earlier that day, he trailed her. This wasn't normal practice for him, stalking a single woman like this, but he might be able to get her to help. As long as she didn't notice him and get scared. For a good while she travelled through the old city with a man twice her age, until he waved a good bye and took a right turn. She walked briskly through the bustling streets, crossing the bridges to enter The Fan and passing through it until she reached the long narrow ferries that crossed back and forth to Spilver.

He was briefly concerned that he had lost her when they had to take different ferries, but luck was with him as he disembarked, turning in the right direction to see her retreating form. Trypp jogged by the people on the street, getting to within twenty feet or so of her without being noticed and followed her all the way to where she disappeared inside a modest house.

This was where he would really see if luck was on his side. If not, his near future would be one standing around outside for the next few hours, only to finally give up in regretful acceptance that she had gone to bed. That or he'd be arrested for sticking out like a sore thumb.

He loved it when his mind contemplated the downsides.

An hour or so passed. As Trypp munched on a dry sausage he had picked up from a nearby butcher's, he saw the door to the house open.

Quickly, Trypp began walking in that direction, his attention seemingly lost in his meat snack, though he sneaked upward glances.

"Oh, I'm so sorry..." said Trypp, as he bumped into the maid. "It's you!" he exclaimed in feigned surprise.

The girl looked momentarily shocked until she saw his face. She laughed infectiously again. "Twice in one day. You are clumsy. But what are you doing here?"

"Er...I live around the corner. I was just going to eat."

She looked dubiously at the sausage in his hand.

"It's just a snack, to tide me over." He paused. "Fine, I was going for a drink." He smiled, as if caught fibbing. "Would you like to join me?"

The maid looked around before answering. "I was just going to get something for my Da..." Trypp's face sunk. "But he's asleep anyway. He's old. I could sneak away for half an hour I guess."

Before she could change her mind, he looped her arm in his and whisked her off in the direction that he had been heading. On the short walk to a local tavern, they shared their names;

Lia for her and Travis for him. He was pleased to discover that she was not the shy or retiring type, eager to ask as many questions as he was. They drank wine and the half hour passed without Trypp mentioning it. He ordered food for them to share and they both drank more. Trypp tallied more expenses against the profitability of this job. But he was also enjoying the conversation with Lia and her eager company. He turned the conversation around to her work, and she was happy to share her dislike for the lecherous Palombi, a surprising confluence with the lie that he had told Luniki just the previous evening.

"I've heard that Palombi has quite the art collection. Have you seen it?"

"Heh. What do you know about art? You spend time thinking about paintings of naked women while you're hauling around fish?"

"I appreciate all manner of beautiful...subjects." He almost cringed at that line, and so Trypp touched her hand as he spoke to cover the reaction. She didn't pull away. He wondered if he would need to display his affection for her in other ways, which as it turned out might be quite enjoyable after all. "Someone told me he had a statue made of solid gold..."

"Likely story." She laughed again. "I don't know about that. But I know he has a room off his study that he doesn't let anyone in. Seriously, what's with all of the question about this stuff?"

Trypp was a little taken aback at the challenge. He wasn't used to women looking past the persona he presented. "I was just thinking that with something like that, someone could make a lot of coin—"

"Ah, now I get it," she interrupted.

"Could get a lot of coin for the future," he continued.

"This might sound quick, but we could get a place of our own. Get a nurse for your father." He let that hang there in the air while he looked into her eyes.

A moment or two passed before she laughed so loud that the nearby tables turned around to stare.

"Fuck off. I just met you." Lia leaned in close and locked gaze with him, adding in a whisper, "You're a good-looking man, I'll give you that. But I'll just take the money, thank you very much."

Trypp leaned back in his chair and smiled. Not exactly how he thought it would go, and he'd probably be spending the night back in the room at Atarah's Hearth with his two snoring friends, but this would do.

"I think I can work with that."

"...COUNTED AT LEAST TWO GUARDS WHEN I WAS FLYING overhead with Per, but the roof seems to be in pretty good shape if we can make it."

"We reckon it's about thirty feet across on a wire from the nearest other building of a similar height. Bit far to walk across. Think we're going to have to go up the outside."

Trypp leaned back in his chair, a smile on his face and a beer in his hand as he listened to Motega and Florian tell him what they had discovered from their day's efforts. They were some of the best in the business in identifying the security weak points of a potential target—Motega's ability to merge his mind with his falcon was invaluable in being able to get overhead and obtain a different perspective on a problem—and Trypp couldn't have asked for a better pair of partners if they happened to walk into trouble.

He was proud of what they had grown into, what he had been able to mold them into. True, they'd both been able to fight when he met them that night in Neenahwi's tower, and that had lended itself well to their initial bouts of crypt diving and monster hunting; but it was extraction where the money lay, and it was Trypp who had taught them the trade.

"There's been no talk about a flashy new bust being on display at the house, so we have to assume that it's hidden away somewhere. And there is no obvious place separate from the rest of the villa, no tower or stretch of wall without windows that would indicate a secure room, so we think there must be something underground..." Motega trailed off as he looked at Trypp. "What are you smirking for?"

"Just wondering how long I'd have to wait before telling you how we're going to do it."

"Don't keep it to yourself then. What have you got?"

"An insider."

"Who? How the actual fuck have you got someone on the inside in just a couple of days?" asked Florian.

"Brains and charm, mate. That's why, of the three of us, only I could have done it." Trypp quickly dodged to the side laughing as he saw Motega's open hand flying toward his head. "Alright, maybe if you'd have done it between you." Motega and Florian looked at each other like they were trying to work out which was which.

"I'm definitely the charm," said Florian. "I can live with that."

"Boys, we need to drink up. We have an early morning tomorrow so our insider can open the back door for us..."

"GET IN, QUICK."

Trypp stepped from the dark, cool, early Iothan morning and into the dimly lit corridor he had been in the day before. "No guard?"

"I sent him to the kitchen for some leftover cake. He'll be back soon," whispered Lia.

Trypp gestured for Florian to come forward and held up one finger to indicate what they had to deal with immediately. The big man nodded and stretched his arms as he moved up ahead of them. Motega came in behind and closed the door silently behind him.

"I've got to go," said Lia. "Do you remember what I told you?"

"Don't worry," said Trypp. "We're professionals. I remember."

"I hope you're professional enough to remember to pay me the other half tomorrow." Lia stood on tip toe, and Trypp thought she was going to kiss his cheek but she whispered into his ear. "I'm very good at remembering faces. Don't forget that." She strode away and he saw Motega and Florian exchange a knowing glance, making assumptions about what she must have said. Trypp grinned for a moment to cover a slight unease.

But it was time to focus.

Silently he crept past Florian and around the corner to the passageway that opened out on to the central courtyard. The light of the moon and the stars cast deep shadows by the wall and that was where he remained, his eyes flicking between the entrance to the kitchen and around the rest of the open space, looking for signs of other guards. He reached into a pocket at his belt and took out a small disc of mirror, being careful to hold it pointing at the ground.

He waited, conscious of his chest rising and falling as he remained at the ready to react.

The boy guard from the day before appeared from the lit kitchen, calling thanks to whoever was inside and closing the door behind him. He munched on something from his hand as he ambled toward them, flicking crumbs from his baggy chainmail shirt in between bites. Trypp flicked the mirror to reflect the light in the direction of the guard and the boy stopped at the entrance to the corridor of his typical post, catching sight of the glint but not able to see what caused it. That was fine. The signal was not for him, it was for Florian—who reached out with both arms and grabbed the kid, one hand around his mouth, the other looping around his neck. Florian hugged the boy tight, like the kid probably did with his blanket at night.

Trypp turned his attention back to the courtyard, looking to see if he could spot the guard by the front entrance, or any others that might be lurking. As he focused on the thin crack of dim light that peeped under the front door, he made out the outstretched feet of someone sitting close by. Sitting in the dark? He'd bet a shiny crown that the man was asleep at his post. *Good.*

Lia had drawn a decent floor plan of the villa, which Trypp had committed to memory. The door on the other side, past the front entrance, was the most direct way up to the study—but he thought it best to let sleeping dogs lie. They'd take the door by the kitchen and work their way through the upstairs. With any luck, given the time of morning and Lia occupying the other maid staff, they wouldn't run in to anyone. Trypp signaled for his friends to follow him and they hugged the wall, creeping past the kitchen entrance, to the doorway. He unlocked it easily and behind it was a sharply turning set of stairs up to the second floor. The stairs opened out onto another long corridor, the left side lined with doors, and the right with windows that looked out on to the courtyard below. Staying away from the windows, they darted past the closed doors one at a time, careful not to have a single floorboard creak.

The corridor wrapped around the empty square of space in the center of the villa and the study was situated on the opposite side. They rounded the first corner and Trypp set off again, Motega behind him. He dashed past the first of two doors and waited a few feet away from it. Motega began to move just as the door opened and out stepped another guard, adjusting his trousers from whatever he had been doing moments before. Motega pulled up short, inches from the guard's face.

"Fuck," said Mot.

The guard lurched back in shock. Not good. *Got to do something.* Without thinking, Trypp pulled a thin stiletto from his side, took one step forward and pushed it through the back of the man's neck. Motega's eyes bulged as the knife neared his face. The guard gurgled as Trypp slowly guided him to the floor. Motega stuck his head inside the open doorway and then jerked a thumb for Trypp to drag the guard inside. A privy. Hopefully no one would come looking for the poor bastard for a while. He'd really been hoping that they could get in and out clean, but he supposed the money from this job was worth getting dirty for.

As Trypp emerged back out into the corridor he was greeted by Florian shaking his head and giving him one of *those* looks. He knew he would hear about this later. But what was he supposed to do? He didn't have the strength to risk that sleep hold that Florian did on the kid. Trypp shook his head indicating that now was not the time, and turned on his heel to continue their quiet advance. The corridor turned to the right again, and if he remembered Lia's map correctly, the door to the study would be the middle one.

He grasped the door handle tightly, opening it enough to peer inside, confident or at least hopeful that no one was inside because there had been no light visible below the door. Inside was a room lined floor to ceiling with shelves of books, except for a small window that was set in the middle of the opposite wall, just big enough for Florian to wriggle through in the event they needed a Plan B. A desk and a chair occupied the middle of the room, one more chair in the corner that they could use to barricade the door in a pinch. Trypp entered; Motega and Florian close behind. Once the door was closed, they each moved to a set of shelves and began to examine the books, flipping them forward to see if anything was hidden behind them. Lia had said she had heard from another maid that there was a secret room attached to the study and somehow the bookshelves were involved in the opening. He had relayed that information to his friends and so they each searched for a hidden lever or something.

"Oh, fuck!" exclaimed Florian.

Trypp whirled to see what was wrong but didn't notice anything immediately. Until he saw what Florian was pointing at.

"I didn't see it there."

"Not a bloody cat," said Trypp. "Not again. Throw it out the fucking window."

"I am not throwing it out the window. It's just sitting there. Big and fat." Florian chuckled and went to stroke it but the cat hissed without moving from its cushioned seat, taking him aback. "I'm still not going to throw it out the window..."

It wasn't the time to argue with the big man, so turning his attention back to the shelf in front of him, Trypp moved quickly along the row of books, flipping them forward, until one of them felt different. There were no pages to it, just a solid block painted to look like a book; when he tipped it, there was a faint click. He tried to pick it up but the book would not move. *Nothing opened, but this has to be it. Maybe there are more.*

Changing approach Trypp started picking up groups of books, a dozen at a time and stacking them on the desk. Soon, four more similar fake books were revealed, all on different shelves. Motega and Florian had stopped to look at what he was doing.

"You think there is a certain order to pull them in?" asked Motega, his eyes narrowing.

Trypp shrugged. "Maybe. Will have to try them to see. Be ready." He took a moment to decide on an order. Middle, down to the bottom, back to the middle and to the top. He pulled the book-levers in turn, a slight click with each one, until with the final one, the set of shelves next to where he stood swung open. "Either there is no order, or I guessed right."

"Or you did it wrong and now all the traps are armed," added Florian, really not helping the situation. Trypp could have listened but chose to go and see what they had found.

The door opened into a square stone room, and he had to admit it, even he was impressed. Hanging from all four walls were paintings of staggering beauty. A few depicted Saints from long ago, beatific faces staring out of gilded frames. There was a dragon, wings outstretched on a canvas larger than he. And there were two that juxtaposed each other; a gathering of people of obvious wealth enjoying wine and conversation, while next to it were the same people engaged in fornication and cannibalism. His eye was drawn to two pedestals in the far corners. On one was a fist sized gem set in a silver surround that Trypp couldn't possibly believe was real, and on the other was the gold bust that he was all too acquainted with.

"I wonder whose this was?" mused Florian, walking over to admire another pedestal in the closest corner on which rested a white shield. His hand waved above it like he was not sure if he should touch it.

Motega laughed and pointed at the sole remaining corner. On its pedestal rested a small wiry terrier, puppy eyes staring up to the ceiling. It was only when it didn't move that Trypp realized that it must have been stuffed.

"Focus!" snapped Trypp, turning his attention back to their prize.

Motega swore behind him and Trypp felt like he was a swiveling weathervane, as he was just about to ask him what had happened to professionalism?

"Cat," spat Motega as a black blur rushed past Trypp, ahead of him into the room. There was a grinding of gears and then an audible click.

He closed his eyes for a moment, hoping that when he turned around, he wasn't going to see what he thought he was going to see.

Unfortunately, he was wrong.

"I told you to throw that fucking cat out of the window. Now, nobody move..."

CALL TO ACTION

Thank you for joining me as we leave the Jeweled Continent and make our way to Alfaria. I hope you enjoyed it. I would appreciate you leaving a few remarks or comments on Amazon or Goodreads, and of course, telling your friends the good old-fashioned way. It's this reader led communication that helps to spread the word and get others interested in trying this book.

You can sign up for my newsletter to be notified of future releases, opportunities to become a beta reader, and behind-the-scenes discussion of what went into the making of all of my books. Also, if you want to drop me a line, please do. My email address is dave@dpwoolliscroft.com.

GLOSSARY

Cast of Characters

ALANA: Special Liaison to the Kingshold Districts
BASHARAAT: King of the Pyxies
BORS: Squad member of the Ravens. Died in the fall of Ioth.
CHALICE (Lady): Managing partner of the Hollow Syndicate, rescuer of Neenahwi and Motega
CHERRY: Squad member of the Ravens
CHITTO: Champion of the Tigereye clan
CRABS: Squad member of the Ravens. Died in the fall of Ioth.
CREWS: Admiral and Sea Marshall
CRULL (CAPT.): Pirate. Murderer. Captain of the *Axe Blade*
DOLPH: Former bodyguard to Mareth
DUG: Squad member of the Ravens. Died in the fall of Ioth.
EGYED: Dwarf, ambassador of the deep people, Keybearer of Unedar Halt
ELKIN: Former chief of the Wolfclaw tribe, Motega and

Neenahwi's great-grandfather

FINABRIA: Originally of Ioth; partner of the Hollow House. Formerly known as Jill.

FLORIAN: Friend to Motega and Trypp, originally introduced by Jyuth. Veteran of foreign wars, including the liberation of Redpool, mercenary for hire. Died in the fall of Ioth.

FOREST: Squad member of the Ravens

FORGER: Elected leader of the dwarves of Unedar Halt

GONAL: Merchant, friend of Mareth, Master of the Merchants Guild

GREY (Chancellor): Lord Hoxteth's widow, financer of Mareth's election campaign, Chancellor of the Realm. Also known as Tarra, wizard under the sway of Llewdon

GREYTOOTH: Shaman of the Wolfclaw clan

GRIMES: Commander of the palace guard and city watch

HUNYG: Freed Alfjarun slave

JOE: Squad member of the Ravens. Died in the fall of Ioth.

JYUTH: Wizard, founder of Edland, adopted father of Neenahwi

KANAVEEN: Wolfclaw champion and protector of Neenahwi and Motega after the flight. Lives in the wilderness of Edland

KARR: Former cabin boy. Pirate. Valet. Sharpshooter.

KHRISTINA TRUEBLOOD (CAPT.):

KOLSEN: Resurrected pirate captain.

KYLE: Chiseler of Unedar Halt. Worm-whisperer.

LLEWDON: Emperor of Pyrfew, wizard, ancient

LOFTY: Lubricator-in-chief of New Port

MARETH BOLLINGSMEAD: Lord Protector. Former bard, former adventurer, former pirate

MIDNIGHT: Squad member of the Ravens

MOLEY: Squad member of the Ravens. Died in the fall of

Ioth.
MORRIS: Sergeant of the Ravens
MORRISSEY: Squad member of the Ravens. Miserable bastard. Died in the fall of Ioth.
MOSI: Childhood friend of Yamaagh
MOTEGA: Warrior and archer of renown from the wild continent, brother to Neenahwi, mercenary for hire
MOUSE: Alchemist. Tamer of Draco-Turtles. Guest of the dwarves of Unedar Halt
MYANK: Wizard, teacher of Jyuth
NANICHITA: Former chief of the Wolfclaw tribe, linked to Motega's spirit animal
NEENAHWI: Of the Wolfclaw clan, wizard, adopted daughter of Jyuth and older sister to Motega
NINI GILSTRAP (CAPT.): Pirate. Captain of *the Icicle*
PETRA: Special Liaison to the Edland Guilds. Died in the fall of Kingshold.
RED TED: First mate to Kolsen
ROSITA: Owner of the Squeaky Tiller
SHAREF: Former chief of the Wolfclaw tribe, Motega and Neenahwi's father
SYD: Squad member of the Ravens
TAWFEEQ BEHLER (CAPT.): Pirate. Captain of *The Gathering Storm*.
THE LIBRARIAN: A wight
THE MATRON: Mystic leader of the Giants of Wespar. Former student of Myank. Known to a select few by her given name of Serenus.
TIVA: Chief of the Tigereye clan
TRYPP: Friend to Motega and Florian, former thief with the Twilight Exiles
YAMAAGH: Spirit warrior of the Tigereye clan

ACKNOWLEDGMENTS

Well, there I was thinking that *Ioth, City of Lights* was tough to write because of some of my favorite characters dying. I did not expect that writing the fallout of those events to be so much harder! Unsurprisingly, the deaths of Petra and Florian have hit our group pretty hard, and as I helped them work through their grief, it definitely brought to mind various losses that I have had in my life. And while our heroes' travels through the dark of Dundenas was occasionally oppressive, I really enjoyed the opportunity to explore the lesser seen side of my world. Who's for more stories of the Myconids?

It was great to visit with some old friends in these stories. Vin Kolsen is still a bastard, and a particularly lucky one at that. And seeing Jyuth once more reminded me how fun he was to write in *Kingshold*. I really did have the intention for him not to appear again in the Wildfire Cycle but we'll just have to see if he pops up again.

If anyone is keeping track of these acknowledgements from one book to another, you will see that I was originally aiming to get this book out before Christmas 2019 and I missed that deadline by a few months. Unfortunately, life got in the way for both me and my editor. But on the plus side, I have books 3, 3.5 and 4 all completely plotted. So I know how this saga is going to end and have a pretty good idea of how many times I'm going to smack you in the face. I'm about 25% of the way through the first draft of book 3 as I write this, a few weeks in to the COVID-19 lockdown. I have the distinct impression that book 3, working title Ajiwiak by the way, will be even longer than *Ioth*, so I'm aiming to get it out to my beta readers before the holidays. Think of that as a plug by the way; if anyone would like to be involved in the future sausage making, please do drop me a line and I'd love to have more beta readers.

Now, time for the fun stuff. Saying thank you to the folks who keep me going. First of all, I want to call out some of the awesome fantasy bloggers out there who have supported The Wildfire Cycle so far; Jason Aycock, Justine Bergman, Briargrey (r/fantasy), Beth Tabler, Nick Borelli, Chrissy (from the returncart), Jay Clementi, Daryl Graves, Olivia Hofer, Kristen Superstardrifter, Jennifer (Bunnyreads), Lukasz, Calvin Park, Jordan Rose, Timy Takács, Esme Weatherwax, Lynn Williams, Wol, Alex at Spellsandspaceships and many others that I may not have remembered in the heat of the moment.

One of the most wonderful things I've encountered is the support from fellow authors; thanks to Jon Auerbach, Angel Boord, Dave De Burgh, Josh Erikson, Bjorn Larssen, Devin Madson, Krystele Matar (hurry up and finish your book!), Richard Nell, Kayleigh Nicol, Carol Park, Kevin Potter, Phil Parker, Clayton Snyder, William Ray, Travis Riddle, Luke

Tarzian, Phil Williams, and a special thanks to Mark Lawrence for organizing the Self-Published Fantasy Blog Off.

As ever, the book in your hands would not have been possible without the help and support of a number of people. Firstly, my wife Haneen and daughter Liberty, supporting me in being able to follow a passion in the limited spare time that is available.

A massive high-five of thanks to my editor, Bethan May. Beth is amazing. I constantly hope that she doesn't get too popular and I'm not able to book her/afford her rates.

Many, many thanks to Matt Barber, Patrick Kansa, James Polledri, Travis Riddle, Andrew Rimmer, Joe Smith, Mark Watkins and Bernie Zimmermann for their immense help as beta readers once again. Once again, their feedback, along with Beth's, has resulted in this book being so much better for you to read than what I put in their hands.

And last, but not least, Jeff Brown my illustrator and cover designer. We've continued the theme that we began in Tales of Kingshold that these editions should look like journals and once again it's really amazing to see how his images of Kingshold, and now Ioth, look in miniature and water colors.

For now, goodbye friends. And I'll see you next year.

D.P. Woolliscroft

April, 2020

ABOUT THE AUTHOR

Born in Derby in England on the day before mid-summers day, David Peter Woolliscroft was very nearly magical. If only his dear old mum could have held on for another day. But magic called out to him over the intervening years, with many a book being devoured for its arcane properties. David studied Accounting at Cardiff University where numbers weaved their own kind of magic and he has since been a successful business leader in the intervening twenty years.

Adventures were had. More books were devoured. And then one day David had read enough that the ideas he had kept bottled up needed a release valve. And thus, rising out of the self-doubt like a phoenix at a clicky keyboard, a writer was born.

David, his wife Haneen, and daughter Liberty all live with their mini goldendoodle Rosie in Princeton, NJ. David is one of the few crabs to escape the crabpot.

Printed in Great Britain
by Amazon

49121422R00177